BITTER GOLD HEARTS

Ogre town was quiet as death—until we sprang our attack on the citadel of the human pug-ugly nicknamed Gorgeous. This cold-blooded killer's pack of ogres had been wiping out some people I'd had a personal interest in keeping alive.

Right from the start the battle seemed to be going just the way we'd planned. Then Gorgeous let loose with a roar that could wake the undead. I jumped him, but the damage was done. The stairs were already drumming to stamping feet. And then the ogre stampede arrived!

There must have been twenty in the first rush. They pushed across the room, into the far wall. Even my grolls, hammering ogre heads from above, scarcely slowed them. And more and more ogres kept coming.

It was looking really grim for my little army as Gorgeous shrieked hysterical, bloodthirsty orders. It was definitely time to try something desperate. . . .

Titles in the Garrett, P.I., Series
by Glen Cook

BITTER GOLD HEARTS

Glen Cook

A ROC BOOK

ROC
Published by New American Library, a division of
Penguin Group (USA) Inc., 375 Hudson Street,
New York, New York 10014, USA
Penguin Group (Canada), 90 Eglinton Avenue East, Suite 700, Toronto,
Ontario M4P 2Y3, Canada (a division of Pearson Penguin Canada Inc.)
Penguin Books Ltd., 80 Strand, London WC2R 0RL, England
Penguin Ireland, 25 St. Stephen's Green, Dublin 2,
Ireland (a division of Penguin Books Ltd.)
Penguin Group (Australia), 250 Camberwell Road, Camberwell, Victoria 3124,
Australia (a division of Pearson Australia Group Pty. Ltd.)
Penguin Books India Pvt. Ltd., 11 Community Centre, Panchsheel Park,
New Delhi - 110 017, India
Penguin Group (NZ), 67 Apollo Drive, Mairangi Bay,
Auckland 1311, New Zealand (a division of Pearson New Zealand Ltd.)
Penguin Books (South Africa) (Pty.) Ltd., 24 Sturdee Avenue,
Rosebank, Johannesburg 2196, South Africa

Penguin Books Ltd., Registered Offices:
80 Strand, London WC2R 0RL, England

First published by Roc, an imprint of New American Library,
a division of Penguin Group (USA) Inc.

First Printing, June 1988
10 9 8 7 6 5 4

1

There was nothing to do after I wrapped up the Case of the Perilous Pixies. Two weeks of living with the Dead Man's grumblings and mutterings would try the patience of a saint. A saint I'm not.

Worse, Tinnie was out of town indefinitely and the redhead refused to share me with anyone she didn't know. It was a trying time to be alive. Nothing to do with my evenings but keep the breweries from going into receivership.

It was early and a devil was doing some blacksmithing in my skull, so I wasn't at my best when somebody came pounding on the door of our battered old house on Macunado Street.

"Yeah?" I snapped when I yanked the door open. It didn't matter that the woman was wearing a thousand marks' worth of custom cloth or that the street was filled with guys in flashy livery. I've seen too much of the rich to be impressed.

"Mr. Garrett?"

"That's me." I lightened up a little. I'd had a chance to give her the up and down, and she was worth a second look. And a third and a fourth. There wasn't a lot of her, though nothing was missing, and what was there had been put together quite nicely. A phantom smile crossed her lips as my gaze drew north again.

"I'm half fairy," she said, and for a moment music broke through the gravity of her voice. "Can you stop gaping long enough to let me in?"

"Of course. Can I ask your name? I don't recall you being on my appointment calendar. Though I'd love to jot you in as often as you want."

"I'm here on business, Mr. Garrett. Save that for your bar girls." She pushed past me a few steps, then stopped and glanced back with mild surprise.

"The outside is camouflage," I told her. "We leave it looking like a dump so we don't strain the honesty of our neighbors." It wasn't the best section of the city. There was a war on, and it was hot, so there were plenty of jobs available, but some of our neighbors hadn't yet given in to the silly notion of personal gain through honest employment.

"We?" she repeated icily. "I wanted to consult with you on a matter that requires the greatest discretion."

Don't they all? They wouldn't come to me if they thought they could solve their problems through the usual channels.

"You can trust him," I replied, nodding toward the other room. "His lips are sealed. He's been dead for four hundred years."

I watched her face go through a series of changes. "He's Loghyr? The Dead Man?"

So she wasn't such a lady after all. Anybody who knows the Dead Man has roots solidly anchored in the downhill end of TunFaire. "Yes. I think he ought to hear it."

I get around and hear a lot of things—some of them true, most of them not. I'd recognized the livery of the Stormwarden Raver Styx outside and thought I could guess what was eating her. It would be fun springing her on the heap of moth-eaten blubber who had become my permanent houseguest.

"No."

I started toward his room. The routine is for me to wake him when I have a business caller. Not everyone who visits is friendly. He can provide powerful backup when the mood hits him. "What did you say your name was, miss?"

I was fishing and she knew it. She could have skipped right around it, but she hesitated in an odd way before confessing, "Amiranda Crest, Mr. Garrett. This is a critical matter."

"They always are, Amiranda. I'll be with you in a minute."

She didn't walk out.

It was important enough that she would let herself be pushed.

He was indulging himself in what had become his favorite pastime, trying to outguess the generals and warlords in the Cantard. No matter that the information he got was scanty, out of date, and mostly filtered through me. He did as well as the geniuses who commanded the armies—better than most of those stormwardens and warlords whose main claim to the right of command was heredity.

He was a mountain of rigid yellow flesh sprawled on a massive wooden chair. The works had been moved several times but the flesh hadn't twitched since somebody stuck a knife in it four hundred years ago. He was getting a little ragged. Loghyr flesh doesn't corrupt quickly, but mice and whole species of insects consider it a delicacy.

The wall facing his chair had no doors or windows. He'd had an artist paint it with a large-scale map of the war zone. At that moment he had hosts of bugs trooping up and down the plaster landscape, re-creating recent campaigns, trying to discover how the mercenary Glory Mooncalled had evaded not only the Venageti out to destroy him, but our own commanders, who wanted to catch and leash him before his string of triumphs made them look more foolish and inept than they already did.

"You're awake."

Go away, Garrett.

"Who's winning? The ants or the roaches? Better watch out for those spiders down in the corner. They're sneaking up on your silverfish."

Quit pestering me, Garrett.

"I have a visitor, a prospective client. We need a client. I want you to hear her outpouring of woe."

You brought a woman into my house again? Garrett, my good nature has limits wider than the ocean, but it does have limits.

"Whose house? Do we have to go back to talking about who's the landlord and who's the squatter?"

The bugs scattered. Some of them jumped on others. That's life in the war zone.

I almost had the pattern.

"He does it with mirrors. If there was a pattern, the Venageti War Council would have spotted it months ago. Finding Glory Mooncalled isn't a hobby for them. It's life or death." The mercenary was picking them off one by one. He had an old score to settle.

I take it this one is not that redheaded witch of yours?

"Tinnie? No. This one works for the Stormwarden Raver Styx. She has fairy blood. You'll love her at first sight."

Unlike you, who loves them all at first sight, I am no longer the victim of my flesh, Garrett. There are some advantages to being dead. One gains the ability to reason. . . .

I'd heard this before—several dozen times. "I'll bring her in." I stepped out, returned to the front room. "Miss Crest? If you'll come with me?"

She glowered. Even angry she was a gem, but there was a quiet desperation in her stance that gave me all the handle I needed. "Amiranda, haunter of my dreams. Please?"

She followed me. I think she knew she had no choice.

2

Amiranda Crest started shaking when she saw the Dead Man. I'm used to him and tend to forget the impact he has on those who never have seen a dead Loghyr. Her cute little nose wrinkled. She whispered, "It smells in here."

Well, yes, it did, but not much, and I was used to that, too. I ignored the remark. "This is Amiranda Crest, who comes to us from the Stormwarden Raver Styx."

Please pardon me for not rising, Miss Crest. I am capable of mental prodigies, but self-levitation is not among them.

Meantime, Amiranda blurted, "Oh, no. Not from the Stormwarden. She's in the Cantard. Her secretary, the Domina Willa Dount, sent me. I'm her assistant. She wants you to see her about something she wants you to do, Mr. Garrett. For the family. Discreetly."

"Then you're not going to tell me what it is?"

"I don't know what it is. I was told to give you a hundred marks, gold, and tell you there is a thousand more if you'll do the job. But the hundred is yours if you'll just come and see her."

She lies, Garrett. She knows what it is about.

He wasn't paying the rent with that.

She had changed strategies while I was alerting the

Dead Man. "That's all? Nothing to tell me why I'm sticking my neck out?"

She had begun counting ten-mark gold pieces into her left hand. I was startled. I'd never met anyone with fairy blood who was right-handed.

"Save yourself the trouble, Miss Crest. If that's it, I'll stay here and help my friend hustle cockroaches."

She thought I was joking. A man of my class turning his back on a hundred marks gold? A man in my line? I ought to be sprinting uptown to find out who they wanted killed. Chances were *she* had run uptown, bartering her good looks for the pretty things she wore.

She asked, "Couldn't you just take me on faith, and for the gold?"

"The last time I trusted somebody from up the Hill I got stuck in the Marines. I spent five years trying to kill Venageti conscripts who didn't know any better than I did what we were fighting about. I didn't figure that out till I came back home, and then I liked your lords and ladies of the Hill even less. Good day, Miss Crest. Unless you'd be interested in some more personal business? I know a little place that serves seafood you could kill for."

I watched her think it over, looking for angles she could use. Finally, she said, "Domina will be very angry with me if I don't bring you."

"How sad. But that's not my problem. If you don't mind? Your boys out front are probably baking in the sun, anyway."

She stomped out of the room, snarling, "You're throwing away the easiest hundred marks of your life, Mr. Garrett."

I followed her to make sure she used the door for its intended purpose. "If your boss wants to see me so bad, tell her to come down here."

She paused, opened her mouth to say something, then shook her head and slipped outside. I caught a glimpse of the sweltering guards jumping to their feet before the door closed. I went back to the Dead Man.

You were a little stubborn, were you not?

"She'll be back."

I know. But what temper will possess her?

"Maybe she'll be ready to lay it out straight, without the games."

She is a female, Garrett. Why do you persist in such unreasonable optimism where that alien species is concerned?

This was one of our running arguments. He was a misogynist to the marrow. This time I refused to play. He gave up.

Are you interested in the job, Garrett?

"My heart won't be broken if it doesn't develop. You know I told the truth when I said I don't have much use for the lords of the Hill. And I particularly have no use for sorcerers. We don't need the money, anyway."

You always need money, Garrett, the way you drink beer and chase skirts.

He exaggerated, of course. His envy was talking. His single greatest regret about being dead was his inability to guzzle beer.

Someone is hammering on the door.

"I hear it. It's probably old Dean, early for work."

The Dead Man would not endure a female housekeeper, and my tolerance for housework is minimal. I'd only been able to find one old man—who moved with the flash and style of a tortoise—willing to come in, pick up, cook, and clear the vermin from the Dead Man's room.

I was surprised to find Amiranda back already. "Quick trip. Come in. I didn't know I was so irresistible."

She strode past me, then turned, hands on hips. "All right, Mr. Garrett. You get it your way. The reason Domina wants you is because my . . . because the Stormwarden's son Karl has been kidnapped. If you insist on getting more than that, we're both out of luck. Because that's all I've been told."

And you certainly are worried about it, I thought.

She started for the door.

"Hold it." I squinted at her. "Give me the hundred."

She handed it over without a smirk of triumph. One point for Amiranda Crest. I decided she might be worth liking.

"I'll be back in a minute."

I took the gold to the Dead Man. There was no safer place on earth. "You heard?"

I did.

"What do you think?"

Kidnapping is your area of expertise.

I rejoined Amiranda Crest. "Let us fare forth, fair fairy lady."

That failed to put a smile on her face.

Not everyone appreciates a great sense of humor.

3

We marched off like a parody of a military outfit. Amiranda's companions were clad in uniforms. That seemed to be the limit of their familiarity with the military concept. At a guess I would have said their only use was to keep their livery from collapsing into the dust.

I tried a few conversational sallies. Amiranda was done talking. I was one of the hired help now.

The Dead Man was right. Kidnapping was my area of expertise, mostly by circumstance. Time and again I get stuck doing the in-between. Each time I deliver the ransom and bring the body home alive the word gets around a little more. Both sides in a swap know where they stand with me. I play it straight, no tricks, and heaven help the bad boys if they deliver damaged goods and my principals want their heads. Which they always do in that case.

I loathe kidnapping and kidnappers. Abduction is a major underground industry in TunFaire. I'd as soon see all kidnappers sent down the river floating facedown, but sound business practice makes me play the game by live-and-let-live rules. Unless *they* cheat first.

The Hill is a good deal more than a piece of high ground looking down its nose at the sprawl of TunFaire, the beast upon whose back it rides. It is a state of mind, and one I don't like. But their coin is as good as any down below, and they have a lot more of it. I register my disapproval by refusing jobs that might help the Hill tribe close their grip even tighter on the rest of us.

Usually when they try to hire me it's because they want dirty work done. I turn them down. They find somebody less morally fastidious. So it goes.

The Stormwarden Raver Styx's place was typical of those on the High Hill. It was huge, tall, walled, brooding, dark, and just a shade more friendly than death. It was one of those places with an invisible "Abandon Hope" sign over the gateway. Maybe there were protective spells involved. I got a strong case of nerves the last fifty feet, the little watchman inside telling me I didn't want to go in there.

I went anyway. One hundred marks gold can shout down the watchman any time.

The inside reminded me of a haunted castle. There were cobwebs everywhere. Amiranda and I, after shedding our escort, were the only people tracking the shadowed halls. "Cheerful little bungalow. Where is everybody?"

"The Stormwarden took most of the household with her."

"But she left her secretary behind?"

"Yes."

Which told me there was some truth in the things I'd heard about the Stormwarden's husband and son, both named Karl. Put charitably, they needed a shepherd.

At first glance Willa Dount looked like a woman who could keep them in line. Her eyes could chill beer, and she had the charm of a stone. I knew a little about her from whispers in the shadows and alleys. She arranged dirty deeds done for the Stormwarden.

She was about five feet two, early forties, chunky without being fat. Her gray eyes matched her hair. She dressed, shall we say, sensibly. She smiled about twice as often as the Man in the Moon, and then without sincerity.

Amiranda said, "Mr. Garrett, Domina."

The woman looked at me like I was either a potentially contagious disease or an especially curious specimen in the zoo. One of the uglier ones, like a thunder lizard.

There are times when I feel like I belong to one of the dying breeds.

"Thank you, Amiranda. Have a seat, Mr. Garrett." The "mister" left her jaws aching. She wasn't used to being nice to people like me.

I sat. So did she. Amiranda hovered.

"That will be all, Amiranda."

"Domina—"

"That will be all."

Amiranda left, furious and hurt. I scanned the clutter on the secretary's desk while she glared the girl from the room.

"What do you think of our Amiranda, Mr. Garrett?" Again she got a jaw ache.

I tried putting it delicately. "A man could dream dreams about a woman with her—"

"I'm sure." She scowled at me. I had failed some test.

I didn't care. I'd decided I wouldn't like the Domina Willa Dount very much. "You had a reason for asking me to come here?"

"How much did Amiranda tell you?"

"Enough to get me to listen." She tried to stare me down. I stared back. "I don't usually have much grief to spare for uptown folks. When the fates want to stick them I say more power to them. But to kidnapping I take exception."

She scowled. I give the woman this—her scowl was first rate. Any gorgon would have been proud to own it. "What else did she tell you?"

"That was it, and getting it took some work. Maybe you can tell me more."

"Yes. As Amiranda told you, the younger Karl has been abducted."

"From what I've heard, there aren't many more deserving guys around." Karl Junior had a reputation for being twenty-three going on a willful and very spoiled three. There was no doubt which side of the family Junior favored. Domina Dounnt had been left to keep it civilized or to cover it up.

Willa Dount's mouth tightened until it was little more than a white point. "Be that as it may. We aren't here to exercise your opinions of your betters, Mr. Garrett."

"What are we here for?"

"The Stormwarden will be returning soon. I don't want her to walk into a situation like this. I want to get it settled and forgotten before she arrives. Do you wish to take notes, Mr. Garrett?" She pushed writing materials my way. I figured she supposed me illiterate and wanted to enjoy feeling superior when I confessed it.

"Not till there's something worth noting. I take it you've heard from the kidnappers? That you know Junior hasn't just gone off on one of his adventures?"

By way of answering me she lifted a rag-wrapped bundle from behind the desk and pushed it across. "This was left with the gateman during the night."

I unwrapped a pair of silver-buckled shoes. A folded piece of paper lay inside one. "His?"

"Yes."

"The messenger?"

"What you would expect. A street urchin of seven or eight. The gateman didn't bring me the bundle till after breakfast. By then the child was too far ahead to catch."

So she had a sense of humor after all.

I gave the shoes the full eyeball treatment. It never works out, but you always look for that speck of rare purple mud or the weird yellow grass stain that will make you look like a genius. I didn't find it this time, either. I unfolded the note.

> We have yore Karl. If you want him back you
> do what yore told. Dont tell nobody about this. You
> be told what to do later.

A snippet of hair had been folded into the paper. I held it to the light falling through the window behind the secretary's desk. It was the color I recalled Junior's hair being the few times I had seen him. "Nice touch, this."

Willa Dount gave me another of her scowls.

I ignored her and examined the note. The paper itself told me nothing except that it was a scrap torn from something else, possibly a book. I could go around town for a century trying to match it to torn pages. But the handwriting was interesting. It was small but loose, confident, the penmanship almost perfect, not in keeping with the apparent education of the writer. "You don't recognize this hand?"

"Of course not. That needn't concern you, anyway."

"When did you see him last?"

"Yesterday morning. I sent him down to our warehouse on the waterfront to check reports of pilferage. The foreman claimed it was brownies. I had a feeling *he* was the brownie in the woodpile and he was selling the Stormwarden's supplies to somebody here on the Hill. Possibly even to one of our neighbors."

"It's always reassuring to know the better classes stand above the sins and temptations of us common folks. You weren't concerned when he didn't come home?"

"I told you I'm not interested in your social attitudes or opinions. Save them for someone who agrees with you. No, I wasn't concerned. He sometimes stays out for weeks. He's a grown man."

"But the Stormwarden left you here to ride herd on him and his father. And you must have done the job till now because there hasn't been a hint of scandal since the old girl left town."

One more scowl.

The door sprang open and a man stomped into the room. "Willa, has there been any more word about . . . ?" He spotted me and pulled up. His eyebrows crawled halfway up his forehead, a trick for which he was famous. To hear some tell it, that was his only talent. "Who the hell is that?" He was renowned for being rude, too, though among people of his class that was a trait the rest of us expected.

4

Willa Dount spoke up. "There hasn't been anything yet. I expect we won't be contacted for a while." She looked at me, her expression making that a question.

"They like to let the anxiety level rise before they come after you. It makes you more eager to cooperate."

"This is Mr. Garrett," she said. "Mr. Garrett is an expert on kidnappers and kidnappings."

"My god, Willa! Are you mad? They said don't tell anybody."

She ignored his outburst. "Mr. Garrett, this is the Stormwarden's consort, the Baronet daPena, the father of the victim."

How he twitched and jerked! Without changing her tone or expression, Domina Dount had hit him with a fat double shot, calling him consort (which labeled him a drone) and mentioning his baronetcy (which wasn't hereditary and purely an honor because he was the fourth son of a cadet of the royal house). She may even have gotten in a sly third shot there, if, as you sometimes heard whispered, Junior wasn't really a seed fallen from the senior.

"How do you do, Lord? He has a good question, Domina." I'd been working up to it when he burst in. "Why bring me in when the kidnappers said don't tell anybody? A man with my reputation, and you sent out what amounted to a platoon of clowns, with the girl dressed flashy enough to catch a blind man's eye. It's not likely the kidnappers won't hear about it."

"That was the point. I want them to."

"Willa!"

"Karl, be quiet. I'm explaining to Mr. Garrett."

He turned white. He was furious. She'd made it clear who stood where, who was in charge, in front of a lowlife from down the Hill. But he contained himself. I pretended blindness. It isn't smart to see things like that.

Willa Dount said, "I want them to know I've brought you in, Mr. Garrett."

"Why?"

"For young Karl's sake. To improve his chances of getting through this alive. Would you say they're less likely to harm him if they know about you?"

"If they're professionals. Professionals know me. If they're not, chances are they'll go the other way. You may have moved too soon."

"Time will tell. It seemed the best bet to me."

"Exactly what do you want me to do?"

"Nothing."

She blindsided me there. "What?"

"You've done what I needed you to do. You've been seen coming here to confer with me. You've lent me your reputation. Hopefully, Karl's chances have been improved."

"That's it?"

"That's it, Mr. Garrett. Do you think a hundred marks adequate recompense for the loan of your reputation?"

It was fine with me, but I ignored the question. "What about the payoff?" Usually they want me to handle that for them.

"I believe I can handle that. It's basically a matter of following instructions, isn't it?"

"Explicitly. The payoff is when they're most nervous. That's when you'll have to be most careful. For your own safety as well as the boy's."

Senior snorted and huffed and stamped, wanting to get his hand into the action. Willa Dount kept him quiet with an occasional touch of her icicle eyes.

I wondered what the Stormwarden had left her in the way of leashes and whips. She sure had the old boy buffaloed.

Karl Senior was still a handsome man though he was running away from forty—if he had not already sneaked past fifty. Time had dealt him a few wrinkles but no extra pounds. His hair was all there, curly and slickly black, the kind that might not start graying for another decade. He was a little short, I thought, but that didn't hold him back. He looked like a fancy man, and word was that he did night work best.

Age had apparently not slowed him down. Those looks, a smooth tongue, his toy title, those magical eyebrows, and soulful big blue eyes all conspired to drop into his lap the sort of soft morsels we ordinary mortals have to scheme and fight just to get near.

It was a certainty he was no use in a crisis. He danced and twitched like a desperate kid awaiting his turn at the loo. He would have panicked if Domina Dount would have let him. He was a member of the royal house, those wonderfully firm and decisive folks who had blessed the Karentine people with their war against the Venageti.

Natural son or not, Karl Junior was a seed that had not fallen far from the tree. He was the image of Karl Senior in body and character, and to that menace to feminine virtue, he had added a generous helping of arrogance based on the fact that his mommy was the Stormwarden Raver Styx and he was her precious one and only, whose misdeeds would never be called to account.

Senior didn't like my being there. Maybe he didn't like me. If so, the feeling was mutual. I've been busting my butt since I was eight and I don't have any use for drones of any sort, and those from the Hill least of all. Their idleness got them into the kind of mischief that resulted in sending a whole generation south to fight over the silver mines of the Cantard.

Maybe Glory Mooncalled would turn on his Karentine employers once he polished off the Venageti Warlords. It wouldn't hurt.

I said, "If you've had your way with me, then I'll be running along. Best of luck getting the boy back."

Her expression said she doubted my sincerity. "You can find your way to the street?"

"I learned scouting when I was in the Marines."

"Good day, then, Mr. Garrett."

Karl Senior exploded the second I closed the door. It was a good door. I couldn't decipher his yells even when I put my ear to the wood. But he was having a good time working the panic and frustration out.

5

Amiranda caught me just before I reached the gate. I caught my breath, then chewed on my tongue a little so I could still fake being a gentleman. She'd changed from the show ensemble she'd worn to fetch me and now, in her everydays, looked like something I find only under the covers of midnight fantasies.

She looked good, but she also looked worried. I told myself this was no time for one of my routines.

My sometime-associate Morley Dotes tells me I'm a sucker for a damsel in distress. He tells me many things about myself, most of them wrong and unwelcomed, but he has me on the damsels. A good-looking gal turns on the tears and Garrett is a knight ready to tilt with dragons.

"What did she say, Mr. Garrett? What does she want you to do?"

"She said a lot of not much at all. What she wants me to do is nothing."

"I don't understand." Did she look disappointed? I couldn't tell.

"I'm not sure I do, either. She said she wanted the kidnappers to see me around the edges of the thing. So my reputation will shade him and maybe give him a better chance."

"Oh. Maybe she's right." She looked relieved. I wondered what her stake was. I'd formed a suspicion and didn't like it. "So do you think he'll be all right, Mr. Garrett?"

"I don't know. But Domina Dount is a formidable woman. I wouldn't want her on my backtrail."

A black-haired looker of the late teens or early twenties variety left a doorway about thirty feet away, caught sight of us, gave me a once-over she followed up with a come-and-get-it smile, then walked off with a sway to still the tumult of battles.

"Who was that?" I asked.

"You needn't pant, Mr. Garrett. You'd be wasting your time. You don't dare touch her with your imagination. That's the Stormwarden's daughter, Amber."

"I see. Yes. Hmmm."

Amiranda placed herself in front of me. "Put your eyes back in, mister. You made a big show of wanting to see me outside of all this. All right. Tonight at eight. At the Iron Liar."

"The Iron Liar? I'm not from uptown. How could I afford . . . ?" I had to put that excuse away. This was the same little gem that had counted the hundred gold marks into my paw a couple hours ago. "Eight, then. I'll spend the rest of the day breathless with anticipation."

I smiled smugly after I hit the street.

I wandered down the Hill wondering why I'd never heard of daughter Amber when the Stormwarden and her family played such a big part in TunFaire's news and gossip. We had obviously been missing the best part.

6

Strange noises were coming from the Dead Man's room.
I went into the kitchen, where old Dean was cooking
sausages over charcoal with one eye on an apple pie that
was about ready to come out of the oven. When he saw
me, he began hoisting a pony keg out of the cold well
I'd had installed with the proceeds of the Starke case.
By damn, I was going to have cold brew whenever the
whim hit while I could afford it.

Dean asked, "A good day today, Mr. Garrett?" as he
drew me a mug.

"Interesting." I tipped my head back and swallowed
a pint. "And profitable. What's he up to in there? I've
never heard him make such a racket."

"I don't know, Mr. Garrett. He wouldn't let me in
to clean."

"We'll see about that after I wrap myself around another one of these." I eyed the sausages and pie. If he
expected me to eat that much, he was more optimistic
than I thought. "Did you invite a niece over again?"

He reddened.

I just shook my head and said, "I have to go out this
evening. Part of the job."

There was a little troll blood on all sides of his family.
I don't have any particular prejudices—who was going

out with a part-fairy girl?—but those poor women had
gotten a double dose of the troll ugly from their parents.
Like they say, personality plus, but horses shied and
dogs howled when they passed. I wished old Dean would
stop matchmaking. I had given up hope that he would
run out of eligible female relatives to parade past me.

Three sausages, two pieces of the world's best apple
pie, and several beers later I was ready to beard the
Loghyr in his den. So to speak. "Food fit for the gods
as usual, Dean. I'm going in after him. If I'm not out by
the weekend, send Saucerhead Tharpe to the rescue. His
skull is so thick he'd never know Old Bones was thinking
at him." I thought about recommending Saucerhead to
Dean's eligibles. But no, I couldn't. I liked Saucerhead.

The Dead Man sensed me coming. *Get away from
here, Garrett.*

I went on in.

It was war in the Cantard again, and this time the god
of the wall had all the hordes of bugdom enlisted in his
enterprise. It was the combined racket of their creepy
little feet and wings that I had been hearing.

"Caught him yet?"

He ignored me.

"That Glory Mooncalled is a tricky bastard, isn't he?"
I wondered if he meant to clean up the entire bug popu-
lation of TunFaire. For a service like that, we should
find some way to get paid.

He ignored me. His bugs got busier. I sat in the only
chair available to me and watched the campaign for a
while. He was experimenting, not re-creating. It was no
campaign I recognized.

Maybe he was even making war upon himself. The
Loghyr can section up their brains into two or three
discrete parts when they want.

"Had an interesting day today?"

He didn't respond. He was going to punish my imper-
tinence by pretending I didn't exist. But he was listening.
The only adventures he truly had were the ones I lived
for him.

I gave him all the details, chronicling even the most trivial. Somewhere down the line I might have to call on his genius.

I finished and watched him play general for a while. I got the feeling there was a hidden pattern that I was too dense to see.

It was nearing time to meet Amiranda. I pried myself from the chair and headed for the door. "See you when I see you, Old Bones."

Garrett. If you get lucky, don't you bring her back here. I will not endure such foolishness in my house.

I seldom did, though occasionally circumstances insisted. It seemed too much like mocking his handicap.

In life the Loghyr are as randy as a pack of seventeen-year-old boys. It was my suspicion that his misogyny was his way of compensating.

I was almost out the door when he sent, *Garrett. Be careful.*

I *am* careful. Always. When I'm paying attention and when I figure I have something to worry about. But how do you get into trouble just walking up the block to buy a bottle of stink-pretty from the neighborhood chemist?

Believe me, it can be done.

It was my lucky day in more ways than one. I smelled weed smoke and that got me curious. Not many in the neighborhood use weed, and this was less of a cloud than a minor storm. I started looking for the source.

Source was five breeds, all with a lot of ogre in them. Ogres are not fast at the best of times and these boys had spent their take getting so high their pointy heads were bumping the belly of the sky. Their professional sins were legion. They hadn't done their homework, either.

One asked me, "Your name Garrett?"

"Who wants to know?"

"I do."

"It's him. Let's do it."

I did it first.

I kicked the nearest in his daydreams, spun and

punched another in the throat—then tripped over my own damned big feet. The first guy bent over and started puking. The second lost interest and wobbled away holding his throat and sucking air.

I rolled and leg-whipped another one, catching him by such surprise that he fell on his back without trying to break his fall. His head bounced off the street. Lights out.

It was a good start. I began thinking I might make it without getting hurt.

The other two stood around trying to get their muggy brains untangled. I got in the finishing licks on the two I had hit already. A crowd began gathering.

The last two decided to get on with the job. They closed in. They were more careful. I was faster but they took advantage of superior numbers to keep me boxed. We waltzed for a while. I got in a few hits but it's hard to hurt guys like that when you can't get in a sucker punch. They got a few in on me, too.

The third such blow murdered my optimism. It left me seeing double and concentrating my considerable intellect on the age-old question: which way is up?

One of them started saying something about me staying away from the Stormwarden's family while the other wound up to finish me off. I grabbed a big gnarly walking stick from an old bystander and smacked the one between the eyes before he could unwind. I went after the talker while the fighter was seeing stars and his hitting arm was flaccid. Yakety-yak did a good job holding me off, stick and all, until I got in a whack that broke his arm.

He was ready to call it quits. So was I. The bystanders were scattering. I returned the old guy's stick and scattered myself. What passed for minions of law and order in TunFaire were coming. I didn't want to get hauled in and charged with intent to commit self-defense, which is about the way the law worked when it worked at all. I left the ogre boys trying to figure out what had happened.

My lucky day indeed.

                    *   *   *

The Dead Man was all enthusiasm when I told him
about the incident. He gave me a good mental grumble
about wishing the ogres had been a little more competent. But when I was about to leave, to get washed up
and changed, he sent, *I told you to be careful.*

"I know. And I'm going to keep that a little more
closely in mind. Watch the cockroaches. They're about
to flank the silverfish at Yellow Dog Mesa."

He detached a part of his attention from his war and
used it to levitate and throw a small stone Loghyr cult
figure. It smacked the other side of the door as I shut it.

I decided to ease up. When he gets that irritable, he's
hot on the spoor of a solution to a problem that has
been bugging him for a long time.

7

Amiranda was waiting and looking uncomfortable when I got to the Iron Liar. I wasn't late, she was early. In my experience a woman on time is a rarity to be treasured. I didn't remark on it.

She asked, "What happened to you? You look like you were in a fight."

"First prize to the lady. You should see the other guys." She seemed excited by the idea of my getting into a fight. Point taken away from Amiranda Crest. I tried the story on her just to see how she would react.

She appeared befuddled and frightened, but got control quickly. "Why would the kidnappers do that?"

"I don't know. It doesn't make sense." Then I turned to more interesting subjects, notably Amiranda Crest. "How did you get hooked up with the Stormwarden?"

"I was born to it."

"What?"

"My father was a friend of her father. They worked together sometimes."

The brain had to run some numbers before I could say anything more. The Stormwarden's father had died before I was born. Fairy folk lived a long time and aged slowly. Could this morsel be old enough to be my mother?

"I'm twenty-one, Garrett."

I gave her the famous Garrett raised eyebrow.

"I've gotten too damned many of those glassy-eyed stares when human men suddenly realize there's a chance I might be older, more knowledgeable, and more experienced than they are. Sometimes it turns into panic or terror."

I apologized where I was guilty, then told her, "You jump to too many conclusions. I suspect the reactions you get don't have anything to do with how old you might be. You're Molahlu Crest's daughter. Even though he's gone, his reputation lingers. And it's got to hang on you like a shroud. People have to wonder if the wickedness is in the blood."

"Most people have never heard of Molahlu Crest."

I didn't answer that. If she wanted to believe it— which she did not for a moment—let her. It could be her way of coping with a difficult ancestry.

The Stormwarden's father (who had taken the name Styx Sabbat), and Molahlu Crest had clawed their ways up from the bottom of the Hill, the former riding a talent for sorcery, the latter an absence of conscience or compassion. A corduroy road of bodies was their route to the heart of the circles of power. They had been takers and breakers and killers, and the only good thing anyone ever said about either was that they had remained true friends from beginning to end. Neither greed nor hunger for power had come between them.

Which is something. How many friends do any of us have that we can count on forever?

Molahlu Crest, they say, had a small talent for sorcery himself, and that had made him doubly deadly. In the old days everyone in TunFaire was scared of him, from the richest and most powerful to the least of the waterfront bums. No one knows what happened to Molahlu Crest, but the conventional wisdom is that the Stormwarden Raver Styx got rid of him.

I wondered if Amiranda knew differently. After a while in my business, professional curiosity becomes habitual curiosity. Then you have to watch yourself so you don't stick your nose in everywhere.

You can get it mashed and have nothing to show for your trouble but a cauliflower schnoz.

We talked of light things and she began to relax. I splurged and ordered the TunFaire Gold with our meal. It helped.

It's a cynical device, but I have yet to encounter the woman who won't loosen up if you buy the Gold. The wine's reputation is such that your buying it makes them feel they're something special.

I like the Gold better than any other wine, but to me it is still spoiled grape juice with a winy taste. I'm a beer man born. I don't begin to pretend to understand wine snobs: to me even the best is nasty.

When the mood was better, I asked, "There been any more word from the kidnappers?"

"Not when I left. I think Domina would have let us know that much. Why are they waiting so long?"

"To get everybody so worried they'll do whatever it takes to get Junior back. Tell me about him. Is he really the kind of guy they say he is?"

Her expression became wary. "I don't know what they say about him. His name is Karl, not Junior."

I pecked at her from a couple directions. She gave me nothing.

"Why are you asking so many questions, Garrett? You did what you were paid for already, didn't you?"

"Sure. Just curiosity. It's an occupational hazard. I'll try not to be a nuisance."

I wondered about her. She was a woman with troubles, very much turned inward. Not my usual sort. But I found myself interested in her for her own sake. Odd.

The meal ended. She asked, "What now? Evil plans?"

"Me? Never. I'm one of the good guys. I know a guy who runs a place you might find interesting, since you're slumming. You want to give it a try?"

"I'm game for anything but going back to that . . ." She was trying to be pleasant company and to have a good time, but she was having to work at it. Thank heaven for TunFaire Gold to support my naturally irresistible charm.

*   *   *

Morley's place was jumping—as much as it ever does. Which means it was packed with dwarfs, elves, trolls, goblins, pixies, brownies, and whatnot, along with the curious specimens you get when you crossbreed the races. The boys looked at Amiranda with obvious approval and at me with equally obvious distaste. But I forgave them. I would be sullen and sour too if I was in a place where the drinks were nonalcoholic and the meals left out everything but the rabbit food.

I went straight to the bar, where I was known and my presence was tolerated. I asked the bartender, "Where's Morley?"

He indicated the stairs with a jerk of his head.

I went up. Amiranda followed, wary again. I pounded on Morley's door and he told me to come in. He knew it was me because there was a speaking tube running from the bar upstairs. We stepped inside.

For a rarity Morley did not have somebody's wife with him. He was doing accounts. He looked worried, but his beady little eyes lit up when he saw Amiranda.

"Down, boy. She's taken. Amiranda, this is Morley Dotes. He has three wives and nine kids, all of them locked up in the Bledsoe mad ward. He owns this dump and sometimes he acts like he's a friend of mine."

Morley Dotes was a lot more to those who knew the underside of the city. He was its top physical specialist, meaning for enough money he broke heads and arms, though he preferred ladies' hearts. He did that for free. He was half human, half dark elf, with the natural slightness and good looks of the latter. He wasn't what I would call a close friend. He was too dangerous to get close to. He had worked with and for me a few times.

"Don't you believe a word this thug tells you," Morley said. "He couldn't tell the truth if he got paid for it. And he's a dangerously violent psychotic. Just this afternoon he whipped up on a bunch of ogres who were minding their own business hanging out on the street smoking weed."

"You heard about that already?"

"News travels fast, Garrett."

"Know anything about it?"

"I figured you'd be around. I asked some questions. I don't know who hired the ogres. I know them. They're second-raters too lazy and stupid to do a job right. You might keep a watch out over your shoulder. You hurt a couple of them bad. The others might not consider that a simple hazard of the business."

"I have been watching. You could pay back a favor when we leave by taking a look at the guy who's following us."

"Somebody's following us?" Amiranda's question squeaked. She was frightened.

"He was with us from the Iron Liar here. He wasn't on me before that. Maybe he picked us up there. But the implication is that he was on you all along."

She got pale.

"Get her a chair, dope," Morley said. "You have the manners and sensitivity of a lizard."

I got her into a chair, not without a glare for Morley. The man was bird-dogging, making his points for the time Amiranda and I went our own ways. Not that I blamed him. I was developing the feeling that she was worth it. On mainly intuitive evidence I'd decided she was a class act.

"What are you into this time, Garrett?" Morley retreated to his chair, came up with a flash of brandy from somewhere behind his desk. He held it up questioningly. I nodded. He produced a single cup. He knew I preferred beer. He didn't touch alcohol himself. I was mildly surprised that he would have it in his place. For his ladies, I supposed.

I took the cup and passed it to Amiranda. She sipped. "I'm sorry. I'm being silly. I should have known it wouldn't be as simple as . . ."

Morley and I exchanged glances while pretending we hadn't heard her murmur. Morley asked, "Is it a secret, Garrett?"

"I don't know. Is it a secret, Amiranda? Might be worth telling him. It won't go any farther if that's what you want, and he might do you some good down the line." I raised a fist to Morley's smirk, silently cursing myself for that brilliant choice of words.

Amiranda pulled herself together. Not a girl for the traditional waterworks. I liked that. I was liking Amiranda more all the time. Damsels in distress were fine, and good for business, but I was tired of the kind who clung and whined. Much better the woman who got up on her hind legs and stood in there punching with you after she put you on the job.

Though in this case I didn't have a job, strictly speaking. I had a dispute with somebody who sent ogres around to thump on me.

Amiranda thought a bit and made a decision. She told the kidnapping story.

She told it so damned good I smelled a rat. She told Morley exactly what I knew, and not an iota more or less.

"It's not a pro job," Morley said. "Have you gotten yourself into something political, Garrett?"

Amiranda looked startled. "Why do you say that?"

"Two reasons. There's nothing shaking in the kidnapping business right now. And the pros wouldn't touch *that* family. Raver Styx may not look as nasty as her father and Molahlu Crest, but she is. In her own quiet way. Nobody who lives on the underside of TunFaire society would think the potential payoff worth the risk."

"Amateurs," I said.

"Amateurs with enough money to hire head crackers and tails, Garrett. That means uptown. And when uptown does dirty deeds, it's always political."

"Maybe. I'm not so sure. It don't have that stink. I'll wait before I make up my mind. There's something cock-eyed in the whole mess. But I can't see where the profit lies. That would clear it up. But I'm not on a job and looking. I'm just trying to watch out for me and Amiranda."

Morley said, "I'll peek in the closets and look under the beds and get back to you tomorrow. Least I can do after the stunt I pulled in that vampire business. You still living with the Dead Man?"

"Yeah."

"You're weird. Let me get back to work." He grabbed his end of the tube connecting with the bar. "Wedge. Send Blood and Sarge and the Puddle up here." I shepherded Amiranda toward the door.

"See you." We went down and out, easing past three high-class bone crushers headed up. I call them high-class because they looked smart enough to be trusted with work more intellectually demanding than skull busting.

My old buddy Saucerhead Tharpe had come in downstairs while we were up. He wanted me to join him for a pitcher of carrot's blood and some yakking up old times, but I begged off. We had to keep moving if Morley was going to do us any good.

I told Amiranda, "You ever feel like you need protecting, you come down here and hire Saucerhead Tharpe. He's the best there is."

"What about the other one? Morley? Do you trust him?"

"With my money or my life but never with my woman. It's getting late. I'd better get you home."

"I don't think I'm going home, Garrett. Unless you insist."

"All right." I do like a woman who can make up her mind, even though I may not understand what she is doing.

The Dead Man would have fits. But that was all right. What did he live for but to chew me out and to march his bugs around the walls?

Only one thing further about that night needs to be reported. When we were slipping into bed, I noted the absence of a gewgaw worn by every woman who doesn't want to hear little voices piping, "Mommy!"

"Where's your amulet?"

"You're a gentleman in your heart, aren't you, Garrett? Most men would have pretended not to notice."

I don't often get caught without something to say. This was one of those rare times. I kept my mouth shut.

She slipped in beside me, warm and bare, and whispered, "You don't have to worry. I can't make you a father."

And of that night nothing more need be said.

She was gone when I awoke the next morning. I never saw her again.

8

Morley himself stopped by to let me know what he'd learned. Old Dean let him in and brought him to the overconfident closet I call an office. I didn't rise and I didn't offer the usual banter. Dean went off to the kitchen to get Morley some of the apple juice we keep in the cold well against those millennial moments when I don't feel like having beer.

"You look glum, Garrett."

"It happens. The strain of being Mr. Smiles catches up."

"Well, you may have good reason. Even though you don't know it yet."

I showed him my eyebrow trick. He wasn't impressed. Everyone knows what familiarity breeds.

"I put out feelers that touched everybody in the snatch racket. Nobody has gone underground. Nobody is scoping out a job on the Hill. I got the personal guarantee of some of the best and the worst that there's nobody in this burg crazy enough to go for the Stormwarden's kid. Not for a million in gold. Gold don't do you any good when you're getting your toes roasted in the sorceress's basement."

"That's what's supposed to give me a sour puss?"

"No. You get that when I tell you about the guy who was tailing you last night. Or your lady, actually. You should have told me she was Amiranda Crest, Garrett. I wouldn't have made remarks about her father."

"She's used to it. What about the tail?"

"He trotted right down here after you, not even thinking somebody might be following him too. Fool. He hung around watching the place for a couple of hours. About the time even a moron would have figured out that she was spending the night he took off and headed—"

Dean stuck his head in through the doorway. "Excuse me, Mr. Garrett. There's a Mr. Slauce here to see you, representing somebody he calls the Domina Dount. Will you see him?"

"I can wait," Morley told me.

"Out that door." I indicated the closet's second exit, which opened on a hallway leading past the Dead Man's room. "Bring Mr. Slauce in, Dean."

Slauce was a blustery, potbellied, red-faced little man who was way out of his element. I think he had me pegged for a professional killer. He worked hard at being polite. It was obvious he wasn't accustomed to that.

"Mr. Garrett?"

I confessed that I was that very devil.

"Domina Dount would like to see you again. She said to tell you she's received another letter from her correspondent and would like further professional advice. I assume you understand what she means. She didn't explain to me."

"I know what she meant."

"She authorized me to offer you ten marks gold for your time."

I wondered what she really wanted. She was throwing one hell of a lot of money around. A laborer, if he got paid in a lump for the time, wouldn't draw ten marks gold for three months of his life.

And right now gold was strong because Glory Moon-called's successes in the Cantard had put several more silver mines into Karentine hands, meaning all their production came north.

Willa Dount might want to climb my leg about Amiranda. For ten marks I would take what she wanted to
hand out. There is never enough money around our
place because of the endless fix-ups.

"Leave word at the gate that I'm on my way. I'll be
there as soon as I take care of a few details and have
lunch."

Slauce's ruddy face got redder. The nerve of me! I was
supposed to frog when uptown said jump. He wanted to
drag me off by the heels. But his instructions held. "Very
well. I'm sure she would appreciate your taking as little
time as possible. She did seem distracted." He counted
five two-mark pieces onto my desk.

"I won't be more than a half hour behind you. Dean?
Will you see Mr. Slauce to the door?" We like to know
that our guests are out when they head out. Some of
them are so slow they might not remember which side
of the door they're supposed to be on when it shuts.

Morley returned to the room. "Better bite those things
to see if they're real, Garrett. Somebody's running a
game."

"How so?"

"That's the guy who was tailing your lady last night."

"Yeah? He looked taller in the dark."

"Maybe he was wearing platforms. I think it's time
you thought about getting out of this."

"I'm not in it."

"I know you, Garrett. You're going to get into it up
to your ears if you don't turn your back now."

Morley is usually not much shakes as a prophet. I paid
him no mind, thanking him and telling him the favor
was a chunk off the account he owed from the vampire
business. I saw him out, then let Dean serve me lunch.

Then I ambled off to earn my ten gold marks.

9

Willa Dount was piqued by my churlish failure to
bounce when she hollered but she hid it well. Everybody
but the Dead Man was hiding irritation with me. I decided I'd best keep my hands covering my pockets.

"Thank you for coming, Mr. Garrett."

"Your man said you'd heard from the kidnappers."

"Yes. Another letter. Delivered much like the first."
She passed it over.

The same hand, with the same poor spelling, told her
that Junior's market value was "200000 Markes gold."
Instructions for delivery would follow.

"Two hundred thou? The kid's in trouble, isn't he?
The Emperor himself might not go for that much."

"The sum can be raised, Mr. Garrett. It will be paid.
That isn't the problem."

"What is?"

"I face a twofold dilemma. Part is that I won't be
able to conceal an outlay of that magnitude from the
Stormwarden. That's my problem and I'll deal with her
displeasure when the time comes. She won't like the
expense but she would like to lose her son far less."

"I gather your own balance scale might not tilt the
same way."

"My opinions are of no moment, Mr. Garrett. This is

the Stormwarden's household and here the Stormwarden's will and whimsy alike are law."

"What do you need me for?"

"Advice on overcoming the mechanical difficulties of delivering that much gold."

"You'll need a big pocket to carry it."

"I'm paying handsomely for your time, Mr. Garrett. Don't waste it on witticisms. I have no sense of humor."

"If you say so."

"Two hundred thousand marks in coined gold weighs four thousand pounds. To move that much weight will require a heavy wagon and at least a four-horse team. Can they possibly expect me to get that someplace where the payoff can't be seen?"

"With a payoff that big they'd set it somewhere way out in the country, after running you along a route they could watch to make sure you aren't being followed."

"They will insist on coined gold; won't they? Bar would be easier for me to get together and handle but harder for them to dispose of. Right?"

"Probably."

"I thought so. I've already started exchanging our bar stock for coin. What else should I know?"

"Don't improvise. Do whatever they tell you, when they tell you. They'll be very nervous and likely to panic and do anything if they see one little thing going different from what they prescribed. If you've got to get some paybacks, wait till everybody is home safe. That much money will leave tracks. Bloody ones, probably."

"I'll worry about that when the time comes. Most probably it'll have to wait till the Stormwarden returns. Thank you, Mr. Garrett. Your expertise has confirmed the soundness of my own reasoning. I would say that we've had an amicable and productive relationship. But there is one thing you could do to make it perfect."

"What's that?"

"Stay away from Amiranda Crest."

"It's been twenty years since I let anybody pick my

friends, Domina. You're a sweetheart, but if I make an exception for you—"

"I'm not accustomed to disobedience."

"You ought to get out into the real world more. You'd get in practice real fast."

"Get out of here before I lose my temper."

I figured that was good advice. I headed for the door.

"Stay away from Amiranda."

I supposed Amiranda had gotten similar advice regarding Garrett.

I nearly trampled the Stormwarden's daughter Amber. I pulled the door shut behind me. "Eavesdropping?"

"She's right."

"About what?" Her ears were sharper than mine if she could make out anything through that door.

"You should forget Ami. I'm much more interesting."

In that instant I decided she was wrong. Amiranda Crest was a woman. This one wore a woman's body but the creature inside was spoiled, vain, snobbish, and probably not very bright. At a snap judgment. "We'll have to talk about it sometime."

"Soon, I hope."

I think I grunted.

"Let me know when."

Persistent little devil.

The office door opened. "What are you doing here, Amber?"

"Talking to Mr. Garrett."

Willa Dount put on a fierce scowl and pointed it my way. It was my fault that the women in the Stormwarden's house tracked me down. "Go back to your apartment, Amber. You know you aren't permitted in this wing."

"Stick your elbow in your ear, you old witch."

The Domina was absolutely astonished. I feared she would begin sputtering. But her footwork was good. "If you wish to contest my authority in your mother's absence, we'll refer the dispute to your father."

"Naturally. He'll say whatever you tell him to say, won't he?"

Domina Dount remained painfully aware of my presence. "Amber!"

"How did you get a hold on him? It can't be because you're a woman. You freeze bathwater when you sit in it."

"That will be quite enough, Amber."

"Excuse me, ladies. I never feel comfortable in these hen sessions. I'll just be running along."

If looks could kill. Domina Dount wanted me deaf to her humiliation. Amber wanted my support.

I walked. I watched for Amiranda, but there was no sign of her.

10

The Dead Man remained engrossed in his war games. He was feeble company at the best of times. When he was like this, with his genius totally committed, he was no company at all. I consoled myself with the suspicion that he was on to something overlooked by the commanders of the many armies in the Cantard. I was spared his irascibility, too.

Old Dean was worse company. Each meal came with its pitch for some deprived and homely female relative who, he hinted, had just the touch the house really needed. Amiranda did not come to visit as I'd hoped. After a few days of that I got to feeling wretchedly sorry for myself and decided to go spend my recent gains buying a few barrels of beer retail, for on-site consumption.

I couldn't get my heart into it. They ran me out of the first two places for doing nothing but taking up space while I nursed a single brew.

The kidnapping kept nagging me. I should have been happy to have my hundred ten marks for doing nothing. But I wasn't. There was a wrongness about the thing, the ring of bad crystal. Look at it as I might, though, I couldn't root out the source of the bad odor.

There wasn't much I could do about it. I didn't have a client. Nobody goes digging around on the Hill just to satisfy a personal curiosity. There was too much potential for pain and none at all for profit.

In the third bar, nearer home, they let me sit and brood. I'd done well by them in the past and would again. When the man sat down opposite me, I presumed they were trying to make the best use of table space. I didn't look at him till he growled, "Your name Garrett?"

I looked. He was a big one, broad, thirtyish, with the air of a tough and clothes you don't find anywhere but on the Hill. But no livery. A hired hand who did his work in the shadows. Nothing gave away who owned him. "Who wants to know?"

"I do."

"I got a feeling you and me aren't going to get along. I don't recall inviting you to sit."

"I don't need an invite from a crumb like you."

He was off the Hill for sure. Their heads swell when they get connected up there. "I know we're not going to be pals."

"Break my heart, smart boy."

"I was thinking more along the line of an arm or leg. What do you want, Bruno?"

Bruno is a derisive generic for a dumb pug. A quick glance around told me he had a couple of buddies along but they were too far away to give him a hand quickly. They were at the bar trying to blend in.

"Word is going around that you been hanging around Raver Styx's place. You got a rep for mixing in where you're not wanted. We want to know what you're up to."

"Who is we?" He was so rude he didn't answer, so I suggested, "Why don't you ask the Stormwarden?"

"I'm asking you, Garrett."

"You're wasting your time. Go away, Bruno. You're interfering with my drinking."

He jabbed a hand out and got hold of my left wrist, started to squeeze. He had a good grip but my right hand fell on his. I buried my thumb in the flesh just behind the root joints of his middle and forefingers. I pressed hard. His eyes got big and his face turned white. I smiled a friendly smile.

"All right, Bruno. You were just going to tell me who you work for and why you're down here trying to convince people that you're somebody scary."

"You go to hell, you cheap—unh!"

"You've got to learn to think before you speak. With a mouth like yours it's a miracle you've lived this long."

"Garrett, you're going to be sorry you were ever—unh!"

"They say pain is the fastest educator. In your case it looks like even that won't help. Yes?"

Someone had come to the table, approached unnoticed because I was watching Bruno's pals slowly develop the suspicion that all was not well with their buddy.

"Mr. Garrett?"

The daPenas were a polite bunch. "Junior. Have a seat. Bruno was just leaving." I let go his hand. He flexed it as he rose, trying to leave me with his best deadly look.

He wanted to pop me one, just to remember him by, but when he went to cock it, I let a foot fly under the table and got him in the shin. His eyes got big again, he made one little whimper of a sound, and decided to go away while he was still fit to limp.

"I see Domina Dount pulled it off and got you back in one piece."

"Yes."

"Congratulations on your good fortune. So how come you're down here slumming?"

The son was the image of the father without the marks of age and dissipation. How had the question of paternity risen? Maybe when he was a baby he hadn't looked so much like his immediate male ancestor. Those notions hang on forever.

"I wanted to thank you personally."

"Thank me? For what? I didn't do a damned thing." The kid had one of those apologetic, whiny voices that made you suspect he wanted to be excused for being alive.

"But you did. At least you appeared to. The kidnappers . . . I overheard them talking. They had somebody watching our place. When they saw you, they talked it over and decided they had to play the whole thing as straight as they could. Because of your reputation. So you see, I owe you a debt of thanks. I might not be here if you hadn't . . ."

In addition to his other charms Junior was a rocker. Whenever he spoke, he jerked back and forth, staring into space. It must have been a joy growing up in the Stormwarden's household.

I got a strong feeling that he had much more on his mind, that gratitude was just an excuse for seeking me out. But you don't have much luck pressing guys like him when you don't have a hold on them. They tend to break for cover. So I leaned back and tried to look pleased with his praise and interested in anything else he might want to tell me.

In a moment it was obvious he was working himself up to something. He started stammering. But he never got the chance to open up.

"Here you are, my lord." And here he was, the Domina's florid flunky, Slauce, wearing an ingratiating smile belied by eyes in which the humor had been extinct for years. "I've been looking everywhere."

I doubted that. He had to have been following Junior to pop up so quickly and inconveniently.

"Courter. I was just telling Mr. Garrett how grateful I am for his help." He rocked.

His eyes gave him away. He was terrified of this character Courter, who had used the name Slauce when he had visited me.

"The Domina needs you right away, my lord." A command cautiously couched for my benefit. Junior flinched.

Across the room Bruno and the boys had been huddled together for a while. Apparently they decided the presence of Junior and his keeper meant there was no more percentage for them there. They went away, though Bruno left me a final dirty look.

Junior got up and Courter took hold of his arm, not

heavy-handed but definitely like he thought his man might try to run. He passed close enough to trip. I thought about giving it a shot to see what would happen, but I left it as a thought.

"See you later, Karl."

His look of despair brightened as he took the notion seriously.

Courter looked at me for the only time during his visit. He had visions of bloodshed echoing through his eyes. I smiled and gave him a big friendly wink. It did nothing for his ulcer.

I gave it the old try but I couldn't get involved in my drinking. I held a caucus with myself, took a vote, and decided to go home and purge my soul by either subjecting it to the torment of old Dean's recitation of the encyclopedia of his eligible relatives, or simply dosing it with a generous helping of the Dead Man's poisonous humors.

They disappointed me. Both of them. I think they had discussed it while I was gone. Dean was whistling when I walked in. "What happened? Your females ambush a troop of hussars and take them prisoners for life?"

He was in too good a mood to take offense. I couldn't get a pout from him. I demanded, "What's going on around here? Why are you grinning like a fox with goosefeathers in his whiskers?"

"It's his nibs. He's ebullient. Exultant. Positively ecstatic."

"All that, huh? This I've got to see."

"It is one for the books, Mr. Garrett."

"What's that you're working on there?"

"A lamb roast."

"Lamb is mutton. I don't like mutton." I had more mutton than I ever wanted while I was in the Marines. We ate it every meal except when we had to make do with rocklike chunks of salt pork or circumstances forced us to eat our horses or, worse, we had to subsist on roots and berries.

"You'll like this. You'll see." He talked cooking technique.

I walked, grumbling, "Mutton is mutton is mutton," figuring I would have to eat the stuff with a big show of appreciation because whenever I get critical of Dean's cooking and he takes umbrage, the next meal is sure to include green peppers. There is no foodstuff in this or any other world quite so hideously nauseating as the green bell pepper. A pig—even a hungry pig—has better sense than to eat green peppers. But not people. It positively astounds me what people will eat.

In such a humor I shoved into the Dead Man's room.

Ah. Garrett. Good afternoon. Good of you to stop in. How is that kidnapping business going?

"The kid came home in one piece." I stepped out of the room, looked around, stepped back inside.

Congratulations. A job well done. You will have to tell me all about it. What was that little dance step?

"Just making sure I was in the right house with the right Dead Man. No Congrats due. I didn't have anything to do with it." I went ahead and brought him up to date, leaving out none of the details but Amiranda's overnight vacation from the household of the Stormwarden.

An interesting situation, infested with anomalies. Almost a pity you have no concern in it. A challenge to crack its shell and lay open the meat within.

"Feeling our genius today, are we?"

Indeed. Yes indeed. The mystery of the magic of Glory Mooncalled is a mystery no more. Subject to observational confirmation, of course.

"You figured out how he does it? When the Venageti War Council can't do better than stumble over their own feet?"

Indeed.

"How?"

Ratiocination, my boy.

My boy? He *was* in a mood to crow.

Cogitation. Induction. Deduction. Repeated experiment manipulating the possible course of events within the known parameters. And from this came a hypothesis bearing the weight of near certainty. I know how Glory Mooncalled did what he did, and with just a bit more information I could predict with some degree of certainty what he will do next.

"So how does he do it? Does he turn invisible? Does he run through secret tunnels to sneak up and sneak away?"

I have to reserve the how for now, Garrett. The hypothesis is insufficiently tested, based as it is on one assumption not yet validated. A bit more observation should confirm it, though, and you will be the first to know.

"No doubt." He would crow like a herd of roosters watching three suns rising. If he was not already. "Why don't you—"

"Mr. Garrett?" Dean had his head in the doorway. "Excuse me. There's a young woman here to see you."

His nose was up and his choice of the word "woman" over "lady" told me he thought her a floozy and probably some playmate of mine not nearly as worthy of me as any one of a dozen of his nieces.

"Who is she?"

"She wouldn't say. She seemed perfectly familiar with you, though." Again with the nose up.

I excused myself and headed for the door expecting Amiranda. *They just can't stay away from you, Garrett.*

It was Amber. She gave me her big teasing smile as I let her in. Dean had instructions to let no one in without consulting me or the Dead Man first.

I scanned the street as Amber brushed past. I didn't see Courter Slauce but assumed he was out there watching.

Amber did some posing, showing off her best features, of which she had several. "Aren't you dressed for the kill today? What's the occasion?" I gave the street another scan. Nothing. But women from the Hill don't wander my end of town unchaperoned. Not unless they're so severely unaware of personal danger that the bad guys shy off as if they were holy madmen.

"A hunt. Of sorts." She did have a promising smile.

"I see. How old are you, Amber?"

"Twenty." She lied. My immediate guess was eighteen going on thirty.

"Uhn. This way." I stalled for time while I led her to my office. There is a side of me that is very fond of women. There is also a side that's wary of those who bring gifts without being asked. When they stand near a center of power and are as changeable and spoiled as this one probably was, I want to play it very carefully. I thought I saw a way.

"I'm a charming scamp, I know. Hurt me to the quick though it does, I'm old enough, plain enough, and poor enough to suspect that maybe my profession has more to do with you being here."

"Maybe." She went on trying to flirt. I had a bad feeling she might be one of those who couldn't deal with a man until she proved to herself she could lead him around by his hopes and fantasies. That kind regards consummation as something to avoid at all costs. She was young but she knew her men well enough to know actually giving in would dilute her power.

I assumed she was playing that game, so I did my best to let her think she might get what she wanted without stretching her virtue.

She did appeal. A whole damned lot. But I'll have to know a Stormwarden's daughter a lot better before I take the risks inherent in such a situation.

"There is one thing you could do," she admitted. "But that can wait. Don't you feel crowded in here? Isn't there somewhere else? That old man could walk in anytime."

At which point I made the mistake of sitting down. My sitter was barely in place when a hundred pounds of potential parked *her* sitter on my lap.

So much for Garrett's infallible estimates of members of the female species.

She had me going for a minute—until she giggled. I don't like my women to giggle. It makes me doubt their maturity.

Still, when the culprit is sitting on your lap, wagging her tail . . .

"Mr. Garrett." It was that old man. "Mr. Dotes is here. He says it's important."

Saved!

Damn it.

11

"Do you have to, Garrett?"

"You don't know Morley Dotes. If he comes here, it's important."

I had Amber about half pried loose when Dotes blew in. He stopped and gawked, then that sparkle flashed in his eye. I'm going to throw pepper in there someday just to get tears to wash it out.

"Down, boy. What's going on?"

Amber made a show of neatening herself up. I guess she knew she had it and couldn't help flaunting it.

"Your pal Saucerhead. He's in the Bledsoe carved up bad enough to kill a mammoth."

"Bound to happen in his line of work." Which was pretty much the same as Morley's less public line, so he gave me a sour look when he could steal a second from appreciating Amber. "How did it happen?"

"Don't have much yet. He staggered in from somewhere way the hell out in the country. They say he shouldn't have made it, but you know him. Too stubborn and stupid to die. They don't think he'll make it."

"Who does, down there? What the hell was he doing out in the boondocks?"

Morley gave me a funny look. "I thought you'd know. He left the place early last night because he had a job. Said you recommended him."

"Me? I never . . . Oh. Damn. I'd better get down there." I had butterflies the size of horses. Amiranda. Had to be.

"I'll stroll along with you, then. I haven't had my exercise today." Far be it from Morley Dotes to admit he had a friend anywhere in the known universe.

As he turned to leave, Amber whispered, "Wait, Garrett." The music was out of her voice.

"Is it critical?"

"To me it is."

"Wait for me at the front door, Morley. So. Tell me."

"My brother came home this morning. They let him go."

"Good for him."

"That means Domina paid the ransom."

"Seems likely. So?"

"So there's two hundred thousand gold marks out there somewhere that belong to my family, that somebody couldn't yell about if it got taken away. Do you think you could find it?"

"Maybe. If I wanted to bad enough. A chunk like that, in the hands of amateurs, would leave a trail like a rogue mammoth. The trick would be getting to it before all the other sharpshooters in town."

"Help me find it, Garrett. You can have half."

"Whoa, girl. That's asking for big trouble with no guarantee of any—"

"This may be my first, last, and only chance to make a hit big enough to get away from my mother. If I could get that money before she comes home, I could disappear so thoroughly she couldn't find me with an army. You could do pretty good with a hundred thousand, too."

"That I could. That I could."

She posed. "And there are ancillary benefits, too."

"Yes. Yes indeed. I'll need some time to think about what I'd need and what I'd have to do. In the meantime, I've got a friend in the infirmary trying to die. I want to see him before he goes."

"Sure." She didn't sound thrilled to hear about obligations imposed by friendship. "I'll come back tomorrow if I can get away from Courter and his bullies. Next day for sure. Maybe you could give that old man the day off." She turned on the smile.

"Maybe I'll think about that too."

She giggled. "You do that."

I patted her fanny. "Come on. Off with you. My friend Morley will be getting impatient." I followed her to the front door. There is nothing I can say to disparage the view from that perspective.

Dean was waiting to bolt up after me, which meant he had been eavesdropping again. I shot him an ugly glare, but it ricocheted like water off the proverbial duck.

Morley was waiting outside. While I stood listening to Dean shoot the bolts, we appreciated Amber's departure.

"Where do you find them, Garrett?"

"I don't. They find me."

"Bull feathers."

"It's true. I just sit here like a big old trapdoor spider and nab them when they walk by. Then I turn on the Garrett charm and they swoon into my arms."

"That one is no swooner, Garrett. The one the other night wasn't, either. High Hill fluff, both of them. Right?"

"Off the Hill. I wouldn't call them fluff."

"No. Probably not." He sighed. "Why doesn't something like that ever turn up at my place?"

"You're doing all right from what I see. Don't get your heart set on this one. You'd be asking for a visit from the whirlwind. Her mother is a Stormwarden."

"Another dream shattered by bitter reality. Still, it's a pity. A pity—that's sweet. Let's go see Saucerhead and find out which way to lay our bets."

12

The Bledsoe infirmary is an imperial charity, meaning it's supposed to provide medical care for the indigent. If you're in the place, though, your chances improve a hell of a lot if you or a friend happen to come up with some cash. Human nature, I guess. I'm not always the biggest fan of my own species.

They weren't going to let me near Saucerhead at first. He was supposedly in real bad shape and would be checking out very soon. Then somebody saw the flash of gold between my fingers and heard a hint or two about metal changing hands if the prognosis improved, and first thing you knew the whole infirmary had a new attitude. Zip! Morley and I were in Saucerhead's ward watching a gang of physicians and healers do their stuff.

Saucerhead looked terrible when they started, paper pale after losing what appeared to be several gallons of blood. He didn't look much better when they finished, but his breathing was steadier, less inclined to the characteristic sighs. I scattered a few marks and showed that I had a few more that might want to keep the others company.

Saucerhead didn't do anything but breathe for a couple of hours. Good enough by me. That put us a few points up on Death.

Morley spoke only once the entire time we were waiting, in a tiny whisper. "If I ever get so desperate I come in here, you come cut my throat and put me out of my misery." The remark illuminated the side of Morley Dotes with a morbid dread of sickness. After this visit he would be on double rations, stoking up on green leafies and whatnot, for weeks.

Not that the Bledsoe was *anybody's* idea of heaven. One look around was enough to curdle a vampire's bones. And this was just a ward to die in. The insane wards are supposed to be ripped straight out of the dungeons of hell.

I couldn't figure why Saucerhead had picked the Bledsoe. He was no tycoon but he wasn't a pauper, either.

We saw only one other vertical human being after the staff left, a priest who was probably the only decent human being working the Bledsoe. I knew him vaguely. He was one of the bigger names in one of the more obscure and bizarre of the several hundred cults hagriding TunFaire. He came over and stared down at the huge slab of muscle that was Saucerhead Tharpe. There was a nobility about Tharpe even in his extremity. It recalled the nobility of the lion or the mammoth. A good guy to have on your side, a bad guy to have for an enemy, simple, trustworthy, and as tough as they make them.

"Has he had his rites?"

"I don't know, Father."

"What gods did he have?"

I put temptation aside. "None that I know about. But we don't need sacraments. This is a life watch, not a deathwatch. He's going to make it."

The priest checked the name chalked on the wall above the head of Saucerhead's cot. "I'll say a prayer for him." Small smile. "It never hurts, even with a sure thing." He went on to those who needed him more, leaving me with the suspicion I had been one-upped.

Saucerhead must have been awake awhile before he let us know. His first remark, a hoarse croak, was, "Garrett, remind me to stay the hell away from your women."

I grunted and waited.

"Getting that one out of the Cantard got me half killed. I thought this one did me all the way."

"Yeah. What the hell did you come *here* for? If you had go-power enough to make it this far, you could have got yourself to somebody who could have done you some good."

"I was born here, Garrett. I had it in my head I was done for and it seemed right it should end up where it started. I guess I wasn't thinking too good."

"Yeah. You big dumb goof. Well, you're going to make it in spite of yourself and these jackals. You got enough energy to tell me what happened?"

"Yeah." His face darkened.

"So? What happened?"

"She's dead, Garrett! They killed her. I got five or six of them but they was too many and they got past me and cut her . . ." And he started by god getting up off that cot.

"Hold him down, Morley. What the hell are you doing, Saucerhead?"

"I got to go. I never blowed a job like that before, Garrett. Never."

Morley put him back down with one hand. Saucerhead was running on spirit alone.

There were tears in his eyes. "She was just a little bit of a thing, Garrett. Sweet as a sugar bun and cute as a button. They shouldn't ought to have done that to her."

"You're right. They shouldn't have." Part of me had known the worst all along, but the part that wishes and hopes was just getting the word.

Saucerhead tried getting up again. "I gotta, Garrett."

"You gotta heal up. I'll take care of the rest. I've got an interest that came before yours. After you give me everything you've got, Morley is going to get you out of here and take you wherever you want to stay. And I'm going headhunting."

Morley gave me a look. He didn't say anything. He didn't have to.

"Don't you start playing devil's advocate, Morley

Dotes, telling me there's no percentage in getting involved. You'd do the same damned thing even if you dressed it up as something else. Come on, Saucerhead. Give it to me. Start from the beginning, the first time you laid eyes on her."

Saucerhead may not be speedy mentally, but his mind gets where it needs to go. And he sees what goes on around him and remembers it.

"The first time I seen her was with you at Morley's place. I thought to myself, How come a runt like Morley Dotes or a homely geek like Garrett always comes up with all the jewels?"

"He isn't dying," I said. "A sick sense of humor is the first thing that comes back. Imagine. Calling me homely. Never mind that night, Saucerhead. When did you see her again?"

"Yesterday afternoon. She tracked me down at my place."

She found him there and told him that I'd recommended him for any bodyguarding she needed done. She had a thing she wanted to do that night but she was nervous and scared and even though she was sure there would be no trouble, she thought it wouldn't hurt to have somebody along. Just in case. Just to make her more comfortable. After Saucerhead agreed to stick with her until she felt she didn't need him anymore. She went away until shortly before dusk, when she came back with a small open carriage.

"She have anything with her?"

"Bunch of cases in the back. The kind women stuff with clothes and things. She wasn't planning on coming back."

"Uhm. She say anything about what she was doing?"

That was the only time he was a little uncertain about what he ought to tell. He decided I needed everything. "She never said what she was up to. But she was going to meet somebody. And she wasn't planning on coming back."

"Then if you hadn't been along, she would've disappeared and nobody would've known what really hap-

pened." Gods. I blind myself with my own brilliance
sometimes.

"Yeah. You going to let me tell it? Or should I catch
a nap while you're jacking your jaw?"

"One more thing, then you can get on. Your payment.
How and when?"

"Up front. I always make them pay up front . . . well,
I almost made an exception for her. I took every coin
she had, and then she was still half a mark short. I forgave her that and told her she should hold out part of
the fee so she wouldn't short herself. But she said there
was no problem, and when we got where we were going,
I'd get my other half mark and maybe a nice bonus for
being such a sweetheart."

"Yeah. That's Saucerhead Tharpe all over. A real
sweetheart. All right. Go on."

They had moved out in the twilight, Saucerhead on
horseback behind the carriage. He was lightly armed,
but that wasn't unusual. He preferred to rely on his
strength and speed. I didn't have to ask if he had seen
anyone watching or following. He was looking for that
and saw nothing. They left the city after dark and
headed north at a leisurely pace, not doing any fancy
switchbacking, not hurrying, and not drawing any special
attention. Because he rode behind the buggy most of the
way, they didn't talk much. But there was a three-
quarter moon and a clear sky, and he was able to tell
she was getting more worried and nervous as the night
wore on. She was thoughtful of him and the animals,
pausing for several rests.

About three in the morning they came to a woodland
crossroad a couple miles from the famous old battleground at Lichfield, where some say the old imperial
bones still sometimes get up and stalk around in search
of the man who betrayed their commander.

As is customary at important crossroads, there was a
central grass diamond with its tutelary obelisk. Amiranda stopped next to the obelisk where her team could
crop grass. She told Saucerhead they would wait there.

As soon as the person she was meeting showed, he could head back to TunFaire.

Saucerhead dismounted. After working the kinks out he just stood leaning against the buggy, waiting. Amiranda had little to say. An hour dragged past. She became more worried by the minute. Saucerhead's feeble attempts to reassure her foundered on his ignorance. She believed her worst fears were coming true.

The moon was about to depart the heavens and the east was lightening when Saucerhead realized they were no longer alone. An absence of the gossip of birds awakening tipped him off. He just had time to warn Amiranda before they charged out of the woods.

The moment he saw them he knew they weren't just road agents.

"There was at least fifteen of them, Garrett. Ogres. Some of them with the pure blood, like you don't hardly never see no more. They had knives and sharp sticks and clubs and big bones and you could tell they was bent on murder. They was cussing in ogrish on account of me being there. They wasn't expecting me."

Saucerhead wasn't clear himself on how it went after that, except that he got himself between the ogres and Amiranda, with his back against the buggy, and went to work with a knife and club of his own, and when he lost those, with bare hands and brute strength.

"I killed five or six, but there just ain't a whole lot any one man can do when he's outnumbered so bad. They just kept piling on me and hitting and cutting me. That girl, she didn't have enough sense to run. She tried to fight, too. But they dragged her down and cut on her . . . I thought I whipped them for a minute 'cause they all ran off. To the edge of the woods. But then I went down and couldn't get up again. Couldn't even move. They thought I was dead. They dragged me over and dumped me in the brush, then they dragged everyone else over, then they started going through the girl's stuff, cussing 'cause there wasn't nothing worth nothing, but they squabbled like sparrows over every piece anyway. And not once even thinking about helping their buddies that was hurt."

Then they heard someone coming. They scurried around cleaning up after themselves, then took off down the road with the buggy and Saucerhead's horse.

About that time Saucerhead got himself together enough to get on his feet. He found Amiranda, scooped her up, and headed out.

"I wasn't thinking so good," he said. "I didn't want her to be dead so I didn't believe it. There's this witch I know that lives about three miles from there, back in the woods. I told myself if I could get the girl to her everything would be all right. And you know me. I get my mind set . . ."

Yeah. I tried to picture it. Saucerhead half dead, still bleeding, stumbling through the woods carrying a dead woman. And after that, he walked all the way back to TunFaire so he'd be in the right place when he died.

I asked a lot of questions then, mostly about the ogres and what they'd said when they'd thought him dead. He hadn't heard anything I could use. I got directions to the witch's hut.

Saucerhead was getting weaker then, but he was working himself up again. I told him, "You just relax. If I don't get it straightened out, you can take over when you're well again. Morley, I want you to get him out of here. Come on. Morley will be back to get you, Saucerhead."

Morley finally spoke when we hit the street. "Nasty business."

"You heard of anybody getting rich since yesterday?"

"No." He gave me a look.

"Got any contacts in Ogre town?" If you aren't part ogre, you can't get the time of day down there. I had a couple of people I knew there but none I knew well enough to get any help on this.

"A few. But not anybody who'll tell me anything about a deal that has Raver Styx on the other end of it."

"That's my problem."

"You going out there to look around?"

"Maybe tomorrow. Got some loose ends to knot up around here first."

"Use some company when you go? I'm way behind on my exercise."

He pretended he was interested in anything but what interested him. "I don't think so. And somebody has to stay here and keep reminding Saucerhead that he's hurt."

"It got personal, eh?"

"Very."

"You be careful out there."

"Damned right I will. And you keep your ears open. I'm interested in news about ogres and news about anybody with a sudden pocketful of gold."

We parted. I went home and wrapped myself around a couple gallons of beer.

13

The Dead Man's mood hadn't soured by the next morning. I got worried. Were we getting to the beginning of the end? I didn't know enough about the Loghyr to be sure what sort of symptom persistent good humor might be. I told him about Saucerhead, leaving out none of the details. "That give you any ideas?"

Several. But you have not given me enough information to form more than one definite opinion.

"A definite one? You? What is it?"

Your little overnight treat was involved up to her cute little ears in the kidnapping of the Stormwarden's son. If not a part of the conspiracy itself, she did at least have guilty knowledge.

I didn't argue. I had formed that suspicion myself. It was good to know I had a mind nearly as agile as his, if not so absolute in its decisions. But him being a genius exempts him from the doubts plaguing us mere mortals.

"Would you care to run through your reasoning?"

It would appear simple and obvious enough for even one of your narrow intellectual focus to unravel.

I gave him a big grin. That was his way of zinging me for having dared entertain overnight in my own home. He couldn't shake his good humor completely, though.

He added, *Troublesome as females are when they step*

out of their proper roles as connivers, manipulators, gossips, backstabbers, and bearers and nurturers of the young, slaughtering them is not an acceptable form of chastisement. I urge you to persist in your inquiries, Garrett. With all due caution. I would not care to see you share the woman's fate. How would I attend the funeral?

"You're just a sentimental fool, aren't you?"

Too often too much so for my own welfare.

"Ha! Dirty truth gets caught with its nose sticking out. If I get scrubbed, you might have to get off your mental duff and do some honest geniusing in order to keep a roof over your head."

I am an artist, Garrett. I do not—

"And I'm a frog prince under a witch's spell."

"Mr. Garrett?"

I turned. Dean was at the door. "What?"

"That woman is here again."

"The one who was here yesterday?"

"The same." You would have thought he smelled spoiled onions in his pantry the way his face was puckered.

"Take her into the office. Don't let her touch you. It might be communicable." I let him get out of hearing before adding, "You might carry it to your nieces and suddenly have them all turn desirable."

You ride him too hard, Garrett. He is a sensitive man with an abiding concern for his loved ones.

"I let him get out of hearing, didn't I?"

I would not want to lose him.

"Me neither. I'd have to go back to cleaning up after you myself." I got out then, ignoring him trying to come up with the last word. We could kill a whole day that way.

Amber was looking her best and sensed that I saw and felt it. She tried starting up where she left off. I told her, "I've decided to find that money for you. I think we're going to have to stick to business and move damned fast if we want to catch the trail before it's cold.

I did a lot of legwork yesterday, poking under rocks. I came up with a sack full of air. I'm starting to think the whole thing was an out-of-town operation."

"Garrett!" She wanted to play. But she could accept two hundred thousand marks gold as a good reason for not, for the moment. I figured her for the type who could get hooked on the challenge. That might be my next problem.

"What do you mean, out-of-town operation?"

"Like I said yesterday, a thing involving two hundred thousand and snatching Raver Styx's kid is going to take big planning and leave big tracks, even when the best pros are working the job. One way to give the tracks a chance to disappear in the mud is to do your design work, recruiting, purchasing, and rehearsal somewhere far away. Then you might take the gold somewhere else, still. In fact, with so much gold involved, you might want to tie up loose ends by erasing any connection between yourself and the kidnap victim."

"You mean kill off the people who helped you?"

"Yes."

"That's horrible. That's . . . that's terrible."

"It's a terrible world. With a lot of terrible people in it. Not to mention things like ogres and ghouls. Or vampires and wolfmen, who see the rest of us as prey, though they used to be human themselves."

"It's horrible."

"Of course. But it's the kind of thing we may run into. You still game? We're partners, you're going to have to carry your half of the load."

"Me? How can I help?"

"You can get me a chance to talk to your brother and Amiranda."

She looked puzzled. Not too bright, my Amber? But decorative. Definitely decorative. "I haven't dug up but one clue yet, and it's not worth squat by itself."

"What is it?"

"Uh-uh. I keep my cards to my chest till I get a better picture."

"Why do you need to talk to Karl and Amiranda?"

"Karl because he's the only one who had any direct contact with the kidnappers—except maybe Domina Dount, when she delivered the ransom. Amiranda because she works for the Domina and might have picked up something useful. I can't go grill Willa Dount. She'd want the gold back herself if she knew we were looking for it. Wouldn't she?"

"Yeah. But Karl would want a cut if he knew what we were doing. He wants out of that house as bad as I do. Amiranda, the same way."

"You get me a chance to talk to them. I'll think of some reason for it."

"All right. But you'd better be careful. Especially with Amiranda. She's a little witch."

"You don't like her?"

"Not very much. She's smarter than me and when she wants she can make herself almost as pretty. Even my own mother always treats her better than me. But I don't think I hate her. I just wish she'd go away."

"And she wants to get away as badly as you and your brother do? When she gets better treatment?"

"Better than awful is still bad, Garrett."

"How soon can you fix it so I can see Karl?"

"It'll be hard. He won't be able to sneak out right now. Domina has Courter watching him every minute. She says the kidnapping won't stay a secret and when the news gets out how much the ransom was, somebody else might try it again. Would they?"

"That happens. There are a lot of lazy, stupid crooks who try to get by imitating success. Your family will be at risk till your mother takes some action to make it plain that folks who mess with her live short and awful lives."

"She probably wouldn't even care."

She would care even if she had no use or love for her offspring, but I had no inclination to illuminate Amber about the symbols and trappings of power and what the powerful have to do to keep them polished and frightening. "The next step has to be your brother. If he can't come to me, I'll go to him. You arrange something. I'll follow you home about a half hour behind you. I'll hang around outside somewhere. You give me a signal when it's all right to come in. Might as well set it for me to see Amiranda, too. What will the signal be?"

I had chosen a conspiratorial tone. It worked. She got into the spirit of doings shadowed and sinister. "I'll flash a mirror out my window. Give me five minutes after that, then meet me at the postern."

"Which window?"

While she explained, I reflected that she had this gimmick too pat to have come up with it on the spur of the moment. I hoped it was a device she used to sneak lovers inside. If she had been getting away with that, the notion might be marginally workable. If she was setting me up . . .

But she had no reason that I could see. It was plain that her only interest was laying hands on her mother's gold.

You get paranoid in this business. But maybe paranoids get that way because of all the people out to get them.

"Better scoot along now," I told her. "Before they miss you up there and start wondering."

"A half hour wouldn't make any difference, would it?"

"A half hour might make all the difference."

"I can get real stubborn when I really want something, Garrett."

"I'll bet you can. I hope you're as stubborn about the gold if we find things getting tight." I guided her toward the front door.

"Tight? How could it get dangerous?"

"Are you kidding? Not to be melodramatic"—like hell!—"but it could get to be a long, dark, narrow valley between your mother and the kidnappers before we get that gold socked away."

She looked at me with big eyes while that sank in. Then she turned on the smile. "Keep that golden carrot dangling out front and this mule won't even see the brooding hills."

So. A little slow, maybe, but gutsy.

Old Dean was watching from down the hall, exercising his disapproving scowl. I patted Amber on the fanny. "That's the spirit, kid. Remember. I'm half an hour behind you. Try not to leave me standing in the street too long."

She spun around and laid a kiss on me that must have curled Dean's hair and toes. It did mine. She backed off, winked, and scooted.

14

I went back and got a big cold one to fortify myself for the coming campaign. I had to draw it myself. Dean had been stricken blind and could hear nothing but ghosts. He was exasperated with me.

I downed the long one, drew another, lowered the keg, then went to tell the Dead Man the latest. He growled and snarled a little, just to make me feel at home. I asked if he was ready to reveal Glory Mooncalled's secrets. He told me no, and get out, and I left suspecting cracks had appeared in his hypothesis. A cracked hypothesis can be lethal to the Loghyr ego.

After depositing my empty mug in the kitchen, I went upstairs and rooted through the closet that serves as the household arsenal, selected a few inconspicuous pieces of steel and a lead-weighted, leather-wrapped truncheon that had served me well in the past. With a warning to Dean to lock up after the ghosts left, I hit the street.

It was a nice day if one doesn't mind an inconsistent hovering between mist and drizzle. Comes with the time of year. The grape growers like it except when they don't. If they had their way, every stormwarden in the business would be employed full-time making fine adjustments in weather so they could maximize the premium of their vintages.

* * *

I was moist and crabby by the time I reached the Hill and started looking for a place to lurk. But the neighborhood had been designed with the inconsiderate notion that lurkers should not be welcome, so I had to hoof it up and down and around, hanging out in one small area trying to look like I belonged there. I told myself I was a pavement inspector and went to work detecting every defect in the lay of those stones. After fifteen minutes that lasted a day and a half, I caught Amber's signal—a candle instead of a mirror—and started drifting toward the postern. A day later that opened and Amber peeked out.

"Not a minute too soon, sweetheart. Here come the dragoons."

The folks on the Hill all tip into a community pot to hire a band of thugs whose task is to spare the Hill folk the discomfitures and embarrassments of the banditry we who live closer to the river have to accept as a fact of life, like dismal weather.

Not fooled for a minute by my romance with the cobblestones, a pair of those luggers were headed my way under full sail. They had been on the job too long. Their beams were as broad as their heights. But they meant business and I wasn't interested in getting into a head-knocking contest with guys who had merely to blow a whistle to conjure up more arguments for their side.

I got through the postern and left them with their meat hooks clamped on nothing but a peel of Amber's laughter. "That's Meenie and Moe. They're brothers. Eenie and Minie must have been circling in on you from the other side. We used to tease them terribly when we were kids."

A couple of remarks occurred to me, but with manly fortitude I kept them behind my teeth.

Amber led me through a maze of servants' passages, chattering brightly about how she and Karl used the corridors to elude Willa Dount's vigilance. Again I restrained myself from commenting.

We had to go up a flight and this way and that, part through passages no longer in use, or at least immune to cleaning. Then Amber shushed me while she peeked between hangings into a hallway for regular people with real blue blood in their veins. "Nobody around. Hurry." She dashed.

I trotted along behind dutifully, appreciating the view. I've never understood those cultures where they make the women walk three paces behind the man. Or maybe I do. There are more of them around arranged like Willa Dount than there are like Amber.

She swept me through a doorway into an empty room and rolled right around with her arms reaching. I caught her by the waist. "Tricked me, eh?"

"No. He'll be here in a minute. He has to get away. Meantime, you know the old saying."

"I live with a dead Loghyr. I hear a lot of old sayings, some of them so hoary the hills blush with embarrassment at his flair for cliché. Which old saying did you have in mind?"

"The one about all work and no play makes Garrett a dull boy."

I should have guessed.

She was determined to wear me down. And she was getting the job done.

Whump! The edge of the door got me as I was bending forward, contemplating yielding to temptation.

The story of my life.

I let my momentum carry me several steps out of orbit around Amber. She laughed.

Karl came into the room spouting apologies and turning red. He might have gone into a hand-wringing act if he had not had them loaded.

"I smell brew," I said. "The elixer of the gods."

"I recalled you were drinking beer in that place the other day. I thought it would be only courteous to provide refreshments, and so I . . ."

A chatterer.

I was amazed. Not only had he managed to come up with an idea of his own, he had managed to carry it out by himself, without so much as a servant to lug the tray.

Maybe he did have a little of his grandfather in him after all. A thimbleful, or so.

He presented me with a capacious mug. I went to work on it. He nibbled the foam on a smaller one, just to show me what a democratic fellow he was. "Why did you want to talk to me, Mr. Garrett? I couldn't make much sense out of what Amber told me."

"I want to satisfy my professional curiosity. Your kidnapping was the most unusual one I've ever encountered. For my own benefit I want to study its ins and outs in case I ever get into a similar situation. The success of the kidnappers might encourage somebody to pull the same stunt again."

Karl looked very uncomfortable. He planted himself on a chair and gripped his mug in both hands. He pressed it into his lap in hopes of steadying it so I wouldn't notice it was shaking. I let him think he had me fooled.

"But what can I tell you that would be of any use, Mr. Garrett?"

"Everything. From the beginning. Where and how they laid hands on you. All the way through to the end. Where and how they turned you loose. I'll try not to interrupt unless you lose me. All right?" I took a long swig. "Good stuff."

Karl bobbed his head. He took a swig of his own. Amber sidled to the tray and discovered that Karl had brought wine, too, though he hadn't bothered to offer her any.

Junior said, "It started five or six nights ago. Right, Amber?"

"Don't look at me. I still wouldn't know about it if I didn't eavesdrop."

"Six nights ago, I guess. I spent the evening with a friend." He thought about it before telling me, "At a place called Half the Moon."

"That's a house of ill repute," Amber said, in case I didn't know.

"I've heard of it. Go on. They got you there?"

"As I was leaving. Going out the back way so nobody would see me."

That didn't sound like the behavior of the hell-raiser he was supposed to be. "Why the sneak? I thought that wasn't your style."

"So Domina wouldn't hear about it. I was supposed to be out working."

That puzzled me. "The word is that she has everyone on a tight leash while your mother is in the Cantard. Yet you two seem to come and go when you want."

"Not when we want," Amber said. "When we can. Courter and Domina can't be everywhere watching all the time."

"I thought you said you wouldn't interrupt, Mr. Garrett."

"So I did. Go on. When last seen you were making a getaway out the back door of Lettie Faren's place."

"Yes. I stopped to say good night to someone, right in the doorway, with my back to the outside. Somebody put a leather sack over my head. It must have had a drawstring sort of thing on it because before I could yell I was being strangled. I was scared to death. I knew I was being murdered and there wasn't any way I could stop it. And then the lights went out." He shivered.

I set my mug down. "Who were you saying good-bye to?" I tried to keep it casual but he wasn't a complete dummy. He didn't answer. I stared him straight in the eye. He looked away.

"He doesn't want to believe it," Amber said.

"What's that?"

"That his favorite little tidbit was in on it. She had to be didn't she? I mean, she would have seen whoever it was over his shoulder. Wouldn't she? And she would have had time to warn him if she wasn't part of it?"

"That's certainly worth a few questions. Does the lady have a name?"

Amber looked at Karl. He tried divining the future from the lees of his beer. Maybe he didn't like what he saw. He grabbed the pitcher off the tray and poured himself a refill, mumbling something as he did so.

I collected the pitcher and pursued his fine example. "What was that?"

"He said her name is Donni Pell."

Put a point down for the kid. If she had wanted, she could have stuck it to him anytime, but she held back until he was ready to surrender the name himself.

Karl started working himself up a case of the miseries. He said, "I can't believe Donni was in on what . . . I've known her for four years. She just wouldn't . . ."

I reserved my opinion of what people in Donni's line would and would not do for money. "All right. Let's move on. You were strangled unconscious. When and where did you wake up?"

"I'm not sure. It was nighttime and in the country. I think. From what sounds I could hear. I was bound hand and foot and still had the bag over my head. I think I was inside a closed coach of some kind but I can't be sure. That would make sense, though, wouldn't it?"

"For them it would. What else?"

"I had a bad headache."

"That follows. Go on."

"They got me where they were taking me, which turned out to be an abandoned farmhouse of some sort."

I urged him to get very detailed. It was in moments of transfer when kidnappers were most at risk of betraying themselves.

"They lifted me out of the coach. Somebody cut the ropes around my ankles. One got me by each arm and they walked me inside. There were at least four of them. Maybe five or six. After they got me inside, somebody cut the rope on my wrists. A door closed behind me. After a long time standing there I finally got up the nerve to take the bag off my head."

He paused to unparch his throat. He could pour it down once he got started. Being a naturally courteous fellow, I matched him swallow for swallow, though I hadn't been working my throat nearly so hard. "A farmhouse, you say? How did you discover that?"

"I'll get to it. Anyway, I took the bag off. I was in a room about twelve feet by twelve feet that hadn't been cleaned in years. There were some blankets to sleep on—all old and dirty and smelly—a chamber pot that never did get emptied, a rickety homemade chair, and a small table with one leg broken."

He had his eyes closed. He was visualizing. "On the table was one of those earthenware pitcher-and-bowl sets with a rusty metal dipper to take a drink with. The pitcher was cracked so it leaked a little into the bowl. I drank about a quart of water right away. Then I went and looked out the window and tried to get myself together. I was scared to death. I didn't have any idea what was going on. Until I got back here and found out Domina had ransomed me, I had my mind made up that some of Mother's political enemies had grabbed me so they could twist her arm."

"Tell me about that window. That sounds like a big lapse on their part."

"Not really. It was closed with a shutter and the shutter was nailed from outside. But the place was old and there was a crack in the shutter big enough to see through. As it turned out, my seeing what was outside didn't matter."

"How so?"

"The way they let me go. They just walked off and left me there. I figured it out when they stopped feeding me."

"Did you ever see any of them?"

"No."

"How did they get food to you, then?"

"They made me stand facing the wall when they brought the food in and took the old platter out."

"Then they talked to you?"

"One did. But only from outside the door and then all he ever said was that it was time to get against the wall. But sometimes I could hear them talking. Not very often. They didn't have much to say to each other."

"Not even about how they were going to spend their shares of the money?"

"I never heard any mention of money at all. That was

one of the reasons I decided the whole thing was political. That and the fact that, after the strangling, they treated me pretty gently. That isn't what I would have expected of kidnappers for profit."

"It isn't customary."

He had his eyes closed and his mind on the past. I don't think he heard me. "The only thing I ever heard that might have had anything to do with the situation was the last afternoon. Before they vanished. Someone came running into the place and yelled, 'Hey, Skredli, it's coming through tonight.' I never heard what, though."

"Skredli? You're sure?"

"Yes."

"You think it was a name?"

"It sounded like one. You think it might have been?"

I knew damned well it was. Skred is the ogre equivalent of Smith, only it is twice as common. Skredli compares with Smitty. Half the ogres in the world are called Skredli, it seems like. So much for the lucky break.

We let it sit that way for a minute while we split the remaining contents of the pitcher. It was a good brew. I wish its like befell me more often. But I usually can't afford the price of a sniff on my own hooks.

"So. We're almost to the end. What happened after Skredli got yelled at?"

"Basically nothing. As far as I know, for those guys that was the end of it."

I waited for him to expand upon that.

"They didn't bring me any supper. By midnight I was hungry enough to bang on the door and complain. That didn't do any good. I tried to sleep. I did a little, then when breakfast didn't come, I got up and pitched a real fit. I pounded the door so hard I broke it open. Then I got so scared they would beat me that I hid in my blankets. But nothing happened. Eventually I worked up enough nerve to go look out the door, then to slip out and explore."

"They were gone?"

"Long gone. The ashes in the kitchen weren't even warm. I ate some scraps they left behind. After those hit bottom I felt braver and decided to do some exploring."

Karl paused to look into his mug and curse because he could see the bottom and there were no reserves to rush into the fray.

I waited.

Karl told me, "That's why I know all about the farmhouse. A pretty substantial place before it was abandoned." He gave me an exhaustive description, not a peasant hovel but not a manor house either. "After I'd looked around awhile I finally got up enough nerve to follow the coach tracks through the woods. After a mile or so I came to a road. A passing tinker told me it was the Vorkuta–Lichfield Road, a little over three miles west of the battlefield."

Amazing. Karl had been sequestered within two miles of the place where Amiranda had bought hers and Saucerhead almost took a slice too many. I was so astonished I may have blinked. "So you just walked on home?"

"Yes. I think I'll go fill this pitcher again. This is taking longer than I thought."

"No need. I'm almost done. Just a couple questions more."

"What do you think? Was it an unusual kidnapping?"

"In some ways. But it went off smooth and you can't criticize success."

"I don't know much about this kind of thing. I was so damned scared while it was happening I didn't study it or think about it. How was it remarkable?"

He had a hook out and wanted to see if he could pull in the name of his friend Donni Pell. Amber had a similar notion. She was alert for the first time in half an hour. I disappointed them both because I had ideas of my own and wanted to save Donni for myself.

"Two peculiarities pounce at you like ogres from ambush. The one that bothers me the least is that they locked you in a room you could break out of without bothering to keep you tied or blindfolded. But that could be explained several ways. No, the big croggle is the way Willa Dount handled her end. She turned over a lot of gold to proven crooks without doing anything to make sure the merchandise she was buying was in good condition. The custom is for the purchaser to insist on delivery at the point of sale. Otherwise there's nothing to keep the kidnappers honest."

Karl mumbled something that sounded like, "I wondered about that, too."

He was in a declining mood and getting restless. I supposed it was time to attack. I went after him hard about timing and movements, and when I noticed Amber looking at me odd and Karl frowning angrily as he stumbled over his answers, I decided I'd gotten too intense. "What the hell is this? I'm doing a professional exercise and I get going like it's the real thing. Thanks, Karl. You've been a lot more patient than I would have been if the roles had been reversed."

"You're done?" He considered the bottom of his mug.

"Yes. Thanks. Drink one for me and think a kind thought while you're at it."

"Sure." He got up and out, trailing one curious glance at his sister.

15

"You got to pressing there at the end, Garrett. Were you on to something?"

"Apparently not. Unless I missed something that was right under my nose, your brother was a waste of time."

"Then why did you spend all that time on him?"

"Because I didn't know what he could tell me. Because you never know what little thing will turn out to be the critical clue. I went hard on the timing because I want to have it pat when we see what Amiranda has to say so we can look at it from the Domina's side."

"I couldn't find Amiranda."

"What?"

"I couldn't find her. She didn't answer her door. When I asked around, nobody had seen her. I finally sneaked into her rooms. She wasn't there. And most of her stuff was gone."

I did me what I hoped was a convincing show of perplexity. "Did she have a maid? Did you talk to her? What did she say?"

"I talked to her. She didn't know anything except that Amiranda is gone. Or so she said."

"Damn! That knocks hell out of everything." I got up and stretched.

"What are we going to do?"

"Start somewhere else. You just keep picking till you

pull a thread loose. You're the inside man here. You find out what you can about Willa Dount's end of things. The how, the where, and the when of the payoff in particular, but anything that sounds unusual or interesting. Keep trying to get a line on Amiranda. And while you're doing all that, try not to attract too much attention. We don't want anybody knowing what we're doing. There's two hundred thousand marks gold at stake and the price is going up. My resident genius says we're about to hear from Glory Mooncalled again."

Her eyes glittered. Each time Glory Mooncalled acted, the Venageti position in the Cantard weakened, the Karentine flourished, the price of silver plunged and that of gold soared. "We're getting richer by the minute!"

"Only in our imaginations. We have to find the gold."

She started toward me with that look in her eye, ready to celebrate. "What will you be doing?"

"The outside stuff. Picking at threads. Talking to this Donni."

"I'll bet. I'm much prettier than she is, Garrett. And maybe just as talented."

"Then I'm going to have my supper, consult the genius, and get on the road so I can be at that farm tomorrow morning. I'll have a whole day to poke around and pick up the trail."

She had gotten in close enough to force a clinch. My resistance was going the way of the dodo. Suddenly, she stiffened and backed away.

"What is it?"

"I just had an awful thought. My mother is going to be home any day. If we don't have the gold found and me out of here before she does . . ." She backed away. "We have to get to work."

Poor little rich kid. Somehow, I couldn't work up a lot of sympathy. If she wasn't miserable enough to walk with nothing but the clothes on her back, she wasn't miserable enough.

The sparkle came back to her eyes. "But once we do, look out, Garrett."

There is a limit to how much you can kid people and

still live with yourself, but also a limit to how much you can kid yourself. "I admire your confidence. *If* we find it."

"*When,* Garrett."

"All right. When we find it, look out, Amber."

We exchanged idiot grins.

"Do I go out the same way I got in?"

"That would be best. Don't let the servants see you. And watch out for the dragoons."

I gave her a kiss meant to be a businesslike sealing of our compact. She turned it into a promise of things to come. I finally peeled her off and fled.

I was distracted. The little witches do that to you. I zipped around a corner and almost plowed into Karl Senior and Domina Dount.

Fortunately, they were distracted too. Very distracted. If they noted a third presence at all, they probably assumed it was a wayward servant. I backed up to consider alternate routes.

Amber had it wrong. Willa Dount didn't freeze bathwater.

Now I knew what hold she had on Daddy. If it turned out to matter.

Reason didn't do me a bit of good trying to get out of there another way. In two minutes I knew I would get lost if I kept on. I found a place where I could look into the real people's world between curtains. I recognized the hallway.

Nothing for it but to march and look like I was about honest business.

It worked fine until I started hiking across the front court headed for the main gate.

Pudgy Courter came in from the street. He started to say something to the gateman, then spotted me. His eyes got big, his face got red, and he started to puff up like an old bullfrog about to sing. "What the hell are you doing in here?"

"Hell, I might ask the same of you. Little out of your

class here, aren't you? Guy like you ought to be slicing vegetables—"

I was close enough. He took a swing. I'm not sure why. I don't think I trampled him hard enough to set him off. I caught his wrist and kept on walking, pulling him along in a stumble. "Tsk-tsk. We should be more friendly to our betters."

I let him go as I stepped outside. He was past the flash point now. He retreated, cursing under his breath, while I glanced around for the four clowns who had been stalking me before Amber let me inside. They were gone.

It was a piece of bad luck, getting spotted like that. I could only hope it would balance out and not get things all stirred up inside. Amber could deal with Willa Dount, especially motivated by visions of gold, but I had my doubts about Junior. He had no strong reason to hide having talked to me.

I figured I'd best get down to Lettie Faren's place right away.

16

I didn't get there as quickly as I'd planned, though the delay lasted only a few seconds. Going down the Hill, I realized that I'd picked up a tail. It didn't take long to discover it was my friend Bruno from the tavern.

Why was he on me?

Five minutes later I knew he was alone. It was personal. I had hurt his feelings and now he felt a need to hurt mine.

I stepped into an areaway when I came to one I knew would suit my purpose. I found a shadow and got into it. He came charging in a few seconds later, apparently wanting to take advantage of my stupidity. But when he got there, he saw nothing. He started cursing.

"But you mustn't blame the gods. All is not lost, Bruno. I'm right here." I stepped out of the shadows.

He was too mad for preliminaries. He tucked in his chin and came after me.

I was in no mood for ego games myself. His first swing I tapped his wrist with my weighted stick. Then I whacked an elbow, putting one arm out of commission. Then I let him set himself up and dropped a couple of good thumps on his noggin. After he was down I put him in the shadows so the street kids wouldn't find and strip him before he woke up. I doubted he would appreciate the courtesy. I hoped he wasn't so stubbornly stupid one of us would have to get killed to end whatever was going on.

Lettie's place was into the lull that comes between the businesslike gentlemen of the afternoon and the revelers of night. I got past the thug at the door without trouble. He didn't know me.

I found Lettie where you always find her, in the back room counting the take. She was a grotesquely obese female of mixed but uncertain antecedents who made the Dead Man look slim, trim, and able to run like a deer.

"Garrett. You son of a bitch. How the hell did you get in here?"

"The sorcery of feet. I put on my magic boots and walked. You're looking as lovely as ever, Lettie."

"And you're just as full of camel guano. What the hell do you want?"

I tried to look hurt by her remarks.

"All right," she snarled. "Out you go."

I clinked coins and showed the face of a dead king on a gold double mark. "I thought the motto of the house was no paying customer is ever turned away."

Gold was talking big talk in TunFaire these days. She eyed the coin. "What do you want?"

"Not what. Who. Her name is Donni Pell."

Lettie's eyes narrowed, hardened. "Shit. You would. You can't have her."

"I know you don't like me, and we'll never run off to become shopkeepers and raise babies together, but when did you ever let personal feelings get in the way of making money?"

"When I was thirteen years old and in the middle of my first big love affair. That's got nothing to do with it, Garrett. I can't sell you merchandise that I don't have in stock."

"She's not here?"

"You figured it out. With a brain like yours, why do you keep that heap of blubber in your front room?"

"Sentiment. And it keeps him off the streets. Where did Donni go?"

"You want her bad, don't you?"

"I want to see her. Don't try to hold me up, Lettie. You've got employees who'll tell me for silver."

"Goddamned human nature. You would, wouldn't you? Give me one good reason why I shouldn't have Leo come in here and twist your face around so you're looking out the back of your head."

"This little crumb that fell from the sun." I flashed the double mark.

"All right. You win, Garrett. What do you want?"

"She's gone, so the why, the when, the how, and the where. Then tell me about Donni Pell the person."

"The why is she got hold of a bunch of money. And that's the how, too. She came in here three, four nights ago and bought out her contract. Not that she was in very deep. She said a rich uncle up north died and left her a fortune. Bull. If you ask me, she got her hooks into some half-wit off the Hill. She had the looks and manners and style for it. She claimed she was off to take over managing the uncle's manor. More bull. She couldn't survive without platoons of men around."

I raised the old eyebrow. Lettie liked me when I did my trick. I used it as often as I could.

"That woman was a freak, Garrett. Ninety-nine out of a hundred of them hate men. She *loved* what she was doing. If she hadn't been selling it, she would have been giving as much away for free."

"A working girl who enjoyed her work? Unusual. She must have brought the clients in."

"In herds. I wish I had a hundred like her. Even if she was a pervert."

I gave her a glim at the other eyebrow.

"You know in this business you got to be tolerant and understanding, Garrett. But it stretches tolerance and surpasses understanding when a perfectly beautiful young human woman prefers ogres for playmates. Even ogre women don't want anything to do with those creeps. I'd let a vampire or wolfman in this place before I'd open my door to an ogre."

She was going good so I let her rant, using up her

hostility on a target other than me, just once throwing in, "Well, there *are* the sexual myths," just to make sure she got all the venom spent.

"Bullshit. That's all bullshit, Garrett. You're talking to an expert, Garrett." And on she raved.

She wound down. I placed the double mark squarely in front of her. "That about the ogres was worth this. Come up with something more and you might get to see some of the old king's ancestors."

Her eyes narrowed. "It's murder, isn't it, Garrett? And a heavyweight client. I know that look. The paladin look. You're after somebody's head. You dumb boy, you keep playing with the lifetakers."

"I'm after a hooker named Donni Pell who might be able to tell me something I need to know."

"You got the works already, Garrett. All I can give you for your money now is a kiss for luck."

"Background her. Her people. You know them all. How long was she here? Where did she come from?"

"She don't have any people. They died in the plague four years ago. That's why I didn't believe the story about the uncle. She was here for about three years. Sometimes more trouble than she was worth on account of stunts she pulled on her johns. She didn't tell a lot about herself but lies, like all the rest, but I usually get their real stories out of them on the bad nights."

"I know you do."

"Her people were country folk with a good-sized free-hold up around Lichfield somewhere."

I muttered, "I'll bet I could go right to it without missing a turn."

"What?"

"Nothing. That chip looks lonely sitting there by itself. What more can you tell me about Donni?"

"You got the load, Garrett." She reached for the coin.

"What about Raver Styx's menfolk? The two Karls."

Her eyes glazed. "Somebody killed one of them?"

"Not yet." I saw she needed to see some color to keep her momentum. I showed her another double.

"The kid was one of Donni's regulars. She said she

felt sorry for him. I think she halfway liked him. He treated her like a lady and he wasn't bashful about being seen with her. The father visited her sometimes, too, but with him it was strictly business. I don't think I want to talk about that family anymore, Garrett. That woman is poison."

"She's out of town, Lettie."

"She'll be back. You got what you came for. Get out. Get out before I start remembering and yell for Leo."

I put the second double mark down beside the first. "We wouldn't want to interrupt Leo's nap, would we?"

"Out, Garrett. And don't show your ugly phiz around here anymore. You'll get it broke."

She loved me, that fat old Lettie.

17

I went by Playmate's stable and smithy yard and told him to send a buggy to the house in a couple of hours, and to load it down with one of every kind of tool he had. He gave me a look but knew better than to ask. I might tell him something he wouldn't want to know.

Old Dean thought he was going to bribe me. He still wasn't talking but he laid on the best spread I'd seen in months. I did right by it. When I went in to see the Dead Man, I was waddling.

I didn't expect another decent meal for days.

Garrett! Dismiss that creature at once! Get him out of my house.

"Good to see you back to your normal cheerful self. What creature? Why?"

That Dean. The fiend brought not one, not two, but three women in here. Get rid of him, Garrett. Throw him out.

So. A fantasy meal explained. Dean wanted me to see what I didn't have to be missing. Him and me, we were going to have to have a little talk, man to man, and get things straight. Real soon now.

I settled in my visiting chair, sipped some beer, then cut loose. The Dead Man sulked and pretended to ignore me, but he took in every word. He had to have

something to distract himself while he waited for Glory
Mooncalled to prove out his hypothesis. I talked for two
hours nonstop, with good old Dean keeping my mug
topped. He enjoyed a little vicarious adventure. And his
coming and going showed just how little depth there was
to the Dead Man's animosity.

I finished my report, having spared no detail.

There is something missing, Garrett.

"I know that. Either that or I know too much and I'm
getting distracted."

You are not getting distracted.

"I keep thinking I've got the kidnap side figured out.
Three different times I've decided that Junior kidnapped
himself. Then I find myself up to my ass in ogres again,
with them perfect for the villains. And if the kid did
kidnap himself, why did he come home? He and his
sister want out of there so bad they can taste it. The
way it went down, with no direct exchange, all he had
to do was take the gold and hike and leave his mommy
wearing weeds."

The ransom money was paid?

"Willa Dount scrounged two hundred thousand and
delivered it to somebody. Junior came home next day.
Amber is digging on that for me. The deep-down root
thing that bugs me can be tied up in one bow. Why did
Amiranda have to die? Real kidnapping or fake, with
her in on it or not, why did she have to be killed?"

*I am certain you will unmask the reason. You have
allowed yourself to become emotionally entangled. Again.*

I saw him sizing up one of his favorite hobbyhorses,
getting ready to mount up and ride. Dean had gone to
answer the door a minute before. I got up. "My transportation is here. You mull it over while you're killing
time. Maybe you'll spot a connection I've missed."

I didn't doubt that he had seen one or two already
but didn't feel obligated to point them out. Neither of us
had a real money interest here, and he had no emotional
investment, so whether he saw something or not he
would just let me exercise my own genius.

I visited the armory. Unlike Saucerhead I don't figure

my hands are my best defense. I tossed a bundle into the buggy, under the seat, and was about to flick the traces when Dean came stumbling out of the house with a hamper.

"Mr. Garrett. Wait."

"What's this?"

"Provender. Victuals. Rations."

"Leftovers?"

"That too. A man has to eat something. What were you going to do out there?"

Hell. I'm a city boy. I don't think about food. "I was going to borrow a page from Morley Dotes and live off roots and bark, but rather than injure your feelings I'll just park that hamper up here beside me and suffer."

He smiled smugly as I pulled away. For however long I subjected myself to this rustication, every bite would remind me that I needed a feeder and a keeper, and the fodder would, for certain, be the best of the best cooked up by his nieces.

The man was obsessed. That is all I can say. He had worked for me long enough to know I wasn't the kind of catch you'd want your female relations stuck with. But he persisted.

Karenta is a kingdom at war. You'd expect some sort of watch to be kept on the entrepôts to one of its most important cities, in case some enterprising Venageti commander decided to try something imaginative. But the war has been going on since my generation were kids, seldom spilling out of the Cantard and the adjoining seas. Any guards who were awake when I left were too busy playing cards to step out and check my bona fides. But our lords from the Hill want the ordinary folk to seethe with fervor against the enemy.

It's a lot easier to seethe against Raver Styx and her ilk. They profit no matter how the fighting goes.

I used the route Saucerhead and Amiranda had followed. The moon was now full. The team didn't mind night travel, even with me at the traces. And the nation

of horses has been out to get me ever since I can
remember.

It was a smooth, quiet ride with very little to see. The
only traffic I encountered was the night coach from
Derry, half an hour ahead of schedule and just lumping
along with its two or three somnolent passengers and
load of mail. Guard and driver tossed me friendly greet-
ings, which showed how worried they were about the
night.

I suppose, theoretically, that I should have had one
hand on a silver blade at all times. There *was* a full
moon. But there hadn't been a confirmed wolfman incident this close to the city since before I went into the
Marines.

Once I did unravel a murder that had been dressed
up to look like a wolfman's work. It's a hell of a way to
make sure your old man doesn't get the chance to write
you out of the will.

I reached the dire crossroad about the same time Saucerhead had. I gave it a look around as it stood, considering the fact that there was more moon than there had
been that night. I didn't see or get a feel for anything,
so I loosened the horses' harnesses, made sure they
couldn't run off, climbed onto the buggy's seat, and
napped.

I did a good job of snoozing, too. I thought first light
would waken me, but the honor went to a ten-year-old
who shook my shoulder and asked, "Are you all right,
mister?"

I counted my hands and feet and purse and discovered
that I hadn't been murdered, mutilated, or robbed. "I
am indeed, son. Except maybe for a case of premature
senility."

He looked at me funny and asked a few kidlike questions. I tried giving reasonable answers and asked him a
few in turn. He was on his way somewhere to help somebody with farm chores, but he let me buy him breakfast.
Which goes to show how tame it really is around Tun-
Faire these days, for all we city people put down the
country. No city boy would have risked hanging around

with a stranger. The real monsters of today live in the city's shadows and cellars and drawing rooms.

He didn't tell me one thing even remotely useful.

Acting on the premise that it is never wise to put temptation into the path of an honest man, I led my team into the woods opposite the area I intended to explore. I made sure the beasts wouldn't have the pleasure of deserting me, returned to the diamond, and checked to make sure they and the rig were invisible, then went across and started looking through the bushes.

It wasn't hard to find where the dead and wounded had been thrown into hurried concealment. The brush was torn and trampled. The corpses had been cleared away but their drippings had been ignored, at least by the cleanup crew. The flies and ants had come and gone. The bloodstains were now the province of a gray-black, whiskery mold that described perfectly every spot and spill. Which didn't tell me anything except that a lot of people had done a lot of bleeding.

My woodcraft was no longer what it had been in my Marine days, but it took no forest genius to follow either of the trails leading deeper into the woods. The first I tried split after about a third of a mile, heavy traffic having turned eastward suddenly. It looked like four or five ogres had been on Saucerhead's trail when they were recalled by their buddies. The other trail ran down into the woods east of where I stood.

I didn't need to follow Saucerhead to know where he'd gone. I turned east.

Five hundred yards along I paused, planted the back of my lap on a fallen tree trunk, and told my brain to get to work. I knew what I would find if I went on a little farther. I could hear the flies buzzing and the wild dogs bickering with the vultures. Much closer and I would smell it, too. Did I *have* to look?

Basically, there was no getting out of it. There was maybe one chance in a hundred that I was wrong and the centerpiece of that grisly feast was a woods bison. If I was right, chances were ten to one against me finding anything that would split things wide open. But you can't skimp and take shortcuts. The odds are always against you until you do stumble across that one in ten.

Still, dead people who have been lying around in the woods for days aren't particularly appealing. So I spent a few minutes considering a spiderweb with dew gems still on it before I put my dogs on the ground and started hoofing it toward a case of upturned stomach.

Five years in the Marines had brought me eyeball to eyeball with old death more times than I cared to remember, and my life since has provided its grisly encounters, but there are some things I can't get used to. Consciousness of my own mortality won't let me.

The conclave of death was being held at the downhill end of an open, grassy area about twenty yards wide and fifty long. Patches of lichened granite peeked out of the soil. I collected a dozen loose chunks of throwing size and cut loose at the wild dogs. They snarled and growled but fled. They have grown very cautious around humans because bounty hunters are after them constantly. Especially farm kids who want to pick up a little change for the fair or whatever.

The buzzards tried to bluff me. I didn't bluff. They got themselves airborne and began turning in patient circles, looking down and thinking, *Someday, you too, man.* In the pantheon of one of the minor cults of Tun-Faire, the god of time is a vulture.

Maybe that's why I hate the damned things. Or maybe that's because they've become identified with my military service, when I saw so many circling the fields of futility where young Karentines died for their country.

So there I stood, a great bull ape, master of the land of the dead. Instead of pounding my chest and maybe forcing myself to inhale some tainted air, I moved as upwind as I could and started looking at what I'd come to see.

There wasn't a woods bison in that mess.

I muttered, "I ought to remember Saucerhead's tendency to exaggerate."

I counted up enough parts to make at least seven bodies. Four or five he said he'd taken. Even torn apart they remained ogre ugly. They'd been buried shallow beneath loose dirt, leaves, and stones. The lazy way, I might call it, but I look at comrades differently than ogres do. They don't form bonds the way humans do. For them a dead associate is a burden, not an obligation.

No doubt they were in a hurry to quit the area, too.

You do what you have to do. I got in and used a stick to poke around, looking for personals, but it took only a minute to figure out that the living hadn't been in too big a hurry not to loot the dead. Even their boots had been taken.

That wasn't the behavior of a band expecting to be in the big money soon. But with ogres you never know. Maybe their mothers had taught them the old saw, "Waste not, want not."

I circled the burial site three times but could find no sign of comings or goings other than by the route I'd followed, and that the second group had taken down from the road.

In places the soil was very moist from groundwater seepage. Such places sometimes hold tracks. I started looking those over, trying to cut the trail of a guy on crutches or one who wore his feet backward; something that would stick out if I happened to be hanging around with a bunch of ogres and one of the bad guys showed up. I didn't expect to find anything, but luck doesn't play for the other side all the time. Got to keep looking for that ten to one.

I found the nothing I expected, though not exactly because there was nothing to be found. It was one of those cases of suddenly deciding you ought to be investigating something somewhere else.

I heard a stir in the woods behind me. Not much of one. Thinking some of the dogs had gotten brave, I turned with the stick I still carried.

"Holy shit!"

A woolly mammoth stood at the edge of the woods, and from where I was it looked about ninety-three hands high at the shoulder. How the hell it had come up so quietly is beyond me. I didn't ask. When it cocked its head and made a curious grunting noise, I put the heels and toes to work according to the gods' design. The beast threw a trumpet roar after me. Laughing.

I paused behind a two-foot-thick oak and gave it a stare. A mammoth. Here. No mammoth had come this close to TunFaire in the past dozen generations. The nearest herds were four hundred miles north of us, up along the borders of thunder-lizard country.

The mammoth ambled out of the woods, laughed at me again, cropped some grass a couple of bales at a time while keeping one eye on me. Finally convinced that I was no fearless mammoth poacher, it eyeballed the vultures, checked the dead ogres, snorted in disgust, and marched off through the woods as quietly as it had come.

And last night I'd been unconcerned because no wolf-man had been seen since I was a kid.

Like I said, luck is not always with the bad guys.

It was time to stop tempting it with the one out of ten and hike on back to my rig before the horses got wind of that monster and decided they would feel more comfortable back in the city. Too bad Garrett had to ride shank's mare.

18

I sat on the buggy seat, beside the crossroads obelisk, and watched a parade of farm families and donkey carts head up the Derry Road. I didn't see them. I was trying to pick between Karl Junior's farm prison and Saucerhead's witch.

The decision had actually been made. I was putting the thumbscrews on myself trying to figure if I was going to the farm first just to delay the pain skulking around the other place. No matter that I had to head the same direction to reach both and the farm was nearer.

You don't alter the past, turn the tide, or change yourself by brooding about your hidden motives. You will surprise yourself every time, anyway. Nobody ever figures out why.

"Hell with it! Get up."

One of the team looked over her shoulder. She had that glint in her eye. The tribe of horses was about to amuse itself at Garrett's expense.

Why do they do this to me? Horses and women. I'll never understand either species.

"Don't even think about it, horse. I have friends in the glue business. Get up."

They got. Unlike women, you can show horses who is boss.

The bout with introspection rekindled my desire to

lay hands on the people responsible for the human
equivalent of sending Amiranda to the glue works.

The exit to the farm was up on a ridgeline where
the ground was too dry to hold tracks, and hidden by
undergrowth. I passed it twice. The third time I got
down and led the team, giving the bushes a closer look,
and that did the trick. Two young mulberry trees, which
grow as fast as weeds, leaned together over the track.
Once past them the way was easy to follow, though it
hadn't been cleared since Donni's departure.

I had to go through a half mile of woods, not a mile.
It was dense in there, dark, quiet, and humid. The deer-
flies and horseflies were out at play, and every few feet
I got a faceful of spider silk. I sweated and slapped and
muttered and picked ticks off my pants. Why doesn't
everybody live in the city?

I ran into a blackberry patch where the berries were
fat and sweet, and decided to lunch on the spot. Afterward I felt more disposed toward the country, until the
chiggers off the blackberry canes started gnawing.

The track through the woods showed evidence of recent use, including that of the passage of at least one
heavy vehicle.

I had a feeling that, no matter what suspicions
haunted me, I wouldn't unearth one bit of physical evidence to impugn Junior's version of what had happened.

I kicked up a doe and fawn near the edge of the wood.
I watched them bound across what once had constituted
considerably more than a one-family subsistence farm,
though now the acreage was wild and heavily spotted
with wild roses and young cedars. The grass was waist
high and some of the weeds were taller. A trampled path
led downslope to what had been a substantial house.
There were no domestic animals in sight, no dogs bark-
ing, no smoke from either chimney, nor any other sign
that the place was occupied.

Still, I remained rooted, giving the wildlife time to
grow accustomed to my presence and return to business.

The Boga Hills loomed indigo in the distance. The
most famous Karentine vineyards are up there. This

country was close enough to have some of the magic rub off, but hadn't been turned into vineyards. I wondered if someone hadn't gotten that idea and had abandoned the place when they found out why. Then I recalled Donni Pell.

A girl who came from some kind of money who went to work for Lettie, on contract, supposedly because she liked the job. A girl who now supposedly owned a place that, a few years ago, had been in satisfactory shape for a quick sale to TunFaire's land-hungry lords. I doubted it was part of the problem at hand, but it might be interesting to unravel the whys.

Ten minutes of pretending I was scouting for the company left me impatient to get on with it. I tied the horses, got down low, and started my downhill sneak.

The place was as empty as a dead shoe. I went for the buggy, turned the team loose to browse while I prowled.

Junior's report was accurate down to the minutiae. The only things he hadn't mentioned were that the well was still good and his captors had equipped it with a new rope and bucket. The horses awarded me a temporary cease-fire after I drew them a few buckets.

There was no doubt that a band of ogres—or a mob equally unfastidious—had spent several days hanging around. Days during which they must have eaten nothing but chicken to judge by the feathers, heads, and hooves scattered around. I wondered how they had managed to pilfer so many without arousing the ire of the entire countryside.

I did a modestly thorough once-over, with special attention to Karl's lockup. That room had the rickety furniture, cracked pitcher, filthy bedding, overburdened chamber pot reported. The chamber pot was significant. I concluded that its very existence meant I must surrender my suspicions of Junior or radically alter my estimate of his intelligence and acting ability. If he had put together a fake, he had done so with a marvelous eye for detail, meaning he had anticipated a thorough investigation despite his getting home healthy and happy, which meant . . .

I didn't know what the hell it meant, except maybe that I had my hat on backward.

Why the hell did Amiranda have to die?

The answer to that would probably bust the whole thing open.

Conscious that I had a passing duty to Amber as a client, I went over the place again with all due professional care to overlook nothing, be that the tracks of a four-hundred-pound ogre with a peg leg or two hundred thousand marks gold hidden by throwing it down the well. Yes. I stripped down and shimmied down and floundered around in the icy water until I was sure there would be no gold strike. My curses should have brought the water to a simmer, but failed. I guess I just don't have the knack.

Four hours and the risk of pneumonia turned up just one thing worth taking along, a silver tenth mark that had strayed in among the dust bunnies against the wall where Junior's blankets were heaped and hadn't been able to find its way home. It looked new but it was a temple coin and didn't use the royal dating. I'd have to visit the temple where it had been struck to find out when it was minted.

But its very presence gave me an idea. It also gave me a bit of indigestion for not having thought to ask a few more questions while I'd had Junior on the griddle. Now I would have to get the answers the hard way—on the trip home. The hard way, but the answers I got were likely to be square.

The sun was headed west. It wasn't going to rebound off the hills out there. I had a call to make, and if I wanted to get it handled before the wolfmen came out to stalk the wily mammoth, I had to get moving.

The horses let the armistice stand. They didn't even play tag with me when I went to harness them up.

19

Saucerhead's directions to his witch friend's place hadn't included the information that there was nothing resembling a road near her home. In fact, any resemblance to a trail was coincidental. That was wicked-witch-of-the-woods territory and anybody who managed to stumble into her through that mess deserved whatever he got.

I had to do most of it on the ground, leading the team. The armistice survived only because they realized they would need me to scout the way back. When we hit the road again all deals would be off.

The last few hundred yards weren't bad. The ground leveled out. The undergrowth ceased to exist, as though somebody manicured the woods every day. The trees were big and old and the canopy above turned most of the remaining light. Lamplight pouring through an open doorway gave me my bearings.

A rosy-cheeked, apple-dumpling-plump little old lady was waiting for me. She stood about four-feet-eight and was dressed like a peasant granny on a christening day, right down to the embroidered apron. She looked me over frankly. I couldn't tell what she thought of what she saw. "Are you Garrett?"

Startled, I confessed.

"Took you long enough to get here. I suppose you might as well come on inside. There's still a bit of water for tea and a scone or two if Shaggoth hasn't got into them. Shaggoth! You good-for-nothing lout! Get out here and take care of the man's horses."

I started to ask how she knew I was coming, but only managed to get the old flycatcher open before Shaggoth came out. And came out. And came out. That doorway was a good seven feet high and he had to crouch to get through. He looked at me the way I'd look at a decomposing rat, snorted, and started unhitching the horses.

"Come inside," the witch told me.

I sidled in behind her, keeping one eye on friend Shaggoth. "Troll?" I squeaked.

"Yes."

"He's got jaws like a saber-tithed tooger. Soobertoothed teegar. The goddamned growly things with the fangs."

She chuckled. "Shaggoth is of the pureblood. He's been with me a long time." She had me in the kitchen then and was dropping a tea egg into a giant mug that I wished was filled with beer. "The rest of his folk migrated because you pesky humans were overrunning everything, but he stayed on. Loyalty before common sense."

I forbore observing that she was human herself.

"They're not a very bright race. Come. By the by, you'll have noted that he isn't sensitive to sunlight."

No. That hadn't registered. Teeth had registered. "How come you know my name?" Great straight line to a witch. "How did you know I was co—geck!"

Amiranda was seated beside a small fire, hands folded in her lap, staring at something beyond my right shoulder. No. Not Amiranda. The essence of Amiranda had fled that flesh. That wasn't a person, it was a thing.

The pain would be less if I thought that way.

"Excuse me?" I glanced at the witch.

"I said Waldo told me you would come. I expected you sooner."

"Who's Waldo? Another pet like Shaggoth? He can see the future?"

"Waldo Tharpe. He told me you were friends."

"Waldo?" There must have been a little hysteria edg-

ing my giggle. She gave me a frown. "I didn't know he had a name. I've never heard him called anything but Saucerhead."

"He's not enthusiastic about being Waldo," she admitted. "Sit and let's talk."

I sat, musing. "So Saucerhead jobbed us. The big dope isn't as dumb as he lets on." I kept getting drawn back to the corpse. It did look very lifelike, very undamaged. Any moment now the chest would heave, the sparkle would come back to the eyes, and she would laugh at me for being taken in.

The witch settled into a chair facing mine. "Waldo said you'd have questions." Her gaze followed mine. "I worked on her a little, making her look a little better, putting spells on to hold the corruption off till she can be given a decent funeral."

"Thank you."

"Questions, Garrett? I went to a good deal of trouble on Waldo's behalf. What will you need to know?"

"Anything. Everything. I want to know why she was killed and who ordered it done."

"I'm not omniscient, Garrett. I can't answer that sort of question. Though I can surmise—which may not stand scrutiny in the light of what you already know—why. She was about three months pregnant."

"*What?* That's impossible."

"The child would have been male had it seen the light of day."

"But she spent the last six months practically imprisoned in the house where she lived."

"There were no men in that house? Hers was a miraculous conception?"

I opened my mouth to protest but a question popped out instead. "Who was the father?"

"I'm no necromancer, Garrett. The name, if she knew it at all, expired with her."

"She knew. She wasn't the type who wouldn't." I'd begun to get angry all over again.

"You knew her? Waldo didn't. Nothing but her name and the fact that you sent her to him."

"I knew her. Not well, but I did."

"Tell me about her."

I talked. It eased the pain a little, bringing her to life in words. I finished. "Did you get anything out of that?"

"Only that you're working in a tight place. A stormwarden's family, yet. Did Waldo tell you that the assassins were ogre breeds?"

"Yes."

"A curse on the beasts. Waldo hurt them, but not nearly enough. I sent Shaggoth to find them. He caught nothing but graves. There was nothing on the bodies to betray them."

"I know. I saw them myself. Tell Shaggoth to watch his step in the woods. There's something out there that's bigger than he is."

"You're making a joke?"

"Sort of. A mammoth did sneak up on me while I was looking at those ogre bodies."

"A mammoth! Here in this day. A wonder for certain." She rose and went to a cabinet while I sipped tea. She said, "I've been considering your situation since Waldo left. It seemed—and does more so now that I know who she was—that the best help I could offer would be a few charms you might use to surprise the villains."

I looked at Amiranda's remains. "I appreciate that. I wonder why you'd commit yourself that way, though."

"For Waldo. For the woman. Maybe for your sake, laddie. Maybe for my own. Certainly for the sake of justice. Whatever, the deed was cruel and should be repaid in coin equally vicious. The man responsible should be . . . But your tea is getting cold. I'll put another pot of water on to boil."

I got fresh tea, this time with fire-hardened flour briquettes that must have been the scones mentioned earlier. I gave them a try. One should show one's hostess the utmost in courtesy, especially when she is a witch.

Shaggoth stuck his head in and grumbled something in dialect that sounded suspiciously like, "Where the hell

did my scones go?" He gave me a narrow-eyed look
when the witch replied.

"Don't you mind him," she told me. "He's just
being playful."

Right. Like a mongoose teases a cobra.

She sat down and explained how I could use the tricks
she'd prepared for me. When she finished, I thanked her
and rose. "If you can get Shaggoth to help me without
breaking any bones in his playfulness, I'll get out of
your hair."

She looked scandalized at first, then just amused.
"You've heard too many stories about witches, Garrett.
You'll be safer here than out in the moonlight. Shaggoth
is the least maligned of those creatures who haven't yet
emigrated. Consider the moon. Consider her ways."

Those who survive in this business develop an intuition for when to argue and when not to argue. Smart
guys have figured out that you don't talk back to
stormwardens, warlocks, sorcerers, and witches. The
place for reservations is tucked neatly behind the teeth.
"All right. Where do I bed down?"

"Here. By the fire. The nights get chilly in the woods."

I looked at what was left of Amiranda Crest.

"She doesn't get up and walk at midnight, Garrett.
She's all through with that."

I have slept in the presence of corpses often enough,
especially while I was in the Marines, but I've never
liked it and never before had I had to share my quarters
with a dead lover. That held no appeal at all.

"Shaggoth will waken you at first light and help you
get her into your buggy."

I looked at the body and reflected that it would be a
long, hard road home. And once I got there I'd have to
face the question of what to do with the cadaver.

"Good night, Mr. Garrett." The witch went around
snuffing lights and collecting tea things, which she took
to the kitchen. She started clattering around out there,
leaving me to my own devices. I asked myself what the
hell the point was of having nerve if I didn't use it,

rounded up a small herd of pillows and cushions, and tried to convince myself they made a bed.

I tossed a couple logs on the fire and lay down. I stared at the ceiling for a long time after the clatter in the kitchen died and the light went with it. The flicker of the fire kept making Amiranda appear to move there in the corner of my eye. I went over everything from the beginning, then went over it again. Somewhere there was some nagging little detail that, added to the maverick coin from the farm, had me feeling very suspicious about Junior again.

Sometimes intuition isn't intuition at all, but rather unconscious memory.

I finally got it. The shoes Willa Dount had shown me first time I went up the Hill.

Those shoes. They deserved a lot of thought from several angles.

In the meantime, I had to rest. Tomorrow was going to be another in a series of long days.

20

Breakfast with Shaggoth was an experience. He could eat. Three of him could lay waste to nations. No wonder the breed was so rare. If there were as many of them as there are of us, they would have to learn to eat rocks because there wouldn't be enough of anything else to go around.

He brought the buggy around front and put the horses into harness with an ease that awakened my envy. Those beasts trotted out docilely and cooperatively and stood there smirking because they knew I would be irked by their easy acquiescence.

Damn the whole equine tribe, anyway.

The witch came out with a lunch she'd packed. I thanked her for that, for her hospitality, and for everything else. She ran through the instructions for using the spells she'd given me. Those instructions were as complicated and difficult to recall as instructions for dropping a rock. But specialists think the uninitiated incapable of falling without technical assistance.

I offered to pay for the help again.

"Don't start up, Garrett. Let me do my little piece for justice in an unjust world. Somewhere out there, there is somebody with the soul of a crocodile. Somebody who ordered the murder of a pregnant woman. Find him.

Balance the scales. If you don't think you can handle him alone—for whatever reason—come see me again."

She was quietly furious about Amiranda. And she hadn't even known the woman. It was curious that Amiranda could find so many allies by getting herself murdered. And a pity none of us had been around when she needed us most. Though Saucerhead had done everything he could.

I didn't argue anymore. "I'll let you know how it comes out. Thanks for everything." I exchanged glares with the horses, putting on a good enough snarl to get my bluff in.

"Watch yourself, Garrett. You're playing with rough people."

"I know. But so are they."

"They probably know who you are and might know you're poking around. You don't know who they are."

"I've had plenty of practice being paranoid." I swung up onto the seat, glanced back at the bundle I'd be taking home, and hollered at the horses to get going. Good old Shaggoth trudged through the woods ahead of the horses, showing them the easy way to get back to the road—the way I'd completely missed coming in. The beasts kept glancing back, silently accusing me of being a moron.

I started with the first farm beyond the road to the place where Junior had been held. No, nobody there had seen a young man on foot the day Karl claimed to have started home. Certainly no one of any breed had come there looking to rent or buy a buggy or mount.

It was what I expected to hear. He wouldn't have done it so close, but the chance had to be covered. It was donkey-work time, grasping for straws. I had nothing concrete to affirm or deny my suspicions.

I got the same response house after house. Some talked easily, some not, the way people will, but the end was always the same. Nobody had begged, bought, borrowed, rented, or stolen transportation of any sort.

Lunch time came and went and I began to consider restructuring my assumptions.

Maybe Karl Junior *had* walked home. Barefoot. Or maybe he'd hitched a ride or had flagged down one of the day coaches running into the city. Or the ogres might have left him some way to get home.

That seemed damned unlikely. Walking, stealing, flagging a coach presented difficulties, too, for reasons of character and obvious traceability. Coachmen remember people they pick up along the road.

Hitching looked like the best and most logical alternative. It's the way I'd have gotten myself to town. But I doubted that a resort to the charity of strangers would even occur to a spoiled child off the Hill.

But had he gotten home that way, my chances of discovering the people who had helped were even more remote than they were by my present, most-favored course. So I stuck to what I was doing. I reasoned that if he had hitched, he would have mentioned it. He'd been careful to mention such details.

I now had a strong attachment to the assumption that Junior had participated in his own kidnapping. I had to caution myself not to get so attached that I began discarding contrary evidence.

The vision sent me back to wartime days. The farmer and his sons and a dozen other men were advancing through the hayfield in echelon, scythes rhythmically swinging. They looked like skirmishers cautiously advancing. I pulled up and watched for a few minutes. They saw me but pretended otherwise. The paterfamilias glanced at the sky, which was overcast, and decided to keep cutting.

All right. I could play it their way.

I slid down, walked to the edge of the field where the hay was down already—just to show how thoughtful a fellow I am—and approached the crowd from the flank. The women and kids raking the hay into piles and getting it onto the backs of several pathetic donkeys were much

more curious than their menfolk. I gave them a "howdy"
as I passed, and nothing more. Anything more would have
been considered a heavy pass by many farm husbands.

I parked myself a cautious distance from the guy who
looked like he was the boss ape in these parts and said
"howdy" again.

He grunted and went on swinging, which was all right
by me. I was trying to be accommodating.

"You might be able to help me."

This time his grunt was filled with the gravest of
doubts.

"I'm looking for a man who passed this way four or
five days back. He might have been looking to rent or
buy a horse."

"Why?"

"On account of what he did to my woman."

He turned his head in rhythm and gave me a look
saying I had no business going around asking for help if
I was not man enough to rule my woman.

"He killed her. I just found out yesterday. Got her
over in the buggy, taking her to her folks. Want to find
that fellow when I get that done."

The farmer stopped swinging his scythe. He stared at
me with squinty eyes that had looked into too many
sunrises and sunsets. The other scythes came to rest and
the men leaned upon them exactly like tired soldiers
lean on their spears. The women and kids stopped raking and loading. Everybody stared at me.

The boss farmer nodded once, curtly, put his scythe
down gently, hiked over to the buggy. He leaned against
the side, lifted the cover off Amiranda.

When he returned, he stood beside me instead of facing me. "Pretty little gal."

"She was. We had a young one coming, too."

"Looked like. Wadlow! Come here."

One of the older farmers came to us. He planted his
scythe and leaned. He looked even more laconic than
the first one.

"You sold that swayback mare to that smart-ass city
boy what day?"

The second farmer considered the sky as though he might find the answer written there. "Five days ago today. About noon." He eyed me like he was suspicious I might want the money back.

I knew what I wanted to know but had to play the game out. "He say where he was headed?"

Wadlow looked to my companion, who told him, "You tell him what he wants to know."

"Said he was going into the city. Said his horse got stole. Didn't say much of nothing else."

"Hope you took him good. Was he wearing shoes?" It was an off-the-wall question but about the only thing left I had to ask. Except, "Was he alone?"

Wadlow said, "Didn't have no shoes. Boots. Pretty rich-boy boots. Wouldn't last a week out here. He was by his lonesome."

"That's that, then," I said.

The older farmer asked, "That tell you what you need?"

"I reckon I know where to look now." And that was true. "Much obliged." I checked the sky. "Thank you, then." I turned to go.

"Luck to you. She was a pretty little thing."

My shoulders tightened and I shuddered in a sudden wash of emotion. I raised a hand and marched on. I had a man's work to do. Those farmers understood better than anybody I knew, except maybe Saucerhead Tharpe.

By the time I settled on the buggy seat, the skirmishers were on the move again and the women and children were back to work. Maybe they would find the time to talk about me over supper.

21

It was late when I entered the city but a sliver of light still remained. I had a brainstorm. It was a long shot but it might stir something.

I had Amiranda's body propped up beside me. The witch's spells were holding their own and the light helped with the illusion. Maybe somebody who knew she could not be alive would see her and think she was.

To that end I made a few cautious forays into the outskirts of Ogre Town, then went up and circled Lettie Faren's place because a lot of the Bruno types from the Hill came there to waste their wages.

The wages of sin is that you get cheated out of them.

Then I headed home, going around to the back so no one would see me take the body inside.

Dean was there despite the hour. He helped with the door and gawked. "What's the matter with her, Mr. Garrett?"

I wasn't in one of my better humors. "She's dead. That's what's the matter with her. Murdered."

He stammered, apologized, stammered some more, so I apologized back and added, "I don't know why. Maybe because she was pregnant. Maybe because she knew too much. Let's take her in to his nibs. He might be able to sort it out."

The Dead Man isn't always as hard and insensitive as

he pretends. He read my mood and saved the usual act. *That is the one who spent the night.* It was the first he admitted knowing about that.

"The same. Let me tell it while I'm in the mood."

He let me run through it up to the moment I carried her in there. Dean ran me mug after mug and hovered solicitously in between. I knew I was doing a good job reporting and had done a good one poking around because he didn't interrupt once and his only questions afterward were about the mammoth. Purely personal curiosity.

Let me mull it over, Garrett. You go get drunk. Watch out for him, Dean.

"Watch out for me? Why?"

You are working yourself up toward a quixotic gesture. You are unreasonable and irrational when you fall into such moods. I caution you to restraint. The information you have gathered is mainly circumstantial and there is not enough to point an accusing finger accurately. Tomorrow I will suggest some courses that may, possibly, produce evidence more concrete.

"More concrete? It's plenty hard enough for me."

You expect to tackle the favorite and only son of the Stormwarden Raver Styx on the basis of a pair of shoes and a horse? When you know there is a high probability that she would shield him even if he were caught cutting the hearts out of babies in the public streets? Further, you may have chosen the wrong villian to be the target of your wrath.

"Who else?"

That is what you will have to discover. It is true, I believe, that there is a reasonable probability that the young daPena and the dead woman were involved in a contrived kidnapping. But that is not a certainty. One simple fact could explain away all the evidence you have adduced as indicting the younger Karl.

"Here you go playing games with my mind again. How are you going to explain everything away?"

Two hundred thousand marks gold. A payoff of that magnitude could waken charity in the heart of a beast as foul as an ogre, perhaps. Perhaps they saw no need to plunder their hostage of pocket money.

Damn him. He could be right. The problem with this thing was that there were too many answers instead of not enough. "I don't believe it," I insisted.

Take this and reflect upon it in your cups, then. What became of the gold?

"Huh?"

Insofar as you know, the gold was turned over. Correct? By the woman Amber's direct statement, and by implication from others, all the young people wanted out of the Stormwarden's household. But the younger daPena returned. Would he have done so if it had been he who had received the gold? Or would he have run? You may have to attack it through the money after all. Or, possibly, through the entertaining girl Donni Pell, who looks like the candidate for the connection with the ogre community.

This time I said it aloud. "Damn you."

He let me have a dose of the mental noise that passes as his chuckle. *Come back in the morning, Garrett. I will suggest an approach.*

I started to go, but there was the thing that used to be Amiranda staring at me with empty eyes. "What about this?"

Leave it. We will commune.

"What's this? Are you a necromancer as well as a mental prodigy? Have you been hiding some of your lights under a bushel?"

No. I expressed myself figuratively only. Go away, Garrett. Even my boundless tolerance has its limits, and you are pressing them.

I went off and got myself rather sloppily wrapped around a few gallons of beer. Faithful to his orders, old Dean hung around and shoveled the pieces into my bed when it was time. Damn the Dead Man, anyhow. Why did he have to complicate things?

22

Old Dean knew how to get me going on the morning after. He bullied me into eating a good breakfast. When he thought I was slackening, he started banging pots and pans until I yielded to the lesser evil and resumed eating.

A good big breakfast with plenty of apple juice and sweets really knocks the edge off my hangover, but food always looks and smells so ghastly I just can't believe it will do any good.

Once I'd stoked up to Dean's satisfaction, he presented me with a huge steaming mug of a smoky-flavored herb tea that had come to us courtesy of Morley Dotes sometime back. It had a mildly analgesic nature. "His nibs is ready anytime you are, Mr. Garrett. You may take the mug along with you."

He was going to trust me carrying something out of the kitchen myself? I gave him a look that he interpreted correctly. He grumbled, "That room was creepy enough with one corpse in it. He can clean up after himself if he's going to keep the other one in there with him."

I rose. From the kitchen doorway I said, "Maybe they'll get married." Feeble, but it wasn't my best time of day.

Dean gave me a black look and reached for the biggest pot he could find.

* * *

The Dead Man was trying to sleep when I stepped into his room. He was long overdue for one of his three-week naps, but now wasn't the time. "Wake it up, Old Bones. You're supposed to have some suggestions for me this morning."

He had several, but none of the first few was fit to record. I observed, "I take it you're sure enough of your Glory Mooncalled theory that you can indulge in a little smug snoozing."

The latest from the Cantard contains nothing contradictory.

"You going to break down and tell me?"

Not yet.

"What about the suggested approach you promised me last night?"

I would have thought that you would have seen the best chance already. You had the night to reflect on next moves.

"I took the night off. Give."

You are allowing yourself to become dependent upon my genius. You should be exercising your own, Garrett.

"We human types are bone lazy. Come on. Pay the rent."

Get the younger Karl. Bring him to me. He appears to be the weakest link in the chain of circumstance. If there is a tumor of guilt in him, I will open him up and expose it. One glimpse of that poor child there should be shock enough to leave him pliable.

"That's all I have to do, eh? Just go drag him out of that fort he calls home and bully him into coming here where you can work him over."

I cannot do your legwork for you, Garrett.

"Bah!" He was getting a sarky tone on him, Old Bones was. Maybe he'd stub a toe on his Glory Mooncalled theory and get dragged down from the heights of conceit.

Oh, how he loves to strut.

There was a foreign object just inside the front door. "Dean!"

He came at a run. "Yes, Mr. Garrett?"

"What the hell is this?"

Actually, I knew what *this* was. It was my old pal Bruno frozen in midstride two steps inside the front door and leaning against the wall. His expression was one of terror and one hand grasped the air before him. Dean had used that to hang up the sweater and knit cap he wears when he comes in early mornings. That showed me a side of him I hadn't suspected.

"He came to the door while you were out in the country. When I answered he just busted in past me. His nibs must have heard the uproar."

Better than a watchdog. "And nobody bothered to tell me."

"You had things on your mind."

"How'd he get against the wall?"

"I pushed him out of the way. I have to get in and out to do the marketing."

I stepped over in front of Bruno. "What am I going to do with you? You just keep coming back. Maybe drop you in the river to see how fast you swim? I'll have to think about it, because you're getting to be a nuisance." I turned to Dean. "Maybe we ought to get a chain so things like this don't happen."

Dean admitted, "His nibs could have been asleep."

The problem of Bruno's ego slipped my mind as I trudged up the Hill. I had a bigger problem. How the devil could I get to Junior, let alone pry him out? Considering the attitudes of some up there, I might not get close to the Stormwarden's place. The hired guards might be waiting for me.

They weren't. Not obviously. I tramped around the daPena place three times, hoping maybe Amber would spot me before Eenie, Meenie, Minie and Moe started closing in and I had to show the Hill the flash of departing heels. It didn't work. I had to go. I decided to take a long walk. Sometimes getting the blood moving vanquishes the gloomier humors and the brain will come up with a thought.

The best I could manage in three hours of marching was the notion of sending Junior a letter saying I knew where the gold was and if he would come down to my place we could talk it over. The trouble with that was it might take a lot of time I didn't have.

He might dither a couple of days. Or he might not be able to slip his leash. Or the letter might not get to him at all, with highly unpredictable results. And Amiranda's body wasn't going to keep forever.

For want of something more constructive to do, I went around to Saucerhead's place to see how he was mending. A girlfriend I didn't know said he was keeping just fine and I should get the hell away before I got my eyes clawed out. She was no bigger than a minute but she had her back up and looked like she would give it a damned good shot.

So much for Saucerhead. Maybe something had fallen into Morley's lap. Besides somebody's wife or an eggplant steak dinner.

Morley wasn't anxious to accept visitors that early in the day but he was awake so I was allowed to go upstairs. He greeted me with a scowl and no banter.

I said, "You look like a guy who isn't getting enough fiber in his diet. What's the matter? Was there a crop failure in the okra forests?"

He grumbled something that sounded like, "Goddim fraggle jigginitz."

"Would you want your virgin daughters to hear language like that?"

"Snacken schtereograk!"

Aha! He was cussing, all right, but in one of the Low Elvish dialects. I've learned that when he goes to grumbling in Elvish he's usually having money troubles. "Been playing the water spiders again, have we?"

"Garrett, are you a curse upon my house?" He actually used a dwarfish idiom equally capable of being translated as "mother-in-law." But I'm such a nice fellow nobody would ever accuse me of mother-in-lawing. "You're the reverse blackbird, you know that? The backward harbinger. Every time I have some bad luck,

I have some more because you turn up right afterward.
I can count on it."

"You don't want me hanging around, stop betting on
the bugs. There's a simple cause-and-effect relationship
there—very much like the one between betting on the
bugs and losing your boots."

He repeated his curse-upon-the-house remark. "What
do you want, Garrett?"

"I want to know if you've heard any news I might
find useful."

"No. Ogre Town is as quiet as a crypt. Those guys
came from somewhere else. And they took the gold with
them when they went back. There hasn't been a whiff
of gold around town. If there was a hint of a pile that
size, you know the hard boys would be as busy as mag-
gots. Saucerhead is doing all right."

"I know. I found out the hard way. He's got some
little she-devil standing gate guard. I thought I was going
to get gutted before I got out of there. Who the hell
is she?"

He gave me the first flash of teeth of the visit. "His
sister, maybe?"

"Horse pucky. Nobody's sister carries on like that."

He grinned. "Actually, I did hear one thing you might
want to know, but I don't see how it would be much
use."

"Well?"

"A drunken sailor off a night boat staggered in here
right before we closed this morning. The gods know why
he came here."

"I was just thinking that myself. Only they know why
anybody does." "Night boat" is a euphemism for smug-
gler. Smugglers account for a third of TunFaire's river
trade.

"You want to hear this or do you want to wisecrack
your way to ignorance?"

"Speak to me, Oracle of the Lettuce."

"He mentioned that Raver Styx's ship entered the
harbor at Leifmold the afternoon they left for TunFaire.
She's on her way home, Garrett. She'll be here in a few

days. If that will make any difference in the way you do what you think you have to do."

"It might. I figure Junior deserves special attention because of Saucerhead and Amiranda. Having Mom around might present difficulties."

"That's the whole barrel, then. Go away so I can feel sorry for myself."

"Right. Next time you got to bet on the bugs, let me know so I can get down the other way and clean up."

"There won't be a next time, Garrett."

"Good for you, Morley." I left the room thinking I had heard it before. He might hang in there awhile, but sooner or later he'd hear about a sure thing and the fever would get him.

I told the barman downstairs, "Send him a couple of turnip tenderloins smothered in onions and a double shot of your high-proof celery juice, straight up. On me."

He didn't crack a smile.

I headed home, my head filled with visions of a steak so rare Morley would die to look at it.

23

Dean had the place sealed up tight. Good for him. Sometimes he forgets. I pounded away. He came and peeked through the peephole. He made a production out of checking to see if I was there under duress. Then he started clinking and clunking as he unlatched latches. He flung the door open.

"Am I glad you're finally here, Mr. Garrett." He did sound glad. He retreated. I went in after him, started to pull the door shut.

"What the hell? What's this?"

We had gained another hall ornament. This one went by the name Courter Slauce when it wasn't in the home-furnishings racket.

"Dean!"

But he was headed for the kitchen at a high-speed shuffle and dared not battle the momentum he had developed. He tossed an answer over his shoulder but it didn't have enough oomph behind it. It fell on the floor before it got to me.

I paused beside Slauce. "Finances take a turn for the worse? You'll never make ends meet housebreaking."

Funny. He didn't answer.

He could hear well enough, though. And I could almost hear the nasty thoughts slithering round inside his

head. I told him, "You'll make great company for
Bruno. He's been dying for a shoulder to cry on."

I stepped past Bruno. Such a quandary. Drop in on
the Dead Man and let him know I hadn't yet found a
way to lure Junior into his lair? Or track Dean down
and find out why we had another statue in the hall?

Dean won the toss. He was closer to the beer.

As I pushed through the door I heard Dean saying,
"There. There, now. It'll be all right. Mr. Garrett is here
now. He'll take care of everything."

Sure he would. He stepped on in to get a better idea
of where to start.

Dean had his arms around an Amber who was shaking
and looked like eighteen going on a terrified ten instead
of thirty. Dean was patting her back and trying to still
her tears. The same Dean who had stamped her with
his scarlet seal of disapproval.

Something had shaken her badly. And the soft heart
inside the old crab's shell had melted to her terror.

"Well?" I asked, sidling to the cold well. "Somebody
want to give me an idea what's going on?"

Amber let out a growl, tore herself away from Dean,
charged into me, opening the floodgates as she came. So
much for having a beer.

Dean had the grace to look embarrassed as he drifted
to the cold well.

I let Amber get the tears out. There is no point inter-
rupting a woman when she is crying. If you don't get it
over in one big chunk, you have to take it in a lot of
little ones that come at unexpected and inopportune
times. Meantime, Dean got me a mug.

When Amber was down to the sniffs and quivers, I
set her in a chair and told Dean to break out the brandy
we keep for special occasions. I settled opposite her, in
hand-touching range, and went to work on my mug. The
first half went down quick and easy.

When I thought she was ready, I asked, "Can you talk
about it now?"

She took a big bite out of her brandy before she nodded. "I have it under control. It was just . . . the circum-

stances, I guess. Domina and my father having a screaming argument that had everybody running for cover. Then the news about Karl. Then when I finally managed to sneak out so I could come talk to you, Courter caught up with me down the street, and when I wouldn't go back home, the look he got made me think he wanted to kill me, too. I went kind of crazy and ran away screaming. But if the whole world has gone crazy, don't I have the right to get a little crazy myself?"

The words tumbled out of her, tripping over one another in their haste to dance in the open air.

"Hold it! Halt! Stop! Good girl. Now take a deep breath. Hold it. Count to ten, slowly. Good. Now tell me what happened. Start from the beginning so it makes sense."

Dean took my mug, which needed filling, and at the same time interrupted. "If you'll pardon me, Mr. Garrett, the most important point comes out of order. Her brother is dead."

I stared at Amber. She shivered, nodded. She was counting well past ten. "How?"

"They say he committed suicide."

That caught me flat-footed. I didn't know what to say. Before I got my mind in order, my permanent motionless houseguest broke all precedent and reached out beyond the bounds of his demesne.

Garrett. Bring them in here.

Dean caught it, too. He looked to me for instructions. "Do what he says, I guess. Amber, come with me. My associate wants us to talk it over in his presence."

"Do I have to?"

"Keep thinking two hundred thousand marks gold."

"I'm not sure I want to keep on . . . Of course I do. I want out of that place more than ever, now. I'll never feel safe there again."

"Let's go, then. Don't worry about him. He's harmless to those who intend him no harm."

I'd forgotten one thing.

24

Amber let out a squeal that was half pain, half horror. I thought she would faint. But she was made of tougher stuff than I suspected. She hung on to my arm a bit while she stared at Amiranda, then got hold of herself, stepped back, looked at me. "What's going on, Garrett?"

"That's what I found instead of the gold."

She stepped over to the corpse.

Bring Mr. Slauce, Garrett. It may be helpful to present him with the same shock.

"What about the other one?"

Dispose of him once we are done here. He should have learned his lesson.

"Want to give me a hand, Dean?" I didn't doubt that I could manage Slauce by myself. If nothing else, I could tip him over and roll him. But why strain myself?

We dragged him inside and per instructions set him down facing Amiranda. Amber seemed in control again. She said, "You have some things to tell me."

"I'll tell you my story if you'll tell me yours."

About then the Dead Man loosed his hold on Courter Slauce. I went to the door to make sure he didn't use it before we were done with him. He shook all over. There wasn't much bluff in him when he looked around. He didn't say anything. That disappointed me. I'd expected some bluster and the invocation of the Stormwarden.

"I want to know some things," I told him. "I think Miss daPena has a few questions, too. It's even possible Miss Crest might want to know why she was killed."

His eyes darted to the corpse. "I don't know nothing about that. Where did that come from? I thought she run off. Domina has been chewing my butt for days because she managed to get out of the house with her stuff. Never mind that I was halfway across town delivering a letter to one of the Baronet's girlfriends when she did it. That wouldn't have done for an excuse anyway, since I couldn't tell her."

He is telling the truth he believes, Garrett.

"Then he wasn't in on it?"

"Not wittingly, though I did not say that, Garrett.

"All right. Slauce. Who kidnapped Junior?"

"What the hell? How should I know? What the hell are you doing sticking your nose in, anyway? You got paid. You're out of it."

"That supposes nobody but Willa Dount would hire me. Slauce, I think you know the answer to the question. Just in case, though, I'll tell you the answer. Nobody kidnapped him. Unless a man can kidnap himself. My main interest, though, is why did Amiranda have to be killed? And who said the word that made it happen?"

Amber opened her mouth. I raised a hand, cautioned her to silence. Slauce didn't need to know her angle.

You are getting ahead of yourself, Garrett. No interrogation or manipulation of this man can be soundly founded—until we have heard everything Miss daPena has to tell us. Have you forgotten what brought her here? Or is her brother's demise too trivial for consideration?

I hadn't forgotten. I was stalling, having to deal with Amber's grief and hysteria and hoping for a breakthrough with Slauce that would give me the answer to my own dilemma. But I wasn't thinking soundly. Not to hear Amber out would be stupid.

Since I'm one of the smartest guys around, it wouldn't do for me to tarnish my image by doing something dumb.

"You win, Old Bones. But upon your head be the rainfall."

It was not I who felt compelled to charge off to the rescue.

It is possible, with great concentration, to shut him out—if he has other things on his minds. He always has to have the last word. There are times he has all the disadvantages of a wife, with none of the advantages.

"Amber. You feel up to telling me what you came to tell? All settled down now?"

Slauce started snarling. "Girl, you don't talk to this guy about nothing. You don't do nothing but march yourself straight home."

I scowled at the Dead Man and said, "You had to let him get his second wind."

Amber told Slauce, "Shove your elbow up your nose, Courter. You don't scare me anymore. In a couple of days you and Domina are going to be hanging out in the wind. Aren't you? Maybe you could bull-smoke your way around Karl, but not Karl *and* Amiranda. And I'm sure not going back there and give you guys a chance to explain to Mother about Karl and Amiranda and *me!*"

"What kind of crazy talk is that, girl? Your brother killed himself."

"Just like Amiranda ran away. Give me credit for knowing my brother. You're not going to sell me that. My mother isn't going to buy it, either. And I'm not going anywhere near any of you people. Not when two out of the three family heirs suddenly turned up murdered."

"Three out of four," I tossed in, just to see how high the water would splash. "Amiranda was pregnant. Three months. The child would have been male."

That was a surprise to both Amber and Slauce. It silenced them. But if it wakened any suspicions, they concealed them well.

I faced the Dead Man, indicated Slauce. "Shut him off, will you? I don't need him shoving his oar in while the lady is talking."

What lady?

Slauce went stiff as a corpse.

Timely revelation, Garrett. You have him rattled and

reflective. But you may have cost yourself your credibility with the girl. She has begun to suspect that you have not been candid about your own motives.

Yeah.

25

I said, "I think the best way would be for you to start right after the last time we talked."

Amber balked. "You aren't interested in anything but Ami."

"Oh?" I admitted an interest. "And I want whoever did this to her. I don't like people who waste attractive young women. But if you think I'm immune to the charms of a share of two hundred thousand marks gold, then you're a lot sillier than I think you are. Listen here. I'd be on this trail just as hot if that was you over there and Amiranda was standing where you are. I want the guy behind it. And I'll bet your mother will, too, once she gets here."

"There'll be hell to pay."

She is going to buy it, Garrett. You slick talker.

I gave the Dead Man the look he deserved. "Amber, right now all I have to work with is what you can tell me."

She stalled long enough to satisfy her ego, then got to it. "Courter saw you when you were leaving. He ran right to Domina. Naturally. And she flew into one of her rages. Only more so. I've seen her angry before but I never ever saw her lose control. She screamed and threatened and threw things and scared Karl so bad he told her everything we said. So it's good we didn't say anything about the gold. He would have told her about that, too. I didn't tell her anything. That made her mad all over again, so she had Courter give me a beating and lock me in my room. They didn't let me out till this morning."

She pirouetted, pranced over to Slauce, slapped him, and danced back. "There."

"They," it turned out, had been Karl, who had come to her while the house was asleep, unlocking her door. He had seemed severely troubled but had refused to explain except to say that he'd had all that he could take and was going away now and wouldn't be back.

"But that didn't mean he was going to kill himself."

I didn't believe he was the type, either. Not enough guts. "You'd better go over what he said. There might be some hint there. Try to recall his exact words and actions."

"I don't know how I could get his words more exact. Except that he asked me to go with him. I told him I wasn't miserable enough yet to give up and run without any prospects. But he was. Really. Something had shaken him badly. He was pale. He couldn't stand still. He was sweating."

"In other words, he was scared."

"Terrified."

"Like he had seen a ghost?"

"That's funny."

"What is?"

"That's exactly what I thought then. That he must have seen a ghost."

"Maybe he did. At least secondhand. Go on. He left?"

"As soon as he knew I wasn't going with him."

"Any hint where?"

"A safe place with an old friend is what he told me when I asked."

"Donni Pell?"

"Maybe. That's what I thought when he said it. The way he said it. Donni Pell or Ami. I just figured he knew where Ami went."

"Why Amiranda?"

"They grew up together. They were close. They always had their heads together. If she ran away, he had to know where she went. She wouldn't go without leaving him a message somehow. Even if he was kidnapped when she went."

The more I saw of them, the more the workings and relationships of the daPena family baffled me. "All right. It could have been Amiranda but it wasn't because she was dead. We have to assume it was Donni Pell. That might not be true but anything else seems unlikely. Given his nature, it would have been a woman. Correct? Who else did he know? No one you or I know about. I guess I'll have to go there and see."

This business was all legwork. Morley would approve of the exercise I was getting. "Go on with the story. Your brother decamped, headed for parts unknown, frightened. Then what?"

"Twenty minutes later, Courter came. They knew Karl was out. They wanted me to tell them where he went."

"They?"

"Courter. It wasn't really they till later. But Courter didn't come on his own. They sent him."

"I assume you gave him valuable advice on the placement of his elbow."

"Yes. So my father took his place. He was as pale and sweaty as Karl had been. And he had a wild look that scared me. Like he was so terrified he was capable of anything. He didn't get anywhere either. He did a lot of yelling. My father yells a lot. I mostly just stayed out of his reach till Domina came in. She tried to keep me from hearing what she said, but I heard part of it. She'd heard from one of the staff that Karl had heard that Mother was in Leifmold. Meaning Mother could show up anytime because she could get to TunFaire almost as fast as the news that she was coming. Father really got excited then."

"And?"

Amber seemed ashamed. "I want you to know, I love my father. Even when he does irrational things."

I tried my raised-eyebrow trick. I hadn't been practicing lately. She wasn't impressed.

"He screamed at Domina to get Courter. They'd beat it out of me. She couldn't calm him down, so she went out, I guess to get Courter. Father came after me. And he actually did hit me. He never did that before. Not himself."

"And?"

"I picked up a shoe and bopped him over the head. He went away. And he didn't come back. A couple hours later I heard him and Domina having a screaming match all the way from her side of the house. But I couldn't tell what it was about. I thought about sneaking over and eavesdropping but I didn't. I was scared to go out of my room. Everybody was going crazy. And then a little while after that, I decided I had to get out of that house. Forever. No matter what. Even if you can't find the gold."

"Why?"

"Because one of the servants told me that Karl had committed suicide. When I heard that, I knew I had to get away. Far away, where nobody could find me. Or I might be dead, too. Only I didn't run fast enough, I guess. Because Courter caught up with me just before I got here. He even tried to come in and drag me back out when your man let me in."

I considered Courter, then the Dead Man. He would be monitoring Slauce's reactions as closely as he could.

The man is a villain for certain, Garrett, but he appears to have no guilty knowledge concerning the death of Karl Junior or his supposed kidnapping. Much of what he has heard here has been news to him. He appears to be slow of wit and it could be that he is considered too stupid to be trusted.

I faced Amber. "You're convinced your brother was incapable of taking his own life?"

"Yes. I told you that already."

"All right. That gives me a new line of attack. Where, when, and how did it happen?"

"I don't know."

"You don't know? You mean you just—"

"Don't you start yelling at me too!" She lifted a foot, snatched off a shoe, and brandished it.

Three seconds later we were shaking with laughter.

I got hold of myself, gave Slauce a look, shifted it to the Dead Man.

He knows.

"Dean, take Miss daPena to the guest room and get her settled. While you're at it, you might as well fix yourself up for a few more nights. We're going to need you here."

"Yes sir." He sounded excited. At least he was in on this thing. "Miss? If you'll come with me?"

She went reluctantly.

26

"I think I have to revise my strategy," I said. "I was going to let Slauce have the works so he could go home and get things stirred up."

I assumed as much. I believe it is time you approached Mr. Dotes on a purely business basis, instead of favor for favor. You need more eyes.

"Right. Things are stirred up enough without me sticking my hand in. Can you make him forget what he's seen and heard here?"

I think so.

"Then let's see what he has to tell about Junior checking out."

The Dead Man released his hold on Slauce.

Friend Courter was vulnerable. When I asked, he answered, and didn't start toughening up for several minutes. He gave me an address and an approximate time of death only two hours after Karl had fled his home.

"How did he do it?" I asked, for Courter's sake going with the suicide fiction.

"He slashed his wrists."

That was the clincher. "Aw, come on! And you believed that? You knew the kid. If you'd said he'd hanged himself, I might have thought it was just barely possible. But even I knew him well enough to know he couldn't cut on himself. He was probably the kind of guy who couldn't shave because he was afraid he might see a speck of blood."

Do not press, Garrett. You will get him to thinking. For him that might prove to be a dangerous new experience.

He just wanted his own job made easier.

You go see Mr. Dotes now. By the time you return, Mr. Slauce will have forgotten this episode entirely. He will be a bit intoxicated. Take that into consideration when you are planning how you will remove him from the premises. And you might as well consider doing the other one while you are at it.

Right. Grumble. I left him to his fun.

Morley rented me five thugs. His discount to the trade left their price only semi-usurious. I assigned one man to keep an eye on my place just in case something happened that the Dead Man couldn't handle alone. The world is filled with unpredictable people.

One man got the job of keeping track of Courter Slauce. The remaining three got the unenviable task of trying to keep tabs on the denizens of the Stormwarden's house. I told them they should report to Morley. Dotes would have a better chance of tracking me down if there was something I needed to know.

Five men weren't enough to do the job the way it ought to be done, but this one was out of my own pocket. The only client I had was one who had retained me on a contingency basis, and while I was willing to grab off a chunk of that ransom, I had a pessimistic view of my chances.

I made a mental note to quiz Amber about what she had learned regarding Domina Dount's handling and delivery of all that gold.

Disposing of Bruno and Slauce was an easy half hour's work with a borrowed buggy. An unconscious Bruno got dumped into an alley where he'd soon waken hungry enough to go into the cannibal business.

Courter wasn't all the way out. He was just roaring drunk. I don't know how the Dead Man managed that.

He never said. I just walked Slauce into a tavern, sat him down with a pitcher, then took the buggy back where it belonged.

Then it was time to go see what could be seen at the scene of Junior's suicide.

27

The wooden tenements, three and four stories tall, leaned against one another like wounded soldiers after the battle. But the war never ended down here. Time was the enemy never to be conquered and there were no reserves to help stay the tide.

It was night and the only light in the street fell from doors and windows open in hopes the day's heat would sneak away. That was a hope only slightly less vain than the hope that poverty would take to its heels. The street was full of serious-faced, gaunt children and the tenements were filled with quarreling adults. The corners, though, lacked their prides of narrow-eyed young men looking for a chance under the guise of cool indifference. No dares issued or taken.

They were all in the Cantard, burning youth's energy in futility and fear, soldiering.

The war had that one positive spinoff. When you wanted to talk about your crime, you had to go find senior citizens who remembered the good old days before the war.

I still had to watch my step—for reasons evoking no romance at all. There were as many dogs in the street as kids. And at any moment the sky might open and spit out a cloudburst of refuse.

There were sanitary laws, but who paid attention? There was no one to enforce them.

The place I sought was one more crippled soldier in the host, three stories that had seen their youth spent before the turn of the century. I planted myself across the way and considered it. Assumption: Junior had run to his friend Donni Pell when he felt the heat. Assumption: Donni Pell had been in on and had helped stage Junior's kidnapping.

The nature of the place where young Karl had died implied that there was something wrong with one or both assumptions. Having collected possibly the biggest ransom ever paid in TunFaire, why would she hole up in such a dump?

If he hadn't run to Donni, then who? No other name had come up. Junior didn't have friends.

Not even one, apparently. Death had sniffed out his hiding place in under two hours.

All the excitement was over, and had been for many hours. In that part of town even the most grotesque death was a wonder only until the blood dried. I began to be an object of interest myself, standing there doing nothing but look. I moved.

There are no locks or bolts on the street doors of those places. Such would only inconvenience the comings and goings of the masses packed inside. I went in, stepped over a sleeping drunk sprawled on the battered floor. The treads of the stair creaked and groaned as I went up. There was no point in sneaking.

Sneakery would have been useless anyway. Getting to the right room on the third floor took me past two others that had no doors. Families fell silent, stared as I passed.

The death room had a door, but not one that would close tightly. It skidded against the floor as I pushed.

It was the sort of place I had pictured—one room, eight-by-twelve, no furnishings, one window with a shutter but no glass. A bunch of blankets were thrown against a wall for a bed, and odds and ends were scattered around. One corner had walls and floor spattered with patches and brown spots. It had been messy. But those things always are. There is a lot of juice in the human fruit.

They must have fastened him down somehow. You don't carve on someone without them putting up a fuss. I kicked around the place but found no ropes or straps or anything that might have bound him. I guess even ogre breeds have sense enough to pick up after themselves sometimes.

Or did they?

Mixed in with the tangle of bedding was a familiar item, from Karl's description. It was a doeskin bag with a heavy, long drawstring. Just the thing to pop over a guy's head and choke him unconscious.

It was stained with dried vomit. I pictured some fastidious thug hurling it aside in disgust.

You might not need to tie a guy if you strangle him before you cut. He could bleed to death before he woke up.

"It's a half-mark silver a week, as is. You want furnishings, you bring your own."

I gave the woman in the doorway my innocent look. "What about the mess?"

"You want cleanup, that's a mark right now. You want fix-up, take care of it yourself."

"Come off the rent?"

She looked at me like I was crazy. "You pay up front, every week. You show me you're reliable, after a few months I might understand if you're one or two days late. Three days and out you go. Got that?"

She was a charmer in every respect. Had she not possessed the winning personality of a lizard, a guy might have been tempted to have her hair and clothes washed. She couldn't have been much past thirty, only the inside had gone completely to seed. But the rest wouldn't be far behind.

"You're staring like you think the place comes with entertainment." She tried a cautious smile from which a few teeth were missing. "That costs you extra, too."

I had a thought. An inspiration, perhaps. What do

hookers do when they get too old or too slovenly to compete? Not all can become Lettie Farens. Maybe this was someone Donni had known before she had become a landlady.

"I'm not so much interested in the room as I am in the tenant." I palmed a gold piece, let her see a flash. Her eyes popped. Then her face closed down, became all suspicious frowns framed by wild, filthy hair.

"The tenant?"

"The tenant. The person who lived in the room. Also the person who paid for it, if they weren't the same."

Still the suspicious eyes. "Who wants to know?"

I looked at the coin. "Dister Greteke." Old Dister was a dead king, of which we in TunFaire are blessed with a lot. We could use a live one—if he'd do something worthwhile.

"A double?"

"Looks like one to me."

"It was a kid named Donny Pell. I don't know where he went. He paid his own rent." She reached.

"You're kidding. Donny Pell, eh? Did you meet him while you were still in the trade?" I put the coin on the windowsill, drifted away. She licked her lips, took one step. She wasn't stupid. She saw the trap taking shape. But she couldn't shake the greed, and maybe she thought she could bluff me. She took another step.

In moments she was at the window and I was at the door. "You going to tell me?"

"What do you need to know?"

"Donni Pell. But female. From Lettie Faren's place. Came here to hide out maybe a week ago. Right?"

She nodded. She had a little shame left.

"You knew her before?"

"I was there when she first came to the place. She was different than the other girls. Ambitious. But kind of decent then. If you know what I mean. Maybe she got too ambitious." The knuckles of her right hand whitened as she squeezed the coin. She'd been out of the trade awhile. It had been awhile since she'd seen that kind of money. Doubtless when it had been easy come she hadn't thought to put any aside. Her gaze strayed to the bloodstains. "She developed weird tastes in friends."

"Ogre breeds?"

That surprised her. "Yeah. How did you—"

"I know some things. Some things I don't. You know some things and you don't know what I don't know." I borrowed a trick from Morley Dotes by getting my knife out and going to work on my nails. "So why don't you just tell me everything you do know about her and the people who visited her here."

Her bluff was a feeble bolt and she knew it. But she tried. "I yell and the whole place will be in here in half a minute."

"I'll bet the fellow in the corner thought the same thing."

She looked at the bloodstain again. "Fair is fair. I was just seeing if you'd pay a little more. All right? What do you want to know?"

"I told you. Everything. Especially who else was here this morning and where she is now." To forestall the next round of delays I added, "I don't mean her any harm. I'm looking for some of her playmates. She's gotten herself caught in the middle of a big and deadly game."

Maybe very deadly for her. If there was to be a next victim in this mess, I'd put all my money on Donni Pell. If I had any chance, I wanted to find her before the villains eliminated the next link in their chain of vulnerability.

"I don't know where she went. I didn't know she was gone till somebody found the mess. That's the gods' honest truth, mister."

She sounded like she was telling the truth. I must have had a ferocious look in my eye. She was getting nervous. But with a hooker you never know. Their whole lives are lies and some of the falsehoods run so deep they don't know the difference.

"Look, mister . . ."

"Just keep talking, sweetheart. I'll let you know when I've gotten my money's worth."

"Only three people ever visited her here that I know about. The one who killed himself here this morning." If she wanted to keep up the pretense on that, it was all right by me. "That was the only time he ever came that I know of. Another one came twice. Both times he was all covered up in one of them hooded cloaks rich guys wear when they go out at night. I never saw his face. I never heard his name."

Inconvenient for me, that, but she was doing all right, considering. "How tall?"

"Shorter than you. I think. I never was very good judging how tall people are."

"How old?"

"I told you, he wore one of them cloaks."

"What about his voice?"

"I never heard him talk."

"When did he come here?" I was determined to get something.

"Last night was the first time. He stayed about two hours. I guess you can figure what they were doing. Then he came back this morning."

I was all over her then, trying to pin down the order of events. But she couldn't get straight who had come when. "I think the cloaked man was first. Maybe not. Maybe it was the one who killed himself. The other one came last, though, I'm pretty sure. Two of them was here at the same time, I think, but I don't know which two."

She wasn't very bright, this woman. Also, she had been very scared. Donni's third visitor, who, it developed, had visited almost every night, had spooked her.

She was sure, almost, that the cloaked man had been the first to leave. Maybe.

"Tell me about this third man. This regular visitor. This guy who scared you so bad. He sounds interesting."

He wasn't interesting to her. She didn't want to talk about him at all. He was bad mojo.

I took that as a good sign. She knew something here. With a little sweet talk . . . "I'm badder mojo, lover. I'm here." A little deft work with the knife . . .

"All right, Bruno. All right. You don't have to get

mean. He can take care of you himself. The guys he ran with called him Gorgeous. If you ever saw him, you'd know why. He was meaner than a wolfman on weed."

"Ugly?" Part ogre, I thought. What else? There had to be an ogre in it somewhere.

"Ugly! So ugly you couldn't tell if he was a breed or not. He came with different guys different times, some of them breeds, some of them not. But always with this one breed he called Skredli."

My eyes must have lit up, and not entirely with joy. She backed away a step, threw up a hand, looked for some place to hide. "Easy, woman. Skredli? Now that's a name I've been wanting to hear. Are you sure?"

"Sure I'm sure."

"You told me only three men ever came here. But now you've got this Gorgeous visiting with a crowd."

"The ones who came with him never came inside. They were like bodyguards or something. Except that Skredli guy did come inside this morning, I think, and maybe one other time. Yeah. That's right. I think he even come here one other time, too, by himself, and stayed with her a couple hours, I forgot about that. Ick." She shuddered. "Doing it with an ogre."

"I want this Skredli. Where do I find him?"

She shrugged. "I don't know. Ogre Town, I guess. But when you find him, you're going to find Gorgeous, too. And maybe the girl. Only she'll probably be dressed like a boy again. Using Donny Pell. Why don't you get out of here? Why don't you leave me the hell alone?"

"Do you know anything else?"

"No."

"Of course you do. Who came for the body? What were they going to do with it?"

"I guess they were his family. Or from his family. Fancy people off the Hill with their own private soldiers and no charity in them for poor people. They talked like they were going to have him cremated."

I grunted. That was the thing to do if you didn't want anybody getting too close a look at the stiff. Like, say, the woman who had given life to the flesh.

Or maybe I was *too* suspicious. This business can do that to you. You have to remember to keep it simple. You don't need to look for the great sinuous, complicated schemes reeking of subterfuge and malice when a little stupidity followed by desperate cover-up efforts will explain everything just as well. And you have to remember to keep an eye out for who stands to gain. That alone will flag your villain eight times out of ten.

That, more than any other facet of the affair, baffled me this time. Not the gold side, of course. However that worked out, the gold was its own explanation. But who could profit from the death of Amiranda Crest? How and why?

I stared at the woman. She wouldn't know. I doubted that she knew anything more worth digging out. "Step back into the corner, please. That's fine. Now sit yourself down."

She grew pale. Her hands, clasped around her knees, were bone white as she fought to keep them from shaking.

"You'll be all right," I promised. "I just want to know where you are while I go over this place again."

I found exactly what I expected to find. Zip. I took the doeskin bag and headed out.

As I passed through the doorway the woman called after me, "Mister, do you know anybody who wants to rent a room?"

28

I found myself a syrupy shadow and installed myself across from the tenement. The street was empty of people now, and of the more honest cats and dogs. The yelling and scuffling inside the buildings had died down. The slum was gathering its strength for tomorrow's frays.

I waited. I waited some more. Then I waited. A band of pubescent marauders swept past, in search of trouble, but they didn't spot me. I waited.

After two hours I gave up. Either the woman had no intention of running to Gorgeous and Skredli or she had left the building another way. I suspected she felt no need to take warning.

I set myself for a long night. First, home to let the Dead Man know what I'd learned, then to Morley's place to find out what his people had reported and to learn what he knew about a thug named Gorgeous. Maybe more after that if anything interesting had turned up.

The interesting stuff started before I got to the house. Despite the hour there were a bunch of guys hanging around out front. I held up and watched awhile.

That is all they were doing. Hanging around. And not trying to hide the fact. I moved a little closer. I could then see that they wore livery. Closer still, I saw that the livery belonged to the Stormwarden Raver Styx.

Not being inclined to cooperate if they were waiting around to do evil when I showed, I slid away and approached the house from the rear. We had no company back there. I rapped and tapped till I got Dean's attention. He let me in.

"What have we got, Dean?"

"Company from the Hill."

"I suspected that. That's why I'm so good in this business. When I see fifteen guys hanging around in the street, I have a hunch that we've got company. What about our guest?"

"Upstairs. Buttoned up tight and keeping quiet."

"She knows?"

"I warned her."

"Good. Where is the company?"

"In your office. Waiting impatiently."

"She'll have to keep on waiting. I'm hungry and I want to let the old boy in on what I picked up. And I wouldn't mind guzzling about a gallon of beer before I face that harpy."

That made two chances I'd given him to ask how I'd guessed that my company was Domina Dount and twice that he'd ignored the bait. He has his little ways of getting even.

"Won't do no good to bother his nibs. He's gone to sleep."

"With an outsider in the house?"

"I suppose he trusts you to handle it." Dean's tone suggested he had a suspicion that the Dead Man's genius had lapsed, that maybe he'd rounded the last turn and was headed down that final stretch toward Loghyr heaven.

It looked like I now had two of them who couldn't keep straight who owned the house and who was the guest or employee. I wouldn't be surprised if Dean wasn't thinking about moving in. He'd reached the occasional nag-about-money stage.

"Be nice, Dean. Or I'll leave you standing at the altar and run off with Willa Dount."

He didn't find that amusing.

"I might as well be married the way things are going around here."

He slapped a plate in front of me like an old wife in a snit. But the food was up to par.

I permitted myself a satisfied smirk.

29

Up north along the edge of the thunder-lizard country there is a region called Hell's Reach. It's not wholly uninhabitable but nobody lives there by choice. Everywhere you turn there are hot geysers, steaming sulfur pits, and places where the raw earth lies there molten, quivering, occasionally humping up to belch out a big *ka-bloop!* of gas.

The lava pools sprang to mind the instant I saw Willa Dount. All her considerable will was bent toward restraining a hot fury. She had an almost red glow about her, but was determined to give it no vent.

"Good evening," I said. "Had I expected a caller, I wouldn't have stayed out so late." I settled myself and my mug. "I hope you haven't been inconvenienced too much." Before I'd left the kitchen Dean had reminded me about sugar, vinegar, and flies, and I'd taken his advice to heart.

It's not smart to go out of your way to make enemies of the Hill, anyway.

"It has been a wait, but my own fault," she replied. Amazing that she would admit the possibility of fault in anything she did. "But had I sent someone to make an appointment, I would have been delayed even longer— if you would have been willing to see me at all. I'm certain you would have refused to come to me again."

"Yes."

"I'm aware that you don't hold me in high regard, Mr. Garrett. Certainly your contacts with my charges have done nothing to elevate your opinion. Even so, that shouldn't interfere with a business relationship. In our contacts thus far you have remained, for the most part, professionally detached."

"Thank you. I try." I do. Sometimes.

"Indeed. And I need you in your professional capacity once more. Not just for show this time."

It was my turn to say, "Indeed?" But I fooled her. I showed her my talented eyebrow instead.

"I'm desperate, Mr. Garrett. My world is falling into ruin around me and I seem to be incapable of halting the decay. I have come to my last resort—no. That's getting ahead of myself."

I told my face it was supposed to look enrapt with anything she might say.

"I have spent my entire adult life in the Stormwarden's employ, Mr. Garrett. Beginning before her father died. It's seldom been pleasant. There have been no holidays. The rewards have been questionable, perhaps. By being privy to inside information, I've managed to amass a small personal fortune, perhaps ten thousand marks. And I've developed an image of myself as a virtual partner in the Stormwarden's enterprises, able to be trusted with anything and capable of carrying any task through to the desired conclusion. In that spirit I've done things I wouldn't admit to my confessor, but with pride that I could be trusted to get them done and trusted not to talk about them later. Do you understand?"

I nodded. No point slowing her down.

"So a few months ago she was called to the Cantard because the course of the war seemed to be swinging our way and it was time to put on all the pressure we could. She left me to manage the household, as she has done a dozen times, and especially charged me with riding herd on her family, all of whom had been showing an increasing tendency toward getting involved in scandals."

"The two Karls, you mean? They're the ones the

rumor mill loved. I never heard of the daughter till the other day."

"She was blind, the Stormwarden. Those girls were the ones who were deserving. Though Amber had begun to show signs of getting wild, just for the attention."

I nodded as my contribution.

She took a deep breath. "Since she's been gone this time, it's been like I've been under a curse. Father and son were determined to circumvent me at every turn. Then that kidnapping business had to come. I had to deplete the family treasury severely, selling silver at a discount, to get that much gold together. It was a disaster, but for a cause the Stormwarden could respect once her temper cooled. I might even have survived Amiranda's having taken flight during the confusion. The girl was restless for some time before she took off. The Stormwarden herself had remarked that it was coming. But putting out two hundred thousand marks gold to ransom Karl, only to have him take his own life, that's insupportable."

Was I supposed to know about Junior or not? Instinct told me to play it cautious. "Did you say that Karl killed himself?"

"This morning. He slashed his wrists and bled to death in a hole of a room in Fishwife's Close."

"Why the hell would he do that?"

"I don't know, Mr. Garrett. And to be perfectly frank, at this point I can't much care. He destroyed me by doing it. Maybe that was his motive. He was a strange boy and he hated me. But Karl isn't the reason I came here. I'm doomed when the Stormwarden returns, which she will very shortly. However, my pride—badly mauled but not yet dead—insists I go on, trying to salvage what I can on her behalf. Amber fled the house this morning. This is where you come in."

I told my face to look interested.

"Amiranda and Amber are at large and therefore at risk. If I can salvage that much for the Stormwarden, I will. I'm going to try. I have gone into my own funds to do so. I want you to find those girls. If you can."

She plomped a sack down in front of me.

"One hundred marks gold, to retain you. I'll pay a fee of one thousand marks gold each if you can return either of those girls before the Stormwarden comes home."

"Your man Slauce can't handle—"

"Courter Slauce is an incompetent imbecile. This morning I sent him after Amber. He turned up just before I left to come here, too drunk to recall where he'd been or what he'd been doing. I console myself with the certainty that he'll starve to death after the Stormwarden chucks the lot of us into the street. Will you look for my missing girls, Mr. Garrett?"

"Give me a few minutes to think." I had to smooth out some dents in my ethics and reach an accommodation with my conscience. I considered myself to be working for three clients already: myself, Saucerhead, and Amber. Though Amber wasn't getting the first-class production. And nobody was paying me.

Willa Dount would be paying, though she wouldn't be getting her money's worth. Still, an experiment had occurred to me.

"Suppose I had a notion where I could find one of the girls right now?"

"Do you?"

"Take it as a supposition. How can I be certain I'd get my fee?"

She levered herself out of her chair, straining like a woman decades older. "I came prepared for that possibility." What might have been a smile tickled the corner of her mouth.

She started digging sacks out of her clothing. In a minute there was a line of ten before me, each a twin of the one offered me as a retainer. I checked the contents of one at random.

It was good.

Eleven hundred marks gold. More than I'd ever had a chance at before. With prospects for another thousand, which I could collect easily. Certainly a temptation to test the dark side of a man's soul.

We all look for the big hit—hope for it, talk about

it—but I don't believe we *think* about it. Not seriously. Because when it's suddenly there, a lot of thinking has to be done.

Amiranda was dead. And what was Amber to me? Morley always says the supply of women is inexhaustible. And who would I have to explain to or make excuses to?

Just to myself. With maybe the Dead Man smirking over my shoulder.

Still, there was the possibility of a useful experiment.

I rose and collected the gold in one big bear hug. "Come with me."

Dean had turned down the lamps in the Dead Man's room. I don't know why he thinks that makes any difference. The Dead Man doesn't care about light one way or the other. When he wants to sleep, he'll sleep through sun, lightning, or earthquake. I hied me down and deposited the take beside his chair.

Domina Dount asked, "Are you going to deliver something or not, Mr. Garrett?"

"Turn around."

For a moment she was human. She let out a little squeak and raised her hands to her cheeks. But she asserted control, taking a full minute to get the parts into the desired order. Then she murmured, "Will the disasters never end?"

She faced me. "I presume you can explain?"

"Explain what?"

She took ten seconds, eyes closed.

I prodded. "You engaged me to find and deliver to you, if possible, Amber daPena and Amiranda Crest. I've done half the job already."

She stared at me and hated me through narrowed eyelids. Her voice remained neutral, though, as she remarked, "I had hoped that you would deliver them in better health. She *is* dead? Not in a trance or ensorcelled?"

"Yes. Amiranda has been in poor health for some time now."

"Your attempts at wit become tiresome, Garrett. I suppose I can assume that you weren't the agent of death. I want to know the who, what, when, where, why, and how."

So did I.

My experiment had flopped. Domina Dount wasn't about to be flustered into giving anything away. If there was anything in her that I didn't already have.

"Well?" she demanded.

Why not? I might still shake something loose. "The day you were supposed to make the ransom payoff, Amiranda hired a friend of mine as her bodyguard. That night he accompanied her into the countryside north of TunFaire. She took several travel cases with her. She went to a crossroad near Lichfield, where she stopped. My friend thought she expected to meet somebody there and that he was supposed to have been dismissed when that somebody showed."

"Who?"

"I don't know. He, she, or it never came. A band of ogre breeds did instead. My friend killed some of them but he couldn't drive them off or keep them from killing Amiranda. He couldn't even save himself, though the ogres thought he was dead enough to throw into the bushes with Amiranda and the other casualties. When they scattered to keep from being seen by travelers, my friend found the strength to pick Amiranda up and carry her three miles to someone he knew who, he hoped, could save her."

"To no avail."

"Of course. My friend isn't very smart. He'd failed. He was outraged and his pride was hurt. Somehow, he got back to Tunfaire, as far as the Bledsoe infirmary, where I got his story in the deathwatch ward."

Willa Dount frowned, uncertain why I'd told her what I had. "You've left something out, haven't you?"

"Yes."

"Why?"

"Because you don't need to know. Because no one

needs to know except my friend's friends—some of them are the kind of guys who eat ogres for breakfast—who figure there's some balancing due for what got done."

You couldn't crack Willa Dount with a hammer. She looked at me straight in the eye and said, "That's why you've been digging around and poking your nose in."

"Yes."

"The Stormwarden resents people who pry into her family's affairs."

"I'll bet she resents people killing her kids even more." Me and my big damned mouth! I'd blown a potful for free there. But she didn't seem to notice.

"Maybe. But those who stick their noses in often become victims of deteriorating health."

I chuckled. "I'll keep that in mind. I'm sure my friend's friends will, too. They might even be so disturbed they'll give the problem enough attention to handle it before she gets home."

I'd abandoned the tactic of experimentation for the strategy of increasing the pressure on Willa Dount. Not that I had her fixed for anything, but she knew things *I* wanted to know. Maybe she would tell me some to get the heat off.

"How about you tell me the how, where, and when of the ransom payment?"

Domina Dount smiled a thin smile. "No, Mr. Garrett." She thought she was covered. If she had any need.

I shrugged. "So be it. Do you need a way to transport the body? I could send my man—"

"I came in a coach. That will do. I'll send my men in to get it."

"No you won't. You have the coach brought. I'll carry it out."

She smiled again. "Very well."

As I looked away from the coach, Domina Dount told me, "You will try to deliver Amber in better condition, won't you?"

I took a count of five, letting my irritation with her

confidence in the power of her gold cool out. I kept reminding myself that it was just business. "I'll do my damnedest."

She climbed into her coach smiling, sure she'd taken the round by getting to me more than I'd gotten to her. I wasn't so sure she was wrong.

I went inside to see what the Dead Man thought of her.

The fat dead son of a bitch had slept through the whole damned thing.

30

I finished a long, cold one and wiped my lips. "I feel like killing the keg, but the night has only just begun. Tell Miss daPena the Domina has gone, but if she has the least sense and regard for her life, she won't even peek out a window. We may have reached a stage where people are cleaning up loose ends, real and imagined. I'm going to see Mr. Dotes. I'll slide out the back in case somebody is watching. You lock up tight. Don't answer the door unless you look first and see that it's me."

Dean scowled, but he'd been around long enough to have seen tight times before. He got out a meat cleaver and his favorite butcher knife, both sharp enough to take your leg off without you noticing. "Go on," he said. "I'll manage."

I went out thinking that someday I'd come home and find the house littered with dismembered burglars. Dean was the sort who would handle an invasion neither calmly nor with the minimum necessary force. Bruno and Courter Slauce were lucky that he'd been surprised and unarmed.

I didn't realize that I'd collected a tail until I was three-quarters of the way to Morley's place. It wasn't that I hadn't checked for one; he was that good. He was so good, in fact, that half a minute after I'd made him he knew it and didn't walk into either of the setups I laid to get a look at him.

I might as well have had a signed confession.

There are only three guys in TunFaire that good. Morley Dotes and I are two of them and Morley had no reason to skulk around behind me.

The other guy's name is Pokey Pigotta and he might even be better than we are. I've heard him accused of being half ghost.

Pokey is in the same line as me. Had Domina Dount hired him to keep an eye on her hired hand?

That seemed unlikely.

Who, then?

By then Pokey would have realized that I'd read his signature. He'd start trying to outguess me.

I resisted my impulse to play that game and call for him to join me. Silliness. Pokey Pigotta had conservative views of what constituted his obligations to a client.

To hell with it, I figured. I headed for Morley's place.

I went in the front door and straight around the bar. The surprised night barman just gawked as I shoved through the door to the kitchen. The rutabaga butchers stopped work and stared. I strolled through like a royal prince assessing the provincials. "Very good, my man. Very good. You. Let's have a little more thought to portion control. That whatever-it-is is sliced too thick."

I made it to the storeroom before the peasants rose and lynched me. The storeroom led me directly to the back door, which I used. I did a quick sprint down the alley and up the side lane to the corner in time to watch the front door swing shut behind Pokey.

Good.

He had decided that since I wasn't going to play games, he wasn't going to either. He'd just trudge after me, not bothering to sneak. And that might suit his client fine, since it would inhibit my more surreptitious ventures.

I watched the door close and grinned, recapturing a view of the customers as I trotted through. It couldn't have been choreographed more beautifully.

"Suckered you, Pokey," I murmured, and ran for the door.

He had scanned the lay and turned to leave. He was a tall guy, without much meat on him—all bones and angles and skin so pale you'd have thought the breed half of him was vampire. He tended to make strangers very nervous.

"Sucked you in this time, Pokey." I peeked over his shoulder.

Saucerhead Tharpe was up and coming, hiding his infirmities well. I had no idea what the hell he was doing there but I was glad to see him.

Pokey shrugged. "I blew one."

"What you up to, Pokey?"

"You say something, Garrett? I been having trouble with my ears."

Saucerhead arrived. "What's up, Garrett?" Every eye in the place was on our get-together.

"Me and Pokey was just headed up to see Morley. I finally got a lead on those fellows you had the run-in with the other day. You're welcome to sit in." I gestured. Pokey surrendered to the inevitable, comfortably certain that I wanted nothing from him badly enough to make an enemy. I would have seen it the same if our roles had been reversed.

I followed Pokey. Saucerhead followed me. All eyes followed us up the stairs. Morley, of course, was expecting us.

"So what do you want to do with him?" Morley asked.

"Since he won't want to say why he's dogging me or who's paying him, I don't know whether to let him tag along or not. So, better safe than sorry. He's got to go into storage."

"How long?"

"A day, maybe."

"Pokey?"

"Sitting or following, it all pays the same."

Morley thought for half a minute, then told one of his

boys, "Blood, you want to politely collect Mr. Pigotta's effects and put them on the table here?"

Pokey endured it.

I knew how he felt. I'd been through it several times myself.

Morley stirred through the take, which included a lot of silver. He examined one piece. "Temple coinage."

I took one. Private mintage, all right. The same as the tenth mark I found on that farm.

"Tell you something?" Morley asked.

"Yeah. Who he isn't working for." Domina Dount never had anything but gold.

So who?

"Put him away," I told Morley. "There's things to talk about and decide and maybe do, and it's late already."

"Blood. The root cellar. Gently and politely. Consider him a guest under restraint."

"Yes, Mr. Dotes."

31

Morley removed his troops from the room. With just two witnesses Saucerhead relaxed and betrayed how uncomfortable he really was. I spent a minute or two telling him what a dope he was. He didn't argue. He didn't go home to bed, either.

Morley told me, "Only thing my boys have told me that you probably don't know is that Junior daPena's body got taken to the crematorium by the Dount woman on her way over to your place. I assume you know he did himself in?"

"I know. Only he didn't kill himself. He had a lot of help from his friends."

"You have that gleam in your eye, Garrett. Does that mean you know who did it?"

"Yep. And one of them was an ogre breed named Skredli, and it just happened that a Skredli was involved in Junior's so-called kidnapping—and most likely in the attack on Saucerhead and Amiranda. And this Skredli runs with a character named Gorgeous, who sounds like he's some double-ugly . . . What's up, Morley?"

"Gorgeous? You did say Gorgeous?"

"Yeah. You know him?"

"Not personally. I know of him."

"I don't like that look in *your* eye."

"Then look at the wall or something while you tell us about it."

While I talked, Saucerhead sat nodding to himself. I pretty much opened the bag and dumped it. Morley got out paper and pen and ink and started doodling.

When I closed the sack up, Morley said, "The Donni Pell trick is like the hub of a wheel. You have connections between her and everyone but the Dount woman. You can't tell about the Crest woman, but you can assume she knew who Donni was since she was good friends with Junior. This Donni is the key. Let's see if we can't lay hands on her."

I exchanged looks with Saucerhead. "The man is a genius, isn't he? Think he's figured out that she's the next one who'll come floating belly-up? If the hard boys are nervous enough to cut the son of Raver Styx . . ."

Morley said, "I think the next casualty will be a guy called Gorgeous. Though maybe I'm wrong." He still had that look.

"Why?" Saucerhead asked. Always direct, friend Waldo.

"Tell me about Gorgeous. I've never heard of him."

"You ought to keep up better, Garrett. He's important."

"I'm trying. If you'll get to it."

"Sure. He hasn't been around long. His real name is Conrad Staley. He came from HasefBro after the kingpin checked out, figuring it was a good time to cut himself a piece of the big city. He's human but he's so damned mean and ugly he ranks with ogres. He brought his own gang to start but I hear most have gone back since he's found local recruits. Keeping the old base secure. There was a hot feud for a while with Chodo Contague but they sorted it out. Gorgeous got Ogre Town. He pays a percentage to keep it in peace. Chodo doesn't want a war because he's having trouble keeping his own people in line."

Chodo Contague was the thug who had taken over as kingpin after the old kingpin's demise. He was more powerful than most of the lords of the Hill, though he lived in the shadows.

"Anything we do that involves Gorgeous, Chodo is going to have to approve." Morley was moving toward the door now. "It could mean war. You guys sit tight. If you need anything, tell them downstairs. I'll be back in a couple hours."

"Where the hell are you going?" I asked.

"To talk to Chodo." He was out.

"You wondering what I'm wondering, Garrett?"

"I'm not wondering, Saucerhead. I know."

Chodo Contague was boss of the TunFaire underworld in part because a certain Morley Dotes had presented the old kingpin with a coffin containing a hungry vampire. The old kingpin had opened the box thinking the thing inside had been killed before delivery. Saucerhead and I had been pallbearers in that shenanigan. Our buddy Morley hadn't bothered to tell us what was going down beforehand.

His reason for the oversight was sound. He had figured we wouldn't help if we knew.

The perceptive little bastard had been right.

I was going to collect favors on that scam for a long time.

"He's in debt again, Saucerhead. The bug races again. But I don't want to try Ogre Town alone, so let him play his game. I'm not going to sit around here waiting for him, though. If I have to kill a couple hours, I'll do it getting something useful done."

Saucerhead just looked at me, a big, tired guy who had been pushing himself too hard. I knew that if we ended up going after Gorgeous—as I would do, one way or another—Saucerhead would go along if he had to drag himself. "You might as well get some sleep. See you in a couple."

I got scowls downstairs but nobody stopped me.

32

I went to Playmate's and pounded around until he got out of bed. He never stopped grumbling and cussing, but he got out the wagon and hitched up a team. He even managed the obligatory refusals when I tried to pay him, though he did end up accepting the money. As he always does. He needs it, no matter how much he pretends.

The Larkin crematorium was one mile away. I pushed, though there was no real need. Junior's body had been delivered late, if I'd heard Morley right, so it wouldn't have been sent to the oven yet. That wasn't permitted at night. Religious and secular law both forbid cremation during the hours of darkness. A soul freed during that time would be condemned to walk the night forever.

There are only three crematoriums in TunFaire. I was sure Junior was at the Larkin place because it was convenient for anyone coming to my home from the Stormwarden's. And the night porter wasn't an honest man.

The world is cancerous with people possessed; some have to vent their sicknesses on the dead and others have to pander to them.

I pulled the wagon into an alley near the crematorium and left the team bound in a spell woven of the direst threats I could conjure. At least I got their attention.

I did it the way I'd heard it was done, going to the

side entrance, tapping a code, and waiting while I was examined through some hidden peephole.

The door opened. I had to grit my teeth to keep from laughing or groaning. The night porter was a character straight out of graveyard spook stories, a hunchback rat-man so ugly I suspected his beauty would undershine that of the creature Gorgeous. Hopefully before the night was done I'd have the opportunity to compare.

If there was a password I didn't know it and he didn't care. I showed him a gold piece and he showed me the room where the bodies were laid out. Like the old joke, people had been dying to get in. Seven of the ten slabs were occupied by the anxiously waiting dead.

Ratman was a born salesman. He lifted a sheet. "This here's the best we got. And you're the only customer tonight." He snickered.

The girl was about fourteen. There was no obvious cause of death.

"She might even be a virgin."

It was one of those times when you want to break bones, but for business reasons you put your feelings on ice and smile, I stepped past him and lifted a sheet at the head of a corpse that looked the right size. Not my man.

Second time was the charm.

"This one. How much to take him with me?"

I've never been looked at like that before and hope never to be again. I saw he was going to argue, so I laid a ten-mark gold piece on an empty slab. I doubt he'd ever seen one before.

Greed touched those hideous features. But caution was just a step behind. "That one came off the Hill, mister. You don't want to mess with it."

"You're right. I don't want to mess with it. I want to buy it."

"But . . . why?"

"For a keepsake. I'm going to have the head shrunk and wear it for an earring."

"Mister, I told you, that one's off the Hill. People are going to come for the ashes."

"Give them ashes. How many of these are city proj-

ects?" TunFaire has a pork-barrel ordinance requiring
unclaimed, found, and paupers' corpses to be distributed
in rotation among the dozen mortuary businesses, paid
for out of the public purse. It's a racket that accounts
for the majority of each business's income. Most families
just bury their dead in the nearest churchyard.

"Four. But I'd have to bring the boss in—"

"How much?" He wouldn't be doing his business
without the silent approval of his employer. "Without
being greedy. I could just take it and leave you in its
place." It was a definite temptation.

The ratman gulped. "Twenty marks."

"There's ten. Ten more when I have it loaded. I'll be
back in a minute." He might have taken his chances and
locked me out, but that was unlikely while ten more
marks were afloat.

He gobbled some but I ignored him. Ten minutes
later I had what was left of Junior daPena installed in
the wagon. I faced the hunchback, gold in hand. "The
same people will bring another one today. Unless they
insist on watching the job, I want that one, too. It'll be
female. The gods help you if it's touched. Do you
understand?"

He gulped.

"Do you understand?"

"Yes sir. Yes sir." Cautiously, he reached for the gold.
I avoided his touch when I let him have it.

Dean answered on the second knock. He was dressed.
"Haven't you been to bed?"

"Couldn't sleep. What is this? Are you collecting bodies now, Mr. Garrett?"

"Just a few that might be useful. I'm taking it into the
Dead Man's room. Get the doors for me. If he wakes
up and wants to know about it, tell him it was Junior
daPena and I'm saving him for his mother."

Dean turned green but handled his part. The corpse
settled, a little shaky. I returned to the kitchen and put
away a couple quarts of beer before leaving.

"You're off again, Mr. Garrett?"

"The night's work isn't done."

"Won't be night all that much longer."

He was right. The light would soon make its presence known.

33

I beat Morley back to his place, but barely in time to waken Saucerhead. Then Dotes came with his men— Blood, Sarge, and the Puddle. He also had two other guys in tow. I didn't know them personally and didn't care to get acquainted. Because I knew who they were: Crask and Sadler, Chodo Contague's first-string life takers. They had been born human. Since then they'd been embalmed and turned into zombies without the nuisance of dying first.

"What the hell are those guys doing here?" I snapped. It didn't help that they seemed equally pleased to see me and Saucerhead.

Morley was up to his old tricks.

"Calm down, Garrett. Unless you want to go after Gorgeous by your lonesome."

I bit my tongue.

Morley said, "This is the way it's got to be, Garrett. Gorgeous holes up in Ogre Town. He's got those people buffaloed down there. But they won't lift a finger if he suddenly turns up missing. Him and his number-one boy Skredli. You want him. Chodo wants him. Chodo will back your play as long as you're the face out front. But he wants first crack at them once they're rounded up. You give him a list of questions you want asked, he'll get the answers."

"Wonderful. Thoroughly wonderful, Morley." I was hot. So hot I didn't trust myself to say anything else.

Morley met my gaze evenly, shrugged. I got the message but I didn't have to like it.

Saucerhead was steamed, too, but he covered it better. He rose, laced his fingers, and bent them back until the knuckles cracked. "You got to live with what you got to live with. Let's do it while they're still asleep." He headed for the door.

"Wait!" Morley said. "This isn't a stroll in the woods with your girlfriend." He stepped behind his desk and fiddled with something. Part of the wall opened, exposing the biggest damned collection of deadly instruments I've seen since I parted with the Marines.

Saucerhead looked at the arsenal and shook his head. It wasn't a shake of refusal, but of astonishment. He joined Morley's thugs in stocking up. Crask and Sadler had brought their own. I had, too, and thought I was adequately outfitted. Morley's scowl told me he saw it otherwise. I selected one knife long enough to be a baby sword and another prissy little thing of the sort ladies (who aren't) carry on their garters. Morley didn't stop scowling but didn't comment, either.

I preferred my head knocker for all but the most desperate situations. And for those I had what the witch had given me.

We trooped downstairs, Morley's boys in the lead, Chodo's headhunters behind. Speculative eyes observed our descent and pursuit of the pathway I'd used on Pokey earlier. But at that hour there were few customers left and most of those were beholden to Morley. There should be no rumors born soon or messages run.

The barman beckoned Morley as we passed. Dotes stopped to trade whispers. He caught up at the door to the alley. "That was the latest from the river. The Stormwarden's boat was spotted at dusk twenty miles down tying up for the night."

"Then she'll be here tomorrow afternoon."

"Late, I'd guess. The winds are unfavorable."

It was something to think about. I didn't have enough to ruminate already.

*   *   *

The alley was filled with the huge black hulk of a four-horse closed coach. And two gargantuan characters with shiny eyes and sparkly fangs grinned down from twenty feet. "Hi, guys."

They were grolls—half troll, half giant, green by daylight, all mean, and tougher than a herd of thunder-lizards. I knew these two. They were two-thirds of triplets who had gone with me into the Cantard to bring out a woman who had inherited a bundle. Despite what we had been through together, I hadn't the slightest notion whether or not I dared trust them.

They had been cursed with unlikely names, Doris and Marsha.

"A little of what I call ally insurance," Morley told me. "You think I'm a raving moron for bringing Chodo in?"

"No. I think you think it'll get you out from under your debts. I hope you're right."

"You're a cynical and suspicious character, Garrett."

"It's people like you who make me that way."

Morley's troops were inside the coach and Saucerhead was clambering aboard. Crask and Sadler were up on the guard's and driver's seats, donning the traditional tall hats and dark cloaks. Each man had immediate access to a pair of powerful, ready crossbows.

Such items are necessary on TunFaire's night streets if you're rich enough to use a coach but not powerful enough to have its doors blazoned with the arms of someone like a stormwarden.

Most high-class folk travel with outriders. We made do with a pair of grolls toting their favorite toys, head-bashers twelve feet long and almost too heavy for a runt like me to lift.

Morley followed me into the coach, then leaned out and told Crask to go. The vehicle jerked into motion.

"I suppose you've made a plan?" I said.

"It's all scoped out. That was one of the reasons I brought Chodo in. His boys know Gorgeous's place. I've never seen it. And neither have you."

I grunted. The rest of the ride passed in silence.

34

Ogre Town was quieter than death at that hour. There seems to be a cultural imperative that sends them to bed very late and brings them out in the afternoon. We were going in soon after most ogres had sacked out. The streets weren't entirely deserted, but it made little difference. Those who were out were scavengers. They made a point of being blind to our presence.

Twelve hours earlier or later we might have been in trouble. The streets would have featured a more treacherous cast.

We swung into a passage between buildings just wide enough for the coach, then continued until we could open the doors. Crask told us to disembark. We tumbled out. He backed the coach into the passage again so we could gather in the shadows, off the street.

"That's the place." Morley indicated a four-story vertical rectangle a hundred yards down the street. "The whole thing belongs to Gorgeous. He had the buildings on either side demolished so nobody could get to him that way. We're going after him that way."

"Wonderful." Light still shone in a couple windows on the top two floors. "You're a genius."

The buildings in Ogre Town are fifty to a hundred years older than the tenements in Fishwife's Close. In many cases that showed. But they had built in brick and stone in those days and Gorgeous's citadel had been kept up. It didn't need to lean on neighbors to remain standing.

There was a ghost of a promise of dawn.

Morley said, "Doris and Marsha are going to climb the buildings on either side. They'll drop ropes. Me, Crask, Blood, and Sarge will go up top the nearer one. The rest up the other. After we get our wind . . ." He droned on with the plan.

"It sucks," I told him.

"You want to march in the front door and fight your way to the top?"

"No. Hell, if I didn't have questions to ask, I'd just go start a fire on the ground floor. Ought to go up that thing like smoke up a chimney."

"But you do want to ask questions. Ready? So let's go." Doris and Marsha were already gone, not bothering to wait out my protests.

We were halfway there when the man came out the front door. His hands were shoved in his pockets and he was looking down. He was human, not ogre. He walked fifty feet toward us before he realized he wasn't alone. He halted, looked at us, and his eyes bugged.

"Bruno," I hissed.

He whirled and headed for the building.

Sadler's crossbow twanged.

It was a damned good try for a snap shot. I think it clipped Bruno's left arm. He veered right and headed up the street, concentrating on speed.

"Let him go. I'll hunt him down later," I said. "He has some answers I need."

While I talked, Crask sped a bolt that split Bruno's spine three inches below his neck. Sadler reached him seconds later and dragged the twitching body into the nearest shadows.

"Thanks a bunch," I snarled.

Crask didn't bother turning that embalmed face my way.

Doris and Marsha reached the roofs of their respective

structures. They anchored ropes and dropped them. Inside Gorgeous's place the lights were dying. Saucerhead and I stood at the foot of the rope. "You going to make it?" I asked.

"You worry about yourself, Garrett. Ain't nothing going to stop me now." He started climbing. I held the rope taut. Saucerhead went up like he was seventeen and had never been hurt in his life. Sadler followed with not one but two crossbows slung on his back, then the Puddle. Lucky Garrett got to do it with no one to tauten the rope.

When I reached the roof, I found that Marsha had already leaped to Gorgeous's roof. Saucerhead was tying off the rope the groll had tossed back. Sadler was leaning on the chimney that anchored both ropes, sighting one crossbow on the top-floor window. Light still leaked through its shutters.

I wondered if Marsha's rooftop landing had been heard below. I didn't see how Gorgeous could help but be forewarned with nearly two tons of groll prancing over his head.

Puddle joined Marsha. Saucerhead and I followed. I pretended the void below was really just water a foot beneath my dangling toes.

The pretense didn't help.

Sadler stayed where he was. He untied the rope so Marsha could haul it across and resumed his lethal posture.

Marsha bent one end of the rope into a harness for me. As I got into it I wondered what was wrong with Gorgeous and his boys. Were they deaf? Or just chuckling as they got a little surprise ready for us?

I was going to find out all too quickly.

There was enough light now to see Morley getting into a similar rig. Doris hoisted him and dangled him over the side.

The universe twisted. An abyss appeared beneath me. I turned at the end of the rope, glimpsing Sadler aiming too close for contentment.

Marsha swung me in against the brick, then over to peek through the cracks in the shutter.

At first I saw nothing. No ambush evidence, no excitement, nobody. Just an empty room. Then an ugly someone opened a door and shoved his face into the room and said something I couldn't hear to someone I couldn't see. The back of the other someone appeared momentarily as he followed the ugly someone out the door. The set of his shoulders said he was aggravated.

I waved. Saucerhead tied the rope to something. They left me hanging.

Evidently the report from the far side was favorable, too. Marsha leaned over the edge and let go a mighty bash with his club. A second later he lowered Saucerhead at the end of a mile of arm and flipped him through the window. Saucerhead grabbed me and dragged me inside. Puddle came through an instant later.

The room was uninhabited except for the insect life infesting the stack of bunk beds. Saucerhead and Puddle headed for the door while I battled ropes like a moth in a spiderweb. There was one hell of a racket going on somewhere else.

A guy came charging through the doorway just as Saucerhead got there. His nose and Saucerhead's fist collided. No contest. The ogre's eyes rolled up. Saucerhead thumped him again as he went down, just for spite.

I got loose and charged after Saucerhead and Puddle, into a narrow hallway that dead-ended to our left. As we turned right a couple of breeds popped out of another bunk-room doorway. They were no more fortunate than their predecessor. Saucerhead was in one of those moods.

In the meantime, heaven put on its dancing shoes and began hoofing it on the roof. The grolls were pounding away with their clubs.

The racket elsewhere revealed itself as a lopsided battle between Morley's crew and Gorgeous and about ten breeds. Several more ogres were down, with quarrels in them, and as we came to the rescue yet another made the mistake of stepping in front of the window. He squealed like a throat-cut hog as he fell. The bolt had gotten the meat of his thigh. Poisoned? Probably.

Being a nice guy, I just whapped a couple of heads with my stick instead of stabbing backs with Puddle. Saucerhead threw ogres around the way us ordinary mortals might work through a pack of house cats. Holes appeared in the ceiling as the grolls kept pounding away, their blows so powerful they smashed through two-by-ten oak ceiling joists.

Our rear attack turned the tide. Suddenly, the numbers were ours.

Gorgeous made a run for the stairs. I flung a foot out and got enough of his ankle to unbalance him. His momentum pitched him into the doorframe.

The fight seemed over but it wasn't yet won. Ogres are tough and stubborn. A few were still upright.

Morley's boys left them to us and went to work finishing the ones who were down. I yelled a complaint that got ignored.

I'd gotten through the worst without a scratch. The others had a few dings and small cuts, except Sarge, who had collected a rib-deep slash across the chest and had taken himself out of the action to tend it.

"Not that one!" Saucerhead roared at Puddle. "You save that one for me." He slammed the last upright ogre into unconsciousness, then explained, "That's the one that was in charge when they killed the girl."

Panting, I asked, "You see any others that were there?"

"Just him." He dragged his ogre out of the mess.

Morley said, "That's the one called Skredli."

I'd suspected as much.

For several minutes there had been considerable racket downstairs. Now Gorgeous levered himself up and roared. Morley and I jumped on him, too late to shut him up.

The stairs drummed to stamping feet.

An ogre stampede arrived.

There must have been twenty in the first rush. They pushed us across the room, into the far wall. Grolls hammering heads from above scarcely slowed them.

And more kept coming.

Sarge couldn't defend himself adequately. Puddle
went down. I thought Morley was a goner. It looked
grim for the rest of us. Gorgeous shrieked hysterical,
bloodthirsty orders.

It was time for something desperate.

35

I dropped the witch's gift and stomped on it. The crystal shattered. I followed instructions and covered my eyes, taking several vicious blows as a result. A thread of fire sliced the outside of my left upper arm.

Hell called the proceedings to disorder.

I opened my eyes. The mob bawled like cows in a panic, flailed wildly, purposelessly. Some howled and clung to the floor. I danced away from the nearer crazies and unlimbered my head knocker.

According to the witch, they were seeing three of everything and their universe was revolving. But that didn't make them easy meat. There were so many of them flailing around. . . .

I watched Gorgeous bang into the wall three times trying to get to the stairs. I tried to reach him before he got away. My luck ran its usual taunting course. I was two ogres short of getting him when he made it out. He went tumbling downstairs, caterwauling in pain and fear.

I wanted that man bad, but not bad enough to abandon friends to fate. I returned to my harvest.

I took a few whacks myself getting the mob done, but lay them low I did. Morley, I saw, had survived after all. He leaned against a wall, pale as death. Saucerhead stood with feet widespread, grinning a big goofy grin. The grolls, who had caught just the edge of the spell, looked in through the ceiling and grinned too. They had helped with the head knocking. Morley's man Blood sat in a corner puking his guts up. Sarge and Puddle were somewhere under the mess.

We all needed patching up.

I stumbled to the window.

It was light out now. And there were sounds outside. People sounds. Ogre Town folks were awake and interested.

It was time to pick up our toys and get out.

"Shut your eyes, you dopes," I told everybody. "Get your hands on the wall and follow it around to the door to the stairwell. Wait for me there."

"What the hell did you have up your sleeve this time, Garrett?" Morley asked in a voice pitched an octave too high. He gagged as he fought to avoid upchucking from the vertigo.

"None of your damned business. Just be glad I had it, you tactical genius. Come on. Get over by the door while I find Puddle and Sarge and Skredli."

An ogre groaned. I gave him a tap on the noggin. There would be plenty of headaches later.

I found Skredli first, dragged him over, and gave him to Saucerhead. Sarge turned up next. "Morley, Sarge checked out. You want to take him home?"

"What for? Hurry up. I smell smoke."

So did I. I started digging for Puddle.

"Oh, hell," Morley said. "What would I tell my guys if I left somebody behind? They'd tell me I was no better than these ogres." He babbled to the grolls in their tongue. They jabbered back. He told me, "Shove Sarge up where Doris can get ahold of him. And hurry. They say there's a mob shaping up. Crask and Sadler have been shooting the boys down when they run out the front door."

I found Puddle. He was alive, and would make it with help. I got him to Morley. "I'm going down first. You guys come as fast as you can." I bounded down the stairs.

Noises rose to greet me. It sounded like somebody dragging himself. . . .

I overtook Gorgeous on the second-floor landing as he was getting ready to head down the last flight. But to catch him I had to jump the fire he had started halfway to the third floor.

He had a broken leg. He wasn't seeing more than double now, and nearly stuck me before I bopped him. I checked for other enemies. The only ones left upright were down at the front door, three or four just inside, arguing about how they were going to get out. That door was the only ground-floor exit. Anybody who used it ran into a crossbow bolt.

I hustled back to help the others past the fire. It was growing, but we managed. Only Morley got singed. I couldn't restrain a chuckle at his pathetic appearance. He's one of those guys who spends hours on his appearance.

The problem of the ogres below solved itself. I went after them behind a bloodthirsty shriek, brandishing my knives, and they flushed like a covey of quail, hitting the street.

Now we'd learn the value of Morley's ally insurance.

I stuck my head out.

No bolt greeted me.

I stepped out carefully, looked around, frowned. What had become of the mob? I saw no one but the flying ogres and the grolls, who had clambered down the outside of the building.

The coach came pounding out of its alley, swung in, and stopped. Crask growled, "Get them in here! There's soldiers coming."

Troops? No wonder the streets were empty.

We tumbled inside, piling on the coach floor. Crask and Sadler took off before we sorted ourselves out. The grolls loped ahead, scouting.

I got myself seated. "This is weird, Morley. They don't call out the troops for squabbles in Ogre Town."

The coach thundered through alleys that *had* to be

too narrow, around corners that *had* to be too tight. Whatever faults the boys up top had, lack of guts was not among them.

Morley grunted in response to my remark.

"They only come out for riots. And there's maybe only eight or ten people who can deploy them."

Morley grunted again. "You figure it out, Garrett. Right now I don't give a damn." He was in pain.

If Bruno hadn't gone down . . . Bruno was off the Hill. Bruno had been visiting Gorgeous. It took a lord from the Hill to order out the army. Maybe Bruno worked for somebody who thought enough of Gorgeous to call out the troops to save him.

The whole affair began to tilt in my head. Maybe Bruno and a few facts I'd ignored needed reexamining. "I've got to find out who he worked for."

Nobody bothered to ask what I was muttering about.

A frightening notion had crept into my mind. Perhaps Junior daPena, his family, and his keeper, were innocent of bloodletting.

The coach careened onto a major street, scattering pedestrians, drawing curses from the other drivers. Around another corner. Then a slowdown to become just another vehicle in the morning flow. I never saw a soldier. Five minutes later we halted behind Morley's place. Sadler growled at us to get the hell out.

I was exhausted and hurt and about as tired as I could get of someone else taking control of what I had started.

"Easy, Garrett," Morley said. "Keep your mouth shut and get inside."

"Stuff it, Morley. I've had it."

"Do what I tell you. It'll improve your long-term health picture." He grabbed me and, with help from Saucerhead, got me through the back door. I was more amenable once I noted that our ally insurance had vanished.

Morley had Saucerhead help get his men inside. Sadler crawled into the coach to babysit Gorgeous and Skredli. The coach rolled.

Morley suggested, "Why don't you go upstairs and

make a list of questions you want asked? I'll have a messenger run it. Then go home and sleep. You'll feel more reasonable afterward."

I supposed if Saucerhead could endure not getting first crack at Skredli, I could live without an immediate shot at Gorgeous. "All right." But I had a feeling I wasn't going to get a lot of rest.

On the way upstairs I glanced out a window toward Ogre Town. A pillar of smoke stood like a gravestone over a ferocious fire. Maybe most of our grim handiwork would be erased, thanks to Gorgeous.

The last thing I needed was to get labeled a tool of the kingpin.

I made my list, pointless exercise that it was. The tricky part was wording questions about two hundred thousand marks gold so that my stand-in would not realize what he was asking and gleefully begin interrogating in his own cause. I solved the problem by mostly avoiding it and entering a plea for direct access to the boys, and maybe even possession of that trifle Skredli.

That done, I went back downstairs, where the survivors were getting patched up and trying to eat breakfast. I was so far gone I didn't comment on the platter they brought me, I just gulped a quart of fruit juice and stuffed my face.

I asked, "Saucerhead, you got anything left? I've got something I want you to do." After I finished with him, I cornered Morley and talked him into turning the tables on Pokey Pigotta. If we let him go and shadowed him he might lead us to some interesting places—if he didn't lead us into deep trouble first.

36

Amber and Dean were in the kitchen when I got home. I went in and collapsed into a chair. Saucerhead thought my example so outstanding he copied it. Dean and Amber stared at us.

"Was it a difficult night, Mr. Garrett?" Dean asked.

"You might say. If you care to understate."

"You look like hell," Amber said. "Whatever it was, I hope it was worth it."

"Maybe. We caught up with the people who killed your brother and Amiranda."

I watched her carefully. She responded the way I had hoped, with no sign of panic or guilt. "You got them? What did you do? Did you find out anything about the ransom?"

"We got them. You don't want to know anything more. I didn't find out anything about the money, but I didn't have a chance. I'm still working on it. How well could you manage if you had a thousand marks to start your new life?"

"Pretty damn good. My needs are simple. You're up to something, Garrett. Spill it."

Dean muttered, "Been around him too long already. Starting to talk like him."

"I love you too, Dean. Amber, Domina offered me a

thousand marks if I could find you and turn you over to her before your mother gets home. I've had word that she'll get here this afternoon. If you want the money, I'll take you home around noon and my friend here will stay with you till you're convinced you're safe."

She eyed me through narrowed lids. "What's your angle, Garrett?" The girl could think when she felt the urge.

"Willa Dount. She knows things she won't tell me. There aren't any sanctions I can threaten to pry them out of her. All I can do is find ways to put the heat on and hope she does something interesting."

"What about the ransom, Garrett? That's what we're supposed to be working on." Her eyes remained narrowed.

"I don't think there's much chance of getting it. Do you? Really? With your mother home?"

"Probably not. But you don't act like you're trying."

Saucerhead began working on a breakfast Dean had offered him. I gawked. He was putting it away like he hadn't eaten in weeks, despite having just eaten at Morley's. But rabbit food will do that.

"Domina offered you that money last night? And you didn't grab it?"

"No." Dean was pouring apple juice. I realized I was dry all the way down to my corns. "Give me about a gallon." Nothing like a good tense situation to sweat you out.

Saucerhead grunted agreement around a mouthful.

"It isn't the money, is it, Garrett?" demanded Amber.

Saucerhead tittered.

"What's with you, oaf?"

"She figured you out, Garrett." He chuckled. "You're right, little girl. With Garrett it's almost never the money."

"You want to talk, Waldo? How rich do you figure on getting in this?"

He gave the name a black look, then shrugged. "There's just some things you got to make right."

Amber knew we meant much more than we said. She scowled. "If you can be noble, so can I. I'll go home. But cut it close. All right?"

"All right."

"What will you do now?"

"Get some sleep. It's been awhile since I've had any."

"Sleep? How can you sleep in the middle of everything?"

"Easy. I lie down and close my eyes. If you want to stay busy and vent some nervous energy, remember everything you can about Karl's friend Donni Pell."

"Why?"

"Because she looks like the common denominator in every angle of what's been happening. Because I want to find her bad."

I had a notion adding Donni Pell might even explain the marvelous appearance of troops in Ogre Town.

My guess was that with Gorgeous and Skredli out of the equation, she stood a chance of surviving long enough to be found and questioned. I hoped she hadn't suffered a sudden and uncharacteristic seizure of smarts and wagged her manipulating tail out of town.

I drank apple juice until I was bloated, then rose. "That's it. I'm putting myself on the shelf. Wake me up at noon, Dean. I've got to go rob a crypt before I sell Miss daPena into fetters. Saucerhead, you can sack out in the room Dean uses."

Dean grumbled and muttered what sounded like threats to revive his interest in finding me a wife among his female kin. I ignored him. He wouldn't learn, and I was too tired to fight.

37

Dean didn't wake me as instructed. Amber pirated that chore with a half hour head start. The brief rest hadn't been enough to restore my resistance. I fear I succumbed.

Amber wasn't a disappointment.

When I ventured into the kitchen, I realized Dean had found his missing scowl mask. It was as ferocious as ever. He has pretensions to gentility, though, so he said nothing. I devoured a few sausages and hit the street.

I listened to the talk around Playmate's place, where the old men hang out. They had a dozen theories about what had happened in Ogre Town. Some were as crazy as the truth, but none were correct.

Collecting Amiranda's corpse was cut and dried. I paid, they delivered, I drove it home, and Dean helped me lug it into the Dead Man's room.

Have you taken up a new hobby, Garrett?

He was awake. I'd thought I might have to start a fire to get his attention.

Or are you getting into a new line?

"Once in a while I like to have somebody around who doesn't get temperamental."

Dean tells me you have been having adventures.

"Yes. And if you'd stay awake and do a little work, I'd have a lot fewer." I brought him up to date.

At last you have begun to understand that several things are happening at once. I am proud of you, Garrett. You have begun to think. I wondered how long you would discount the repeated appearances of the Bruno person. Particularly in view of your first collected fact having been that the younger Karl left his house to investigate a pilferage problem that the Dount woman suggested might have another Hill family at its root.

"You figured there might be a connection, eh?"

Of course.

"But you didn't bother to mention it."

You have become too dependent upon me. You need to exercise your brain yourself.

"The reason you're here at all is so I don't have to strain my brain. We humans are born bone lazy. Remember? With innate ambition and energy levels only slightly above those of a dead Loghyr."

Do not make a special effort to irritate me, Garrett. You have done adequately with your collection of corpses and your parade of frenzied females. If you have a question you cannot handle yourself, spit it out. Otherwise, relocate yourself in some demesne where the mentality is sufficiently naive to appreciate your wit.

"All right, genius. Answer me this. Who killed Amiranda Crest? Is that something else you've been holding back, waiting for me to get my head bashed in while I tried to find out the hard way?"

I suppose you mean do I know who gave the order that resulted in Miss Crest's death at the hand of the ogre breed Skredli and his henchmen?

"To be precise."

We must be precise, Garrett. An intelligent mind is not ambiguous.

I could have talked about that for hours, but I resisted. "Do you know who's responsible?"

No.

"Do you know why?"

Chances are if we knew that, we would know who as

*well, Garrett. I can render at least three plausibilities im-
mediately, though I will discount the pregnancy as motive
till such time as you produce evidence that she told someone. She did not tell you except by the most ambiguous
implication, and young women empty the darkest corners
of their souls into your ears.*

"You know, with two marks and all the help you've
given me I could buy a barrel of beer."

*Find Donni Pell. Bring her to me. Find out who
Bruno's master was. Look for any connections with the
daPena family. Look into the pilferage at the daPena
warehouse. It might open new avenues. Now begone. I
cannot endure your vexatious importunities any longer.*

"Right. I'll just conjure the Pell woman out of thin
air."

You will not learn anything sitting here drinking beer.

"You have a point, I admit. But before I fare forth
to keep my date with destiny, how about you clue me
in on how Glory Mooncalled manages his magic show.
Or hasn't the hypothesis withstood the test of time?"

*The hypothesis has stood quite well, Garrett. But not
enough time has passed to set it in concrete. I should not
risk contradiction by events, but I will present you with
the key. Glory Mooncalled has not found the secret of
prolonged invisibility. He has invented invisibility by
treaty. When you cannot escape the seeing eye, you convince the eye that blindness is in its own best interest.
Begone. Take your tart back to her family.*

"You ready to go?" I asked Saucerhead. I didn't have
to ask Amber because I knew she wasn't—either emotionally or intellectually. She was scared to death. But
for the thousand marks she would give it a shot.

Saucerhead grunted and got to his feet slowly. His
exertions of the night before were exacting their price.
I hoped he hadn't drawn too heavily on his reserves.
Even the most stubborn will has its final limit.

"Let's do it, Garrett," Amber said.

38

Courter Slauce himself was on the daPena gate. He looked grim, still showing the effects of his carouse. I supposed he was being punished. He stared at me with a mixture of anger and uncertainty. I said, "Tell Domina Dount I'm out here with the other package she ordered."

He eyed Amber and Saucerhead, frowned puzzledly, as if a memory ghost were slithering around somewhere behind his eyes, too elusive to catch.

"You can go on in to her office. She left standing orders to the gate."

"Uhn-uh. Not that I don't thrust her, but you know how it is. There's a payment due, and if she brings it down here, chances are a lot better that I'll actually get it."

That look again. I had a feeling the Dead Man hadn't done as good a job as he thought. Some of Slauce's memories might return.

"Have it your way." He called to somebody in the court, told them to get Willa Dount and why. When he turned to us again, he was frowning, straining after that fugitive memory.

I figured I could distract him and find out something at the same time. I described Bruno and asked if he knew the man.

Slauce was more cooperative than I expected. "The guy sounds vaguely familiar. But I can't pin a name on him. Why?"

"I thought he might be connected with that pilferage problem you people were having at your warehouse. I don't know. Just something I heard. I don't know who he is, either, except he's supposed to be from up here somewhere. He had a job like yours, they say."

Slauce shook his head, trying to clear the cobwebs. Amber and Saucerhead both stared at me, wondering what the hell I was up to.

Just stirring the pot, friends. With the Stormwarden on the horizon, looming like a grandmother tornado, anything was likely to panic somebody and break something loose.

But not from Courter Slauce. He just stood there with a dumb look, trying to get both oars in the water.

Domina Dount came stomping across the courtyard wearing that contrived and controlled face that had become so familiar. "Garrett comes through again," I told her.

She glared at Amber so fiercely the girl stepped behind Saucerhead. "It's about time."

"It took more doing than you think."

"Get in here, Amber. Go to your suite."

Amber didn't come out of hiding.

I said, "There's a fee due."

"Yes. Of course. You're a parasite, Garrett."

"Absolutely. But unlike the ruling-class sort of parasite, I relieve pain instead of creating it." I winked, grinned. "Is the honeymoon over?"

She almost smiled back. "In about a minute." She produced several fat doeskin bags. I let her plunk their weight into my folded arms, then turned.

Amber came out of hiding, took a sack, counted out Saucerhead's fee, whispered, "You take care of this, Garrett. I'll pick it up as soon as I get away from my mother."

I lent her only enough ear to follow what she said. I asked Domina Dount, "Just as a matter of personal curiosity, did you ever tie the knot on that warehouse trouble?"

"Warehouse trouble?"

"Back when you first called me out here, you told me the younger Karl disappeared after you sent him out to check on a pilferage problem. I just wondered if you'd put the wraps on that yet."

"I haven't had time to worry about it, Mr. Garrett."

Amber and Saucerhead pushed past us while we talked. The Domina realized that Saucerhead was going inside.

"Hey! You! Come back here. You can't go in there." Saucerhead ignored her.

"Who the hell is he, Garrett? What is he doing?"

"He's Amber's bodyguard. DaPena youngsters have been dropping like flies. The reason she ran away was she was afraid she might be next. To get her to come back I had to fix her up with a bodyguard so mean and ugly and stubborn he'd take on the gods themselves. Also one who has a lot of friends willing to get revenge if anything happens to him."

"I don't like your tone, Garrett. You sound like you're accusing me."

"I'm accusing no one. Not yet. But somebody had Amiranda and Junior murdered. I'm just letting people know it's going to get gruesome if it's tried on Amber."

"Karl took his own life, Mr. Garrett."

"He was murdered, Domina. By a man named Gorgeous. *I* think at the instigation of a third party. I'm going to be talking to friend Gorgeous later. One of the questions I'm going to ask is who put him up to it. Thanks for this. Enjoy your day."

I left her looking flustered and maybe—hopefully—frightened.

The name of the game was Garrett opens his bag of little horrors and lets out some of what he knows, hoping that knowledge looks like a thick and deadly wall against which the onrushing Stormwarden might crush the guilty. Maybe somebody would panic.

As I moved away, looking around to see if any of

Morley's boys were lurking, I heard footsteps behind me. I looked back.

Courter Slauce was hurrying my way, an odd expression on his fat face. All the color was gone. "Mr. Garrett. Wait up."

Had my bolts pinked something in the bushes already? He obviously had something on his mind.

"Courter! Where are you? Come here! Immediately!"

Domina Dount sounded like a fishwife. I couldn't see her, so I assumed she couldn't see me. Slauce threw up his hands in despair and trotted back home.

What had he wanted to tell me?

Morley was waiting at the house when I got there. He hadn't been waiting long.

39

"What's up, Morley?"

"Chodo wants to see you. Right away."

"Now I'm not happy. What brought this on?"

Morley shrugged. "I'm just relaying a message Crask left with me. I'll say this. He didn't look like he thought his boss was going to feed you to the fishes."

"That's very reassuring, Morley."

"Chodo is an honorable man, in his own way. He wouldn't chop somebody down without warning."

"Like Gorgeous?"

"Gorgeous had plenty of warnings. Anyway, he put himself on the bull's-eye. Then he stood there with his tongue out. He begged for it, Garrett."

"What do you think? Should I go?"

"Only if you don't want the kingpin pissed at you. A time might come when you'd want him to give you a little leeway."

"You're right. Let's go. Lock it up, Dean."

Dean grumbled, I told him it wouldn't last much longer.

Chodo had set himself up in a manor house in the suburbs. The place beggared the Stormwarden's in size and ostentation, a commentary on the wages of sin if you're slick.

Sadler was waiting at the gate, a commentary on the confidence Chodo had in the terror of his name, I suppose. He said nothing, just let us follow him across the professionally barbered grounds. Having that kind of eye, I couldn't help but study the security arrangements.

"Don't step off the path," Morley cautioned. "You're only safe inside the enchantment."

I then noticed that in addition to the expected and obvious armed guards and killer dogs, there were thunder-lizards lazing in the bushes. They were not the tenement-tall monsters we think of, but little guys four or five feet tall, bipedal, all tail, teeth, and hind legs built for running. They were the reason for the enchantment on the path. Unlike the dogs, those things were too stupid to train. All they understood was eating and mating.

"Nice pets," I told Sadler. He didn't respond. Wonderful company, the kingpin's boys.

But the grimness ended at the front door.

Chodo knew how to do it up royal. I've been inside several places on the Hill. None could match Chodo's.

"Don't gawk, Garrett. It's impolite."

A platoon of nearly naked cuties were playing in and around a heated bath pool three times bigger than the ground area of my whole place. We passed through. I muttered, "Business must be good."

"Looks like." The man who had cautioned me not to gawk was looking back, the gleam in his eyes a conflagration. "Never saw them before." He walked into a pillar.

The part of the house where we met the kingpin was less luxurious. It was, in fact, your basic filthy, miserable dungeon—except it was located on the ground level. The kingpin himself was a pallid, doughy fat man in a wheelchair who didn't look like he could whip potatoes until you met his eyes. I had seen eyes like those only a few times, on some very old and hungry vampires. They were the eyes of Death.

"Mr. Garrett?"

The voice went with the eyes, deep and dank and

cold, with hints of awful things crawling around its underside.

"Yes."

"I believe I owe you a considerable debt."

"Not at all. I—"

"In your fumbling and poking after whatever it is you're seeking, you presented me with an opportunity to rid myself of a vicious pest. I seized the chance, trampling your interests in my rush, a presumption you'll have found close to intolerable. But you've been gracious about it. You participated in the operation which delivered me despite having little hope you would get what you were after. So I believe I am in your debt."

Were it not for his voice from beyond the grave, I might have been amused by his pedantic manner. When I didn't respond, he continued, "Mr. Dotes didn't make much sense when he tried to explain what you're doing. If you can satisfy me that your interests don't conflict with mine, I'll do what I can to help you."

I wanted to demur, quietly, still preferring to avoid any chance of becoming identified with him. But Morley gouged me gently, and the fact was, he had two of the people I most wanted to question. I explained as concisely as I could, carefully sliding around the matter of two hundred thousand marks gold floating free.

Sadler continued, "One of Gorgeous's enterprises was the fencing of goods stolen from the warehouses along the waterfront, sir."

"Yes. Continue, Mr. Garrett."

"Basically, I need to question Gorgeous and Skredli so I can define their sector of the web of intrigue." Does that top you, you villainous slug? "I need to ask them who told them to kill Amiranda Crest and the younger Karl daPena."

"I knew Molahlu Crest when I was a young man. You might say I was one of his protégés." He crooked a finger. Sadler went to him, bent down. They whispered.

After Sadler backed off, Chodo asked, "The questions

you want answered are the ones Raver Styx will ask with a great deal less delicacy?"

"No doubt."

"Then not only must I pay my debt to you, I must move to avert the attention of the mighty. But I have erred, and today I demonstrated my fallibility to myself in no uncertain fashion. I'm able to give you only the lesser part of what you want. I overestimated Mr. Staley's endurance and he's no longer with us. He couldn't take it."

I sighed. I should have expected the grave to slam another door in my face. "He wasn't in very good shape the last time I saw him."

"Perhaps his injuries were more extensive than they appeared. Whatever, I learned very little of value. But the other, the ogre breed, has survived and is amenable. The trouble is, he doesn't seem to know much."

"He wouldn't."

Morley gouged me. "Donni Pell, Garrett."

"What?"

Chodo raised a plump, almost white caterpillar of an eyebrow. He was as good at it as I was.

"You said the hooker was the key, Garrett. And you don't even know where to start looking."

"Who is Donni Pell?" Chodo asked.

"The she-spider in this web." I gave Morley a dirty look. "She used to work for Lettie Faren, but ran out on her the day Junior was snatched. She could be related to Lettie. Human, but supposedly with a thing for ogres." I ran through the whole thing, how every way I turned the name Donni Pell popped up. I finished, "She could be masquerading as a boy but using the same name."

Chodo grunted. He stared at the nails on one plump pink hand. "Mr. Sadler."

"Yes sir?"

"Find the whore. Deliver her to Mr. Garrett's residence."

"Yes sir." Sadler left us.

"If she's in the city, she'll be found, Mr. Garrett,"
Chodo told me. "Mr. Sadler and Mr. Crask are nothing
if not efficient."

"I've noticed."

"I suppose it's time I took you to my ogrish
houseguest. Come." He spun his wheelchair and rolled.
Morley and I followed.

40

The first thought that entered my mind when I walked in on Skredli was *drowned sparrow*. He looked very small, very weak, very bedraggled, and like he'd never been dangerous to anything bigger than a bug. Curiously, I recognized him now. I hadn't during the excitement in Ogre Town or later in the coach. He was one of the gang who had waylaid me the afternoon of my date with Amiranda, while I was on my way to the chemist for some stink-pretty.

Skredli was seated on a rumpled cot. He glanced up but showed no real interest. Ogres tend toward fatalism.

Morley held the door for Chodo, then stepped aside. The kingpin backed his chair against the door.

I studied Skredli, wondering how to get to him. A man has to have hope before he's vulnerable. This one had no hope left. He was deader than the Dead Man, but his traitorous heart kept pumping and his battered flesh kept aching.

"The good times always come to an end, don't they, Skredli? And the better the times are, the bigger the fall when they end. Right?"

He didn't respond. I didn't expect him to.

"The chance for the good times doesn't have to be gone forever."

His right cheek twitched, once. Ogres and ogre breeds

may be indifferent to the fates of their comrades, but they aren't indifferent to their own.

"Mr. Chodo has gotten what he wants from you. He doesn't have any outstanding grievance. Mine isn't with you at all. So there's no reason you shouldn't be let out of here if you give me what I need."

I didn't bother checking to see how Chodo took me putting words into his mouth. It didn't matter. He would do what he wanted no matter what I said or promised.

Skredli glanced up. He didn't believe me, but he wanted to.

"The whole scheme is in the dump, Skredli. And you're down at the bottom. No way to go but up or out. The choice is yours." I had asked Chodo only one question coming to the cell: did Skredli know Gorgeous was out of it? He did. "Your boss is gone. No reason to stay loyal to him or be afraid of him. Your fate is in your own hands."

Morley shifted his weight against the wall, gave me a look that said he thought I was laying it on too thick.

Skredli grunted. I had no way of telling what that meant. I took it as a go-ahead.

"I'm Garrett. We had a run-in once before."

One bob of the head.

I had him. For a moment, though, I feared it had been too easy. Then I reflected that it was the ogrish way. When you've got nothing you've got nothing to lose.

"You recall the circumstances?"

Grunt again.

"Who put you up to that?"

"Gorgeous." That in a dry-throated croak.

"Why? What for? I'd never had anything either of you."

"Business. We had a thing going on in the daPena warehouse and they thought you were going to horn in and spoil it."

"Who is they?"

"Gorgeous."

"You said they. Gorgeous and who?"

He'd reached his next point of decision. He decided

to tell a warped truth. "A guy named Donny something who set up the deal."

"You mean a hooker named Donni Pell who worked for Lettie Faren and had a thing for ogres. Don't do that again, Skredli."

His shoulders sagged.

I took a moment to reflect. There was a question of timing that deserved it. Skredli had been in town, leading that pack, after Junior was snatched. But then he'd been at that farm the afternoon before Junior walked away, and the next morning he'd led the crew that did in Amiranda.

I tabled that for the moment. "I'm interested in that warehouse scheme. All the petty little details."

I'd caught him on Donni Pell, so now he was determined to spin me a good tale. "That was one of Donni's ideas. She was always bringing us things she'd dreamed up from stuff her johns told her. Some of them we went with, and she got a cut. This one was real sweet. Raver Styx had left town and Donni had a foreman that would let us siphon off ten percent of everything that went through. We took it on a fifty-fifty split with Donni, on account of she was the one keeping the daPena side in line, but the foreman's cut and expenses had to come out of her half. We moved a lot of stuff. As much as we were doing from the rest of the waterfront, practically. But then Donni warned us that people were getting suspicious. Raver Styx's woman Dount sent the kid to nose around. Then there was you, starting to snoop just when we had decided to close the thing out by cleaning out the warehouse in one hit. So they had me try to discourage you."

Interesting. Not worried about me and my reputation for getting into kidnap cases? "When we hit the place in Ogre Town, we saw a guy leaving. A Bruno off the Hill. Who was he?"

"I never heard his name. A guy Donni knew. He worked for the guy who was taking the stuff from the warehouse. The guy was worried. He hired some other guy to keep track of you and you grabbed him, he thought. He wanted us to do something about you. There was a big panic about covering tracks because Raver Styx had been seen in Leifmold and could turn up anytime."

I turned to Morley. "Pokey?"

"Probably."

"What became of him?"

"I turned him loose. He went home and sat tight. He knew I was watching."

"Uhm. Skredli. Who did the Bruno work for?"

"I don't know. I don't even think Gorgeous knew. Donni or the Bruno delivered all the messages."

"A cautious man. And wisely so, considering who he was stealing from. But the goods had to be transferred somehow."

"We had our own warehouse, partly legit. The Bruno hired teamsters to pick up the stuff there."

There was an opportunity for some legwork if I decided I really wanted to know where the Stormwarden's goods had gone. I wondered if I ought to ask what goods a Stormwarden dealt in that were so attractive to thieves, but decided ignorance might prove beneficial at a later date. I needed whos and whys but not many whats.

"Let's talk about the younger Karl daPena. One night as he was going out the back door of Lettie Faren's place, somebody popped a bag over his head, choked him, and threw him into a carriage. And after that the story gets confusing."

Skredli had come around to where I wanted him. He was able to volunteer information without upsetting whatever minuscule conscience resides in an ogrish heart.

"That whole mess started out as a fake. The kid wanted to run out on his old lady and rip her off at the same time. He fixed it up with Donni to make it look like a snatch and he'd split the payoff with her and start traveling. Donni was going to split her half with us for making it look good. It wasn't the kind of thing Gorgeous usually got into, but it looked like money for nothing, so he sent for the old gang and we did it."

"Only it didn't come off that way. What happened?"

"I don't know. Honest. The same night after you and me go around in the street, Gorgeous calls me in and says there's a big change of plans. I seen Donni leaving, so I know where the change came from. Anyway, he told me I had to go out where the kid was hid out and turn it into the real thing. And when the payoff came through, we was supposed to be a whole lot better off than with the old plan. We was going to leave the kid twisting in the wind."

"Uhm." I thought a moment. "What about Donni's cut of the fatter pot?"

"We got that whole wad. All the kid's share."

Something told me Donni Pell had gotten her share somewhere else.

"So that's that? You just went out, got the money, and headed north?"

My tone warned him.

"No. You know that, don't you?"

"You had to kill a girl to get that extra chunk."

"Gorgeous said it had to be done. I didn't like it."

"Why?"

"I don't know. Look, no matter what you do, I'm going to tell you that a lot. Because I *don't* know. I wasn't his partner. Gorgeous told me to do things and I did them and he paid me good. And part of what he paid me for was not asking questions. You want to know who wanted something done and why, you got to find Donni Pell and ask her."

"What you say is probably true, but you have eyes and ears and a brain. You saw things and heard things and you thought about them. Why do you *think* the girl had to die?"

"Maybe she knew too much about something. She knew the kidnap was a fake because she was supposed to run off with the kid and the money. Maybe she found out the fake turned real. Maybe she just did something to make Donni want to get her. Maybe it was just because she was set to take the frame for the kidnapping and Gorgeous didn't want her turning up saying it wasn't so. I know we was supposed to make her disappear forever. Only when we showed up to do it she had some son of a bitch with her and he turned out to be a goddamned one-man army. And by the time we got him down, there was traffic coming and we had to throw them in the bushes and make it look like nothing happened. When we got back, we found out that big ape wasn't dead at all. He'd grabbed the girl and took off through the woods. I never thought he'd get far, cut like he was. And he left us with a lot of cleaning up to—"

"That's enough of that. Tell me about the payoff. Where. When. How."

"On the Chamberton Old Coach Road four miles south of where it runs into the Vorkuta-Lichfield Road, just north of the bridge over Little Cedar Creek. Set for midnight the night before what we was just talking about, but the delivery was two hours late. I guess Gorgeous wasn't pissed because he never complained."

I didn't know the place. On the map the Chamberton Old Coach Road cuts up through woody hill country four miles west of the route I'd taken when I'd gone out to explore. "Why that spot?"

"The road runs straight for a mile either way from the bridge. There's never any traffic at night, but if there was, you'd spot it coming in plenty of time. And you can look off northeast and see the ridge the Lichfield road runs on. I was up there to watch in case there was any tricks. I was supposed to light one signal flare if everything was all right and two if it wasn't."

"Did you expect trouble?"

"No. We had them by the short hairs. But you don't take chances with those people."

"And the delivery was late?"

"Yeah. But I guess that was just because the damn fool woman didn't know what she was doing. Any idiot should know a covered wagon with a four-horse team won't make time like a buggy or carriage."

Oh? "You weren't there for the actual payoff, then?"

"No. But Gorgeous said it went down exactly the way it was supposed to."

"Which was?"

"The wagon came down and stopped in the road. Gorgeous and Donni had their coaches off to the side. Gorgeous and Donni had their drivers transfer the moneybags, half and half. The woman and her wagon headed on south. Donni stayed put for an hour, then headed south too. Gorgeous came up where I was and gave me my cut and enough to pay off the boys so they could go home after the business in the morning. We didn't want them coming to TunFaire, getting drunk, and shooting their mouths off."

"They knew what was happening?"

"Not the payoff. But they were in on a killing."

"There was no concern about just following the woman?"

"She wasn't told what to do about going back till she turned over the ransom."

"I see." Not very bright, this Skredli. "She didn't have anything to say when she didn't get the kid after the payoff?"

"I don't know. Maybe she did. Gorgeous never said."

"I guess you came out pretty good on the deal personally, eh?"

"Yeah. Look at me. Living like a lord. Yeah. I got my usual ten percent of Gorgeous's fifty percent. A big hit to you, maybe, but I did better on the warehouse business, even if it took longer to come in."

"You stripped the warehouse, then?"

"Yeah. I didn't think it was smart, but Gorgeous said we already had such a big investment we might as well finish it off."

"Uhm." I began to pace, to think. We'd been at it a long time. He'd given me a lot to think about. We were almost there, but I needed that moment to reflect, to reorder my forces.

"Where is Donni Pell, Skredli?"

"I don't know."

"She was there when we came after you, wasn't she?" He nodded.

"And she ran out behind us and went for help."

He shrugged.

"It's going to be interesting, finding out who called out the troops. That was a stupid mistake. Very stupid. Panic thinking. Raver Styx will have his hide. Where's Donni Pell?"

"How many times I got to tell you I don't know? If she's got the sense of a cockroach, she's done got her butt out of TunFaire."

"If she had that much sense, she would have headed out of town as soon as she had her share of the money. She seems to have a certain low cunning, an ability to manipulate men, and complete confidence in her invulnerability, but no brains. I'll take your word. You don't know where she is. But where might she run? Who would hide her?"

Skredli shrugged. "One of her johns, maybe."

I'd had that thought already. I suspected Skredli was mined out on the subject. And he was relaxed enough for the next stage.

"Why did the Stormwarden's kid have to be killed?"

"Huh? Killed? I heard he committed suicide."

"We're getting along fine, Skredli. I'm starting to feel kindly toward you. Don't blow your chance. I know you and Gorgeous and Donni and somebody were in and out of the room where he died. And I knew him well enough to know he couldn't kill himself that way—if he could ever find guts enough to kill himself at all. I figure you used the choke sack on him and Gorgeous cut him himself. I think Donni—but what I think doesn't matter. The thing I can't figure is why he went within a mile of that woman after what she did to him."

"You don't know Donni Pell."

"No. But I intend to get acquainted. Go ahead. Tell me about that morning."

"You aren't going to spread it around, are you? I don't need no Raver Styx breathing down my neck."

"None of us do. But you don't worry about Raver Styx. You worry about me. I'm the only chance you've got to walk out of here. You've got to make me happy."

He shrugged. He wasn't counting on me. But he did have new hopes that he hadn't had a while ago.

"All right. What started it was you parading around with that dead woman. Somebody seen you by Lettie Faren's place. They told Donni and Donni must have told everybody in town. She sent a messenger to us. Gorgeous had a fit, but he believed me when I said she had to be dead and you was just trying to stir something up.

"But you did get Donni stirred. Like you said, she ain't too smart. She thought she had her handle on the daPena kid. She sent him a message that told him where to find her, that she had to see him. The dope went there. I don't know what she thought she was going to get him to do. He wasn't having none of her finger-wrapping no more. He'd figured some of it out, and like a dummy she told him the girl was dead.

"That did it. He was going to hike out of there and blow the whole thing wide open. And he would have, too, only me and Gorgeous showed up. On account of Gorgeous was worried about Donni maybe getting too excited and doing something really stupid."

"It wasn't planned, then?"

"I gotta be careful with that. I don't think it was. I wasn't in on no planning, which I usually was because I was the guy who had to go out and do things. But it did have a funny feel. Like maybe Donni rigged it so it would come out the way it did."

"You keep contradicting yourself. Is Donni Pell stupid or not?"

"She's good at coming up with schemes and playing them out, long as she's got the reins in her hands. You catch her by surprise, she don't do so good. She thinks slow, she gets flustered, she does dumb things. So Gorgeous figured we better get over there and sit on her till she calmed down and whatever was bugging her blew away."

"And Karl was there."

"There and throwing a fit. He figured some of it out

and he was going to tell the world. Donni even tried to buy him off, saying she'd give him his share after all. Dumb. After the way she screwed him over, and him just about sure what was going on. We didn't have no choice. He wouldn't back down. Even with me and Gorgeous there. It was our asses or his. I thought we made it look good."

"You did. You just didn't know he was so chicken nobody would believe he did it himself. Who was the other guy who was there?"

"What other guy?"

"A man in a hooded black cloak."

"I never saw one."

"Uhm." I paced. There were more questions I wanted to ask, but most had to do with the money. I didn't want Chodo getting interested in that. And Skredli had given me plenty to untangle, anyway. Probably close to enough. Donni Pell would put the cap on it. She would throw some light into the hearts of some shadows. She would cast the bones of doom for somebody.

"I played it straight for you," Skredli said. "Get me out of here."

"I'll have to talk Mr. Chodo into it," I replied. "What will you do?"

"Head north as fast as I can run. I don't want to be anywhere around when Raver Styx hits town. And there ain't nothing here for me anymore, anyway."

"You'd keep your mouth shut?"

"Are you kidding? Whose throat would the knife bite first?"

"Good point." I wagged a hand at Morley, indicating the door. He moved to open it. Chodo rolled out of his way. Morley stepped aside. Chodo and I followed.

"Where do you stand?" I asked the kingpin, indicating the door with a jerk of my head.

"I got rid of the bloodsucker bothering me. That's just a hired hand. You can have him."

"I don't know if I want him. Maybe he swung the knife but didn't give the order." We walked for a while. I said, "You know Saucerhead Tharpe?"

"I've heard the name. I know the reputation. I've never had the pleasure."

"Saucerhead Tharpe has a grievance against Skredli. It supersedes mine. I think he deserves first choice in deciding."

We traveled through that vast room where the naked ladies played. Again Morley had trouble steering. To Chodo they were furniture. He said, "Tell Tharpe to come out if he wants a piece." And, "If I don't hear by this time tomorrow, I turn him loose." And, at the front door, "Sometimes you let one go so word gets around how it goes for those who don't get out."

"Sure." Morley and I stepped outside and waited for an escort. We didn't speak until we were on the public road. Then I asked, "You think Chodo will let him go?"

"No."

"Me neither."

"What now, Garrett?"

"I don't know about you. I'm going home to sleep. I had a late night last night."

"Sounds good to me. You let me know if anything comes of all this."

"How's your financial position these days, Morley?"

He gave me a dark look, but replied, "I'm doing all right."

"Yeah. I figured you would be. Listen, knothead. Stay away from the damned water-spider races. I'm not getting killed in one of your harebrained schemes for getting out from under."

"Hey, Garrett!"

"You've done it to me twice, Morley. This time maybe not as hairy as last time, but that crap down in Ogre Town was too damned close. You hear what I'm saying?"

He heard well enough to sulk.

41

I needed a sixteen-hour nap, but I devoured a roast chicken with trimmings and downed a couple quarts of beer instead. I went into the Dead Man's den, being careful not to trample on the bodies, and tiptoed over to the shelves on the short north wall. Among the clutter I found a fine collection of maps. I dug out several and settled in my reserved chair.

I see you had a productive day.

He startled me. I hadn't known he was awake. But that's the sort of game he likes to play—sneak and scare. Near my heart I nurture a suspicion that malicious and capricious spirits are dead Loghyr disembodied.

I didn't answer immediately.

A productive day indeed. You are smugly certain you have a handle on everything and no longer need badger me to do your thinking for you.

Just to be contrary—though that's probably what he wanted—I gave him a blow-by-blow of everything that had happened since my last report. He seemed amused by my having chewed Morley out.

While I talked, I ran my right forefinger along lines on one of the maps, trying to visualize points of interest barely noticed in the real world.

Looking for a place someone unfamiliar with the terri-

tory might have felt safe squirreling a pile of gold when pressed for time?

"I'm thinking about going for a ride in the country tomorrow, maybe stopping to go swimming under a few bridges."

An interesting notion. Though you may never get to put it to the test.

"Why not?"

You still need me to explain to you the consequences of your actions? The Stormwarden Raver Styx was due home today. She should, in fact, have been home for some hours now. She should be howling at the moon. And who has had his nose deep into the thing, from several angles? Who is she going to drag in to answer questions right beside Domina Dount and the Baronet daPena?

I suppose that had been lounging around in the back of my mind, overshadowed by the puzzle. And maybe by a touch of gold fever. "Dean!"

He looked a bit exasperated when he stuck his head in. "Yes sir?"

"Don't answer the door tonight. I'll do it. In fact, why don't you go on home and put yourself out of harm's way? You haven't left for days. Maybe a few of your nieces have roped some men."

Dean smiled. "You aren't closing me out now, sir. I'll stay."

"It's your funeral."

As if conjured by the conversation, someone began pounding on the door. I went and peeked through the peephole. I didn't recognize any of the crowd, but they wore Raver Styx's colors. I shut the peephole and went for another beer.

Her men? the Dead Man asked when I returned.

"Yes." I turned to the maps again.

You ignore her at your peril.

Yours too, I thought. "I know what I'm doing."

You usually think you do. Occasionally you are correct.

I ignored him, too.

It wasn't ten minutes before someone else knocked. This time when I peeped I found Sadler on the stoop.

"Chodo said tell you what we come up with," he said when I opened the door, making no move to come inside. "We asked around, places. Somebody got word to her we were looking. She took off. Out of town. Nobody knows where she landed. We asked."

I'll bet they did.

"Chodo says tell you he still owes you the favor."

"Tell him I said thank you very much."

"I don't say much to civilians, Garrett. But you done all right down in Ogre Town. You maybe pulled us all out with your trick. So I'll tell you, don't waste that favor on nothing silly."

"Right."

He turned away and hiked. I shut the door and went back to the Dead Man.

Good advice, Garrett. A favor due from the kingpin is like a pound of gold squirreled away.

"I don't like it anyway. I just hope he stays alive long enough for me to collect." Kingpins have a habit of turning up dead almost as often as our kings do.

It was quiet for an hour. So quiet I dozed off in my chair, the maps sliding out of my lap. The Dead Man awakened me with a sudden strong touch. *Company again, Garrett.*

I heard the knocking as I tried to get the body parts moving in unison. When I peeked, I saw Morley on the stoop. He was alone. I opened up and he slipped inside. "I wake you?"

"Sort of. I thought you were going to crap out. What's up?"

"I just heard something I thought you should know. They found that guy Courter Slauce in an alley a couple streets from here. Somebody busted the back of his head in for him."

"What?" I tried to shake the groggies. "He's dead?"

"Like the proverbial wedge."

"Who did it?"

"How should I know?"

"This don't make sense. I have to get some tea or something. Wash the cobwebs out."

"For that you'll need the high water of the decade. Sometimes I think the only substance inside your head is the dust on the cobwebs."

"Ain't nothing will perk you up like a vote of confidence from your friends. Dean. Tea."

Dean had water on. He always does. He favors tea the way I favor beer. He brewed me a mug thick enough to slice. In the meantime, I asked Morley, "Did you keep anyone watching the Stormwarden's place?"

"For all the good it did. Till today."

"And?"

"There's no way to do a decent job when you spend eighty percent of your time dodging security patrols."

"They got nothing?"

"Zippo. Zilch. Zero. Armies could have marched in and out and they would have missed them."

"It was a long shot anyway. What about Pokey?"

"What about him? Why keep on him?"

"He might have trotted off to somebody interesting."

"You're grasping, Garrett. Pokey Pigotta? You're kidding."

"There's always a chance."

"There's a chance the world will end tomorrow. I'll give you fifty-to-one odds it does before Pokey Pigotta does something unprofessional."

"I don't want to hear bet or odds from you."

He gave me a narrow-eyed look. "I laid off you and your poisonous diet, Garrett. I laid off your self-destructive knight errantry. You lay off me. I'll go to hell in my own way."

"I don't care how you go to hell, Morley. That's your business. But every time you head out you throw a rope on me and try to drag me along."

"You feel that way about it, quit pulling me into your quests."

"I pay you to do a job. That's all I want done."

"Somebody ought to profit. If you're so damned lily

pure, you're willing to get paid off in self-satisfaction for righting deadly wrongs—"

Dean interjected, "You kids want to whoop and holler and call each other names, why don't you take it out in the alley? Or at least get it out of my kitchen."

I was about to patiently explain again who owned that kitchen and who just worked there, when someone else came pounding on my door and hollering for me. "Saucerhead," I said, and headed that way. Morley followed me. I asked, "Who killed Slauce?"

"I told you I don't know. I heard he was dead. I came to tell you. I didn't go turn out his pockets to see if he left a note naming his killer."

I peeked through the peephole, just in case. I was in one of those moods.

Saucerhead, all right. And Amber. And several of the Stormwarden's men, including a couple who had been around before. I let Morley peek. "You want to be here for this?"

"No. I'm done. With you, with them, with the whole damned mess."

"Have it your way." I opened the door as Saucerhead wound up to start pounding again. Morley shoved out, grumbled a greeting. I said, "You two can come inside. The army stays where it is."

42

"What's a matter with Morley?" Saucerhead asked. He had a glazed look, but I suppose even a statue would be numb after an exposure to the Stormwarden Raver Styx.

"He tried to take a bite out of something that bit him back. Or maybe it was the other way around. What're you two up to, with your private army out there?"

"Mother wants you," Amber said. "You should have seen Mr. Tharpe stand up to Domina and Mother. He was magnificent."

"I've heard him called a lot of things but magnificent was never on the list."

"I didn't do nothing but stand there and pretend I was deaf except when they absolutely had to have me say something. Then I just sounded stupid and said they had to talk to her on account of I was working for her."

"And what was it all about?" I asked Amber.

"They wanted him out. They really got mad because he wouldn't go and I wouldn't tell him to go."

"It'll do them good. So your mother wants me to come running."

"Yes."

"Why did she send you?"

"Because she sent Courter and he didn't even come back. Then she sent Dawson and you wouldn't open the door."

Courter? She sent him to get me?

"Dean! Come Here a minute." He came in. "Did anybody come to the door today? Before I told you I would answer it myself?"

"No. Just the boy who brought the letter."

"What letter?"

"I put it on your desk. I assumed you'd seen it."

"Excuse me for a minute." I went to the office. The letter was there, all right. I gave it a read. It was from my friend Tinnie. Out of sight, she had slipped out of mind.

"Anything important?" Saucerhead asked when I returned.

"Nah. Red's headed for TunFaire."

He looked at Amber sidelong, smirked. "That ought to put some life back in this town."

"Amber, does your mother think I'll just hike out there because she crooked her finger?"

"She's the Stormwarden Raver Styx, Garrett. She's used to getting what she wants."

"She isn't getting it this time. I'm tired and I've been playing with thugs so much lately another one isn't going to bother me none. Tell her if she wants to see me, she knows where to find me. During normal business hours. If she comes down now, I won't answer the door."

Amber said, "I'm not going to tell her anything, Garrett. I'm not going back. I forgot how bad it could get till she came storming in. As far as I'm concerned, she can take it out on Father and Domina from now on. She's seen the last of her unbeloved daughter. . . . You did mean it when you let me have that gold, didn't you?"

I was tempted to say no just to see how quick she could turn in her tracks, but forbore. "Yes."

"Then I'm going upstairs. You can go home, Mr. Tharpe."

"Just a minute, girl. You're going to declare your independence, you're going to declare your independence. You can stay tonight because it's too late to do it now but tomorrow you go shopping for a place of your own."

For a moment she was stunned. Then she looked hurt.

I tried to soften it. "This is a dangerous place and I'm in a dangerous line."

"And I have a dangerous family."

"That, too. When you relay my message to the troops out there, tell them to tell your mother that Courter didn't run away after all. Somebody lured him into an alley and smashed his head in. She can sleep on that."

Amber gawked. She opened and closed her mouth several times.

"You look like a goldfish."

"Really? Courter was murdered too?"

"Yes."

"Why would anyone do that?"

"I assume because he was coming to see me."

"Damn them!"

As I hoped, the anger I'd aroused now became a white righteous fury. She stomped to the door.

I raised a hand, delaying Saucerhead. "Chodo had me out to his place today. He still has that character that killed Amiranda. He offered him to me. I told him you had more claim. He said if you're interested, get your butt out there because tomorrow he's going to turn him loose."

Saucerhead pursed his lips and touched himself a couple of places where he still hurt. He grunted.

"I'd also like you to come back tomorrow. I'm figuring on taking a trip and I want you to keep on keeping an eye on Amber."

He nodded. "Yeah. They ain't getting this one, Garrett."

"Fine. I'll see you when you get—"

Amber's yell sent us hustling out front, me unlimbering my skull buster. Saucerhead picked up a couple of the Stormwarden's men and cracked their heads together. I thumped two behind the ears. That left three and two of those had all they could handle with Amber. Saucerhead peeled them off while I held their leader at bay. "What the hell you trying to do, shithead?"

"Take her home."

"I'm not going to argue. I'm just going to tell you she

said she don't want to go. She's old enough to make up
her own mind. Pick up your buddies and leave."

He looked at me like he wanted to tell me what it
meant to get into the Stormwarden's way, then just
shrugged. Saucerhead let go of the two he had. The
bunch began getting themselves together.

Amber started to say something. I told her to go inside. We would talk after the crowd thinned out. She
went, and Raver Styx's thugs did the same, leaving me
with a flock of promising black looks.

"You're starting to catch on, Garrett. Talk *after* you
kick ass. They're more inclined to hear what you have
to say."

That was Morley Dotes talking from a perch on the
stoop next door. He got up and came down, stood with
us watching the Stormwarden's boys stumble off. I said
nothing, not knowing what might set him off. He offered
me a folded piece of paper. I looked him in the eye for
a moment. His expression remained bland.

There was nothing on that paper but a name:
Lyman Gameleon.

"I've heard of him. Big bear on the Hill, and so forth.
What's the significance?"

"Just thought I'd save you some trouble, Garrett.
That's the man who sent the soldiers into Ogre Town.
A man who, coincidentally, happens to be your
Stormwarden's next-door neighbor—and bitterest
enemy, politically and personally. Not to mention being
her husband's older half-brother."

"Hey! Very interesting. Thanks, Morley."

"No big deal, Garrett." He waved one hand as he
marched away.

The tidbit was Morley's way of extending the olive
branch.

Saucerhead said, "It's time I was going, too, Garrett.
Take care of Miss daPena."

I considered his broad back as he went. Had he said
more than he had said? With Saucerhead it's hard to
tell if he's just being a dumb goof or a mild cynic.

I went inside and locked up. I looked around for Amber, didn't see her. "Amber?"

"In your office."

I went in. She had parked herself in my chair and seemed to be sulking.

"Cheer up. You were marvelous."

"You manipulated me."

"Of course I did. Would you have stood up to those thugs if you weren't mad?"

"Probably not."

I settled on a corner of the desk. "One piece of news that might perk you up. I think there's a small chance we can lay hands on some of the gold."

"You're stringing me along again, aren't you?"

"No. It's a long shot but a real chance. I didn't think there was one before. It depends on how distracted your mother is by the emotional side of what's happened. I think I know what happened to some of the gold, but finding it is going to be like scratching through the proverbial haystack. We'll need time."

"You mean it, don't you?"

"Yes. Though I admit I'm riding a hunch." Dean brought beer and wine. We thanked him. I told Amber, "I can't stay awake much longer. I'm going to turn in. I'll see you in the morning."

She flashed me a wicked smile.

I understood the smile soon enough.

I didn't latch my door. Who does, inside his own house? Amber took that as an invitation. Not only did I see her sooner than I expected, I got less sleep than I hoped. Repeated clamors at the front door, ignored by the entire household, also interrupted my rest.

43

I staggered out when the smell of breakfast overpowered my laziness. As I descended the stairs another hurrah broke out at the front door. I slipped over and peered through the peephole. An ugly face, bloated and red, bobbed outside. A mouth filled with bad teeth gaped and bellowed.

I closed the peephole and went to breakfast.

I leaned back and patted my belly. "Dean, of all the several geniuses infesting this place, I think you're the most valuable. Where the hell did you find strawberries?"

"My niece May brought them. They've been in the cold well for three days."

Nieces again? At that rate of regression the Dead Man would soon be interested in Glory Mooncalled again. "I'd better see if his nibs is awake." Sooner or later that front door was going to have to open. "Amber, your mother is bound to come. You going to want to be scarce?"

"I can face her as long as I've got a place to run when it gets gruesome."

"You're all right, then. Dean, I'll take a mug of tea while I rattle Old Bones."

Dean scowled and grumbled, not at all inclined to let

me take matters into my own hands. He prepared the tea with such care and deliberation I was ready to do without before he finished. Tea is tea. Making a religious ceremony of fixing it doesn't improve it a bit.

There are those who would consider me a barbarian— the same ones who aren't civilized enough to appreciate good beer.

The Dead Man was awake. He wasn't in a mood to be interrupted. He knew we'd have company soon and was working himself up for it. I believe he had visions of using the Stormwarden—who had been in the Cantard for months—as a chamois to buff up his Glory Mooncalled theory.

I followed Amber's example and went to my room to groom myself for the hours ahead.

That done, I settled at a window and watched the street. It wasn't quiet out there. The Stormwarden's men remained at their posts but weren't watching the house. Their carrying on had drawn a crowd.

The lords of the Hill can get away with a lot. They usually remain above the laws that keep the rest of us from preying on each other. But the invasion of a home without the prior approval of the judges is something people won't tolerate.

Had the Stormwarden's men tried to break in during the night, they might have gotten away with something— had the Dead Man allowed it. Now it was too late. If they tried, the crowd would tear them apart. Our overlords have to exercise a delicate touch when they violate the sanctity of the home.

I hoped the uptown boys didn't get stupid. I had worked myself into a tight enough place already.

They kept me there. And company, when it came, did so from an unexpected quarter. From the corner of my eye I caught a stir coming from downtown. What to my wondering eye should appear but Saucerhead Tharpe in convoy with Sadler and Crask. The bunch looked like they had breakfasted on bitterbark soup at Morley's place.

I sighed. "I knew things were shaping up too damned well."

I ran into Amber in the hallway. She asked, "Is she here?"

"Not yet. It's Saucerhead and a couple guys you don't even want to know by sight. And I'm not going to be able to find out what they want if you don't let me get to the stairs."

"Oh." She stepped aside. "Grouch."

"You're probably right. You might warn Dean so he can get something ready. They look like they'll need it."

I was three steps from the door when Saucerhead knocked. I glanced through the peephole and opened up. As my guests entered I gave the Stormwarden's red-faced boy a glare and said, "Don't even think about it." He got redder, but I didn't have to watch. I shut the door on him.

I seated them in the small front room next to my office. Dean appeared with tea and sweetcakes just as though they were expected. I said, "Well? What is it? How bad is it?"

Saucerhead glanced at the other two. They were willing to let him do the talking. I couldn't quite tell what the threesome were up to. There was no tension between them, just a commonality of undirected disgust. Tharpe said, "Skredli got away."

"Skredli? Got? Away? What did he do? Sprout wings and fly? Was he some kind of werebuzzard?" I'd never heard of such a beast, but nothing in this world surprises me anymore. If a man can turn into a wolf, why not an ogre into a buzzard? Both transformations seem singularly fitting. Perhaps even symbolic.

Prejudiced? Who? Me?

The gods forfend.

"No, he didn't fly, Garrett. He just took off running."

I started to express my incredulity, but it struck me that I might learn a little more a lot faster with my mouth shut. I admit I don't often have these epiphanies.

Saucerhead explained. "It was just getting light when I went out there. They took me up to the front porch and told me to wait. Then they went in and brought

Skredli out. And all of a sudden, like that was all he was waiting for, he took off like a bat out of hell.''

Crask said, "It was chilly up there last night. The lizards get sluggish when their blood cools down.''

Sadler added, "Dogs won't run an ogre 'less they're specially trained. Anyway, Chodo's mutts are supposed to keep people from getting in, not from getting out.''

And Saucerhead, "It happened so sudden, and he was gone so fast, nobody had time to do nothing but gawk.''

No point in whining. It wasn't my problem, anyway. Or was it? "You didn't come down here just to let me in on that, did you?''

Saucerhead hit me with the news. "Chodo thinks you're going to stick on what you're after till you find Donni Pell. He figures that when you find her, you'll find Skredli again, too.''

"That sounds plausible.''

"He wants Sadler and Crask to be there when you find them.''

"I see.'' I can't say I was disappointed. I foresaw any number of potentialities right down the path. Those three guys would be handy if the fur began to fly. "All right. I'm expecting heavyweight company sometime today. Raver Styx.''

"We know the game and the stakes, Garrett.''

"Indeed?'' Had Amber been running her mouth? No. Saucerhead just *thought* he knew the stakes.

Which alerted me to the fact that there would be no gold hunting until Skredli and Donni Pell turned up. Unless I decided I didn't mind Chodo's thugs hanging around when I turned it up.

"Go about your routine,'' Sadler told me. "We'll stay out of your way.''

Sure they would. As long as it wasn't in their interest to do otherwise.

44

We killed time playing cards. Dean was in and out, laying scowls on me. I knew what he was thinking: I ought to whip all these bodies into a rehabilitation frenzy and get some work done on the house. He doesn't understand that characters like Saucerhead, Sadler, and Crask get no thrill out of domestic triumphs.

Amber popped in once, decided she couldn't handle all the joviality, and retreated upstairs. The Dead Man remained alert in his quarters. My neck prickled each time his touch passed through the room. He would never admit he was nervous, though.

Amber came back awhile later. "She's coming, Garrett. I thought she'd at least send Domina once first." She hesitated for a split second. "I think I'll stay upstairs."

"I was sure you'd want to suggest she learn to pick her nose with her elbow."

"I'm not quite ready for that yet."

"And if she insists on seeing you?"

"Tell her I'm not here. Say I ran off somewhere."

"You know she won't believe that. She's a stormwarden. She'll know where you are."

Amber shrugged. "If I have to face her, I will. Otherwise, just leave me out of it."

"Whatever you say."

The future began hammering on the door. Dean looked in to see if I wanted him to answer. I nodded. He headed out at a reluctant shuffle. I rose and went after him. Amber scurried up the stairs. Saucerhead and the boys folded their hands and strolled into the hallway.

I was five feet behind Dean when he swung the door inward. The Dead Man's attention was so intense the air almost crackled. I had one hand in my pocket, gripping one of the potencies given me by Saucerhead's witch, knowing that if I employed it, Raver Styx would notice the spell about as much as she might notice the whine of a mosquito.

She had come to the door alone, though she'd been accompanied on the journey from the Hill. A coach and small army cluttered the street behind her. My neighbors had made themselves scarce.

She was a short woman, heavy and gnarly, like a dwarf. She'd never had anything like Amber's beauty, even at sixteen, when they all look good. Her face was grim and ugly. She had bright blue eyes that seemed to blaze in contrast with her tanned, leathery skin and graying hair. If she was angry, though, she concealed it very well. She seemed more relaxed than most people who come to my door.

Dean had frozen. I moved forward. "Do come in, Stormwarden. I've been expecting you."

She stepped past Dean, glancing at him as though she was puzzled by his rigidity. Could she be that naive?

"Close the door, Dean."

He finally moved.

I led the Stormwarden into the room where we'd been playing cards. The office was not large enough for the crowd. As I seated my guest, I asked, "Can Dean get you anything? Tea?"

"Brandy. Something of that sort. And not by the thimbleful. I want something to drink, not something to sniff at."

Her voice was gravelly and as deep as ever I'd heard from a woman. It had a timbre that made her sound like she was used to being one of the boys.

That was the way they talked about her. I had no
direct knowledge. I'd never crossed paths with her
before.

"Dean, bring a bottle from that bunch the Bahgell
brothers sent me."

"Yes sir."

I considered Raver Styx. That I might have grateful
clients of the Baghell caliber didn't impress her.

"Mr. Garrett . . . You are Mr. Garrett?" she asked.

"I am."

"These others?"

"Associates. They represent the interests of a former
protégé of Molahlu Crest."

If that news amazed or dismayed her or in any other
way impressed her, she didn't show it. She said, "Very
well. I've studied you briefly. I understand you carry on
your business your own way or you don't do business.
You get results, so you can't be faulted for your ways."

I examined her again while Dean delivered her bottle
and glass. I wasn't sure how to play her. She was disap-
pointing my expectations. I'd been steeling myself for a
storm of imperial rage. I said, "I did say I was expecting
you, having been drawn into the periphery of your
family's affairs. But I'm not quite certain why."

"Don't be ingenuous, Mr. Garrett. It's wasted effort.
You've been nearer the heart than the periphery. Maybe
nearer than you know. My first question of you would
be why."

"Representing a client or clients, of course."

She waited a moment. When I didn't add anything,
she asked, "Who?" Then, "No, strike that. You won't
tell me if you think it's to your advantage to reserve it.
Let me think a moment."

After she'd reflected a moment, she continued. "Disaster after disaster has trampled my family the past few
weeks. My son kidnapped, to be redeemed for a ransom
so huge the financial future of the family is in doubt.
And my adopted daughter decided she had to fly the
nest and for her trouble got herself slaughtered by
bandits."

I wagged a cautionary finger at Saucerhead.

"My son, after being freed, killed himself. And my natural daughter, despite your efforts and those of Willa Dount, fled home not once but twice."

"Not to mention trivia like Courter Slauce getting himself killed on his way down to see me last night, or the fact that thieves have stripped the daPena warehouse."

Her face shaded with the faintest cloud of emotion, the first she'd shown. "Is that true?"

"Which?"

"About the warehouse."

"Yes."

"I hadn't heard."

"Maybe Domina has been too distracted to keep track of what's happening on the commercial side."

"Horsefeathers. Domina is feeding me disasters in tidbits in hopes I won't have her flayed and use her hide for bookbinding."

It was a sour, trite remark, not meant to be taken seriously. Witches and sorcerers had stood the accusation so long it had become a joke of the trade.

Having done my dance to show off, I waited, leaving the next play in her hand.

"I'd suspected you possessed knowledge not at my command, Mr. Garrett. Now you've told me as much, for whatever motives move you. All right. We both know I want the rest. You want something for yourself. Can we arrive at a peaceful middle ground?"

"Probably. I doubt if our goals are too far apart."

"Indeed? What do you want, then?"

"The man or woman who gave the order that got Amiranda Crest murdered."

I guess when you play for stakes as high as she had for so long, you learn to keep yourself controlled. That face would have made her a deadly cardplayer. "Go on, Mr. Garrett."

"I want the person no matter who it is. That's what I want."

She surveyed my companions. Sadler and Crask were

blanks, but Saucerhead had leaned a little toward us. "It's obvious you know a great deal that I don't."

Saucerhead couldn't restrain himself. "Skredli and Donni Pell, Garrett. We get them, too."

The Stormwarden looked at me. I said, "My friend was there when Amiranda was murdered. He tried to save her and failed. He feels obligated to restore a balance. He also has a personal score to settle. Show her."

Saucerhead understood. He started stripping. The wounds he exposed still looked nasty. The deeper cuts wouldn't lose their purplish-red color for months.

"I see," the Stormwarden said. "Would you care to tell me how it happened?"

Saucerhead put his shirt back on. I said nothing. Raver Styx muttered, "So that's the way it's going to be."

All the while I stared smoke and fire at Saucerhead. He had to mention Donni Pell in front of the wife! I'd wanted to reserve Donni Pell for the moment of maximum impact.

She hadn't reacted to the name at all.

"I suppose the thing to do is hire you, Mr. Garrett. Then you might be more responsive."

"Maybe. Maybe not. I do my job my own way. Between the hiring and the results I don't put up with meddling from my principal. I'm the specialist. If I can't be trusted to do the job without interference, I shouldn't be hired in the first place." I don't think my voice squeaked. I sure hoped it didn't. "What did you want to hire me for, anyway?"

She looked at me like I was a moron.

"I don't mind having multiple clients, but I don't take them on when their goals conflict."

She continued to stare. Serpents of temper had begun to stir beneath the surface of her calm. No more pushing permitted.

"Before we go on there's something I've got to show you, Stormwarden. I warn you up front, you're not going to like it. You're going to be upset. But you need to see it so you don't walk into anything with the web of illusion across your eyes."

The Dead Man brushed me with a touch of approval.

The Stormwarden rose, her face carefully composed. I said, "You ought to finish that glass and pour yourself another before we go."

"If it's that tough, I'll take the bottle along."

Just one of the guys. "Come on, then."

I crossed the hall to the Dead Man's room, stepped inside, stepped aside. The parade followed, the Stormwarden first. The boys lined up against the wall beside the door. Crask and Sadler stared at the Dead Man and went gray around the edges.

Seeing is believing.

"A dead Loghyr!" The Stormwarden enthused, sounding like she'd just spotted a cute fairy toddler peeking out of the bushes. "I didn't know there were any around anymore. What do you want for it?"

"You wouldn't want this one. He's a social parasite. My personal charity project. He does nothing but sleep and amuse himself by playing with bugs."

"Laziness is a Loghyr racial characteristic. But even the dead can be trained to harness when you use the right lash."

"You'll have to explain that to me sometime. I can't get any work out of him. What you need to see is over here. Dean! Get some decent damned lamps in here!" He was supposed to have done that already.

He came sidling in with the necessary and stammered apologies. He was shaking all over, and I didn't blame him. This was the moment that could explode.

She stood there staring at the bodies, not a hairline cracking her composure. She raised a hand, beckoned Dean, took the lamp, knelt. She studied Karl for a long time, taking him in inch by inch. Finished, she took a long pull on the brandy bottle, then did it all over again with Amiranda. Amiranda didn't get a second's less attention. In fact, she got a moment more.

The Stormwarden grunted, then set her bottle aside and rested the tips of two fingers on Amiranda's belly. After a minute she muttered, "So!" and reclaimed the bottle. She drew another healthy draft.

She rose. "I owe you a debt of gratitude, Mr. Garrett." She returned the lamp to Dean. "Can we talk now? Seriously? The two of us?"

"Yes. Dean, take these guys into the kitchen and feed them. Bring me a mug and a pitcher. In the office."

"Yes sir. Gentlemen?"

They didn't protest. I guess Chodo had given them orders to cooperate.

45

I settled behind my desk. The Stormwarden sat opposite me, devoting herself to her bottle and her inner landscape. Finally, she said, "Karl was murdered."

"He was. By a man named Gorgeous and an ogre breed named Skredli. Gorgeous is dead. Skredli is on the loose but we intend to find him. He also led the gang that killed Amiranda. But he was just a hired hand. Someone paid for the blood."

"You have a great deal to tell me."

"If I take you as a client."

She thought for a while. "Your task now is to find the person responsible for Amiranda's murder. Correct?"

"Yes."

"I have a great deal of power, as you're aware. But I don't know how to go about rooting out a killer. Suppose I hire you to find Karl's murderer?"

"That might work. Assuming we agree on precedence of claims if the same hand directed the blades in both murders."

"There'll be no problem of precedence if you meet one condition."

"Which is?"

"You may take precedence for yourself, your friends, and your client—if you'll permit me to be present when you handle your end of it. It won't matter what you do.

Not even death will be an escape for whoever did that in there."

I felt a surge of elation, wondered why, then realized that most of it came from the Dead Man. He knew something, or had something. "I think we can deal."

"I'll stay out of your way, Mr. Garrett. I'll give you whatever aid and assistance you require."

Dean brought the beer in. I poured my mug full, damned near drained it. The Stormwarden did likewise with a second mug Dean thoughtfully provided.

The Stormwarden said, "I expect you're out of pocket considerably for the bodies. You wouldn't have gotten them cheaply."

"That's true."

"Add that to what you need for a deposit against your expenses and fee."

"Let me make sure we understand one another. You're willing to take me on and turn me loose, without shoving your hand in, as long as you're there for the showdown?"

"Yes."

"And you'll lend me your authority along the way?"

"If that's necessary."

"It will be in a few cases."

"I have one goal only, Mr. Garrett. Laying my hands on the person or persons responsible for what happened to my children. Cost is no obstacle. Neither is the emperor himself. Do you understand me?" Those ice-blue eyes were ablaze now. "You do what you have to do to deliver. I'll back you to the gates of hell itself."

"Pact?"

"You want a witch's oath, written in blood?"

"The sworn word of the Stormwarden Raver Styx will do."

She did the whole formal thing after allowing me to word the undertaking.

"Settled," I said. "We're on. I owe you a story." And I began telling it from the moment it intruded upon my life. I gave her the crop, reserving only my personal interactions with Amber and Amiranda. I don't think she was fooled.

I reserved a couple thoughts about the gold, too. I did have a client, after all.

It took several hours. She didn't interrupt. Dean kept the pitcher full and brought in food when he felt it was time.

She didn't immediately comment when I finished. I gave her a few minutes, then asked, "Am I still retained?"

She gave me a don't-be-stupid look. "Of course." She thought awhile longer. "It doesn't make sense."

"Not from where we stand now. It probably looked slick at the start. Before people started doing unto one another and things started going wrong. Before the terror set in."

"It doesn't make much sense from that perspective, either. Not to me."

"Don't go closing your mind now."

She came into the real world for the first time in hours, fixing me with a basilisk's stare. "What?"

"You're ignoring the centerpiece at this hell's feast. The shadow that falls upon it all. The Stormwarden Raver Styx."

"Explain yourself, Mr. Garrett."

"I will. By example. Suppose everyone involved was exactly who he or she is, but you, instead of being the dread Raver Styx, were the heiress to the Gallard wine fortune, that what's-her-name. Would anyone have done what they did if you were her and she'd gone out of town for six months? Would anyone have been tempted? Donni Pell and her gang, maybe, but they were motivated by greed going in. Who you were or weren't didn't matter till the double crosses and foul-ups started and asses had to be covered."

She didn't like it a bit, though I'd barely skimmed the edges. But that woman had to be the most hard-hearted damned realist ever to cross my trail. She swallowed her ego. "I see." She made Willa Dount look like a kitten.

She took time out for more reflection. Then, "What do you plan to do, Mr. Garrett?"

"I'd like to interview your husband and Willa Dount in circumstances where they can't evade questions or avoid answering them."

"It can be arranged. When?"

"The sooner the better. Today. Now. That old man with the black sword has been busy enough. Let's not give him time to sniff out anybody else." Old Death is supposed to be blind but I've noticed he never misses.

"That's probably wisest. How do you want to set it up?"

We talked about it for fifteen minutes. I said I'd play it by ear, making sure she understood I wanted to be given my head. Then she rose. "I'll have the bodies taken away now, Mr. Garrett."

"Out the back would be best. They're supposed to have been cremated already. Nobody outside this house knows they haven't been."

"I understand."

I followed her to the front door, where she paused before she allowed me to let her out. "Take very good care of my daughter, Mr. Garrett. She may be all that I have left."

"I intend to, Stormwarden."

We locked gazes for a moment. We understood one another.

It is a pitiful truth that people like Raver Styx cannot express their love in any way that their beloved will find meaningful.

46

The door shut. I leaned against it and let out a long, heartfelt sigh of relief. I shook for about a minute while the tension drained away. I wanted to let out a big old war whoop.

Saucerhead leaned out of the kitchen. "She finally go?"

"Finally."

He counted my arms and legs. "Guess you worked something out."

"Yeah. We'll see how it stays together."

"What's the game?"

"First thing is, some of her boys are going to come to the back door to pick up those bodies. You guys can hand them over. I'm going to set a fire under the Dead Man."

Saucerhead gave me a dirty look, grumbling about "them that puts on aristocratic airs," but he went and got Sadler and Crask. I waited while they removed the corpses.

There, now. That was not so bad after all, was it, Garrett?

"A snap. So why the hell are you sweating?"

That startled him. I could almost see him checking to see if, by some miracle, some of life's processes had resumed.

Point for Garrett.

"You had some kind of epiphany while I was talking to her. What was it?"

I realized that by taking a short trip upcountry you could probably put the cap on the affair. He was all set to do some crowing about his genius.

"You mean by going out to that farm and rounding up Donni Pell?"

You reasoned it out!

"You've been telling me I have to use my own head. Using yours is too much like work. All the kingpin's hounds and all the kingpin's men couldn't catch more than a few whiffs of old backtrails. She'd used up her friends here in town. Where else would she go?"

Very good. Though we do rely on the assumption that she has not taken the proceeds of her multifarious treacheries and gotten herself somewhere where she can become a new and possibly even respectable person.

"I don't think she has the sense or character to make the clean break. If she did, she would've gotten out days ago."

You are going to return to that farm?

"I'm still formulating strategy," I fibbed. "Meanwhile I'll go up to the daPena place for a chat with the Stormwarden's old man and Willa Dount—maybe even her staff if it looks like that'll do any good. And in the back of my head I'll be trying to decide if Skredli is smart enough to have scoped it out himself."

I had not thought of that.

"Because you don't think like a thug. I guarantee you, the first thing Skredli did after he decided it was safe to stop running was start looking for somebody to blame for the fix he's in. It would be easy for him to get all righteous about Donni. And look what a great target she makes. She's got no friends left. No protector or avenger. And she's got buckets of money that can be taken without any comebacks. And on top of that, she's a woman."

You pity her?

"Not much. She's the one who decided to play with the hard boys."

Saucerhead was in the doorway, waiting for me to stop talking. I beckoned him inside. "They off?"

"Gone."

"You know what I was saying?"

"I heard your side."

"You heard everything worth hearing." I got the maps I'd studied after my talk with Skredli and opened one. "You see this? That's the crossroads where you and the girl had your run-in with Skredli's gang. If you head west to about here, you come to two young mulberry trees hiding the end of an old road. About a half mile down that road is an abandoned farm. The place where they took Junior back when this mess was just a kidnapping. I think that's where we'll find Donni Pell."

"You want me to go drag her back here?"

"Oh, no. I want her right where she sits. I'm going to organize a family outing to convene out there. But when I get there, I want to know what I'm walking into."

"You want me to go scout it out, then."

"Can you handle it?"

"No problem. When?"

"Soon as you can. Don't come at the place down that road."

He snorted. "Give me *some* credit, Garrrett."

"Meet me at the crossroads tomorrow. I'll try to be there as close to noon as I can. I'll have some stops to make along the way."

Tharpe jerked his head in the general direction of the kitchen. "What about those guys?"

"I don't care. Let them tag along if they want. Or they can stick with me. If they decide to go with you, make sure they don't start playing their own game. I've got to head up the Hill in a few minutes. Go find out what they want to do."

What are you planning, Garrett? The Dead Man sounded suspicious.

"I don't know. I'm making it up as I go along."

It feels like you're setting something up.

"I wish I was. There're tags and threads that're going to hang loose after this's over and they could cause problems."

For instance, a certain Garrett getting caught in a collision between a young woman used to getting what she wants and a somewhat older, no-nonsense redhead who feels she has a certain proprietary interest in the man?

"That one hadn't occurred to me. I was thinking more along the lines of the Stormwarden wanting to get me for my presumptions and disrespect after she no longer has any use for me. Amber won't have any interest in me if she gets her meat hooks in that ransom money."

Garrett, you are, for the most part, an unusually sound-thinking representative of your species. But where members of the opposite sex are concerned, you are often a fool.

"A congenital weakness. My father was subject to it too. I'm working on it."

You will break your beer habit first, I am certain.

"Speaking of Amber, I should let her know what's going on."

One piece of advice, since you wish to avoid a prime position on the Stormwarden's get-even list.

"What's that?"

Try to restrain that part of you which insists on being sarcastic, abrasive, and confrontational.

"I'm working on that, too. I think I'll clear that up right after I get straightened out about women."

I went to the kitchen doorway and stuck my head in. Saucerhead said, "They decided to stick with me." His smirk said that was because they weren't interested in doing anything that would bring them to the attention of Raver Styx.

I winked and headed upstairs.

47

I tapped on Amber's door. "You there?"

"It's not locked."

I went inside. She was seated on the edge of her bed, looking pale and tired. "Is she gone?"

I settled into the room's sole chair. "She left. We managed to work something out."

"How heavily did she outbid me?"

"I don't like your mother, Amber."

"What does that mean?"

"People I don't like never outbid people I do like. Though sometimes I'll let them think they can."

"Thanks." She didn't sound cheered.

"What's the matter?"

"It's almost over, isn't it?"

"I expect to put the noose around somebody's neck tomorrow."

"Do you know who?"

"Not for certain. Not yet."

"It's not going to make anybody happy, is it?"

"No. Murder never does. Not for long."

"Then I won't be seeing you. . . ."

I had an impulse to trot down and give the Dead Man a swift kick. He was listening in and snickering, probably. Why is the old blubber boat always right?

"Who knows? Look, I'm just about to go up to your

mother's house to question your father and Domina
Dount. How's your nerve? You want to go along and
stand silent witness? Maybe pick up a change of
clothes?"

"Do I smell bad, or something?"

"What?"

"Never mind. What's a silent witness?"

"Somebody who just stands there and makes people
stick to the truth because they know the silent witness
can contradict them."

"Oh." She frowned. "I don't know if I'm up to that.
My own father. . . ."

"It'd be a chance to see Domina Dount pick her nose
with her elbow."

She rose immediately. "All right."

"My god. What enthusiasm."

"I don't want to hurt my father, Garrett. And I know
you'll back him into a corner where things will come out
that my mother won't be able to forgive."

Something in her tone suggested she was ready to spill
family secrets. "Maybe if I didn't ask certain questions,
your mother wouldn't have to know. As long as the answers don't have any bearing on what—"

"I don't know!" There was agony in that, and a plea
for help.

"Tell me."

"Ami . . . He *has* to the father of the baby she was
carrying."

"I'm not surprised to hear that, Amber. I even suspect
that your mother already entertains the possibility too."

"I guess she would. But even if she did, she wouldn't
understand it." Pure misery, Amber. This was gnawing
her good.

"It isn't exactly incest."

"It could've been."

"What? How so?"

"Ami . . . She wasn't a willing partner."

"He raped her?" I couldn't believe Amiranda would
have tolerated that from anybody.

"Yes. No. Not the way you're thinking. He didn't hold

a knife at her throat. He just . . . *coerced* her, I guess. I don't know how he did it. She never told me about it. Only Karl. But Karl told me. It started when she was thirteen. When you're that young it's hard . . . It's hard to know what to do."

"Not you too?"

"No. But . . . But he tried. Twice. When I was fourteen. Almost fifteen. It was hard, Garrett. Maybe a man wouldn't even understand. The first time I just ran away when I realized what he wanted. The second time he made sure I didn't have anywhere to run. I . . . He . . . He wouldn't let me alone till I said I was going to tell mother."

"And?"

"He went into a panic. A psychotic panic. That's why . . ."

"Did he threaten you? Physically?"

She nodded.

"I see." I settled back to ruminate. I understood her fears. This didn't do Karl Senior any good at all. I already had him down as murder suspect number one, but I was still a little nebulous on motive.

"They were both dumb, Ami and Father. They had to realize it would happen sooner or later. There's too much free-floating residual energy around any place used by someone like my mother not to interfere with the spells on a contraceptive amulet."

"If she could see it coming—"

"Don't start, Garrett. You don't know what it was like. You aren't a woman. You aren't a daughter. And you've never been in a squeeze anything like it."

"You're right. All right, here's what I'll do. I'll talk to him without your mother being there. If it's not germane, she won't have to know."

"She won't allow that."

"I'll insist. I'll also insist that you be there with us."

"Oh! Do I have to?"

"I want him in a corner so tight he's got to think his only way out is the truth. He can't lie with you standing there ready to blurt, 'Remember the time when you—' "

"I don't like it."

"Neither do I. But you have to use the tools at hand."

"He couldn't *do* something like you're thinking."

"Amiranda would've begun to show soon. Your mother is inquisitive. And when she asks, she gets answers. How would she have reacted—"

"I know what you're going to say, Garrett. He'd panic. He'd go crazy out of fear. But not that crazy."

"Maybe you're right. If we get him deep enough into that corner, maybe we'll find out for sure." It seemed a good idea to forget that the Stormwarden had discovered Amiranda's pregnancy on her own.

"Garrett. Do we have time . . . ?"

I shook my head slowly.

"It's a pity, really."

"I'm sorry."

As we started down the stairs, she said, "I'll bet you he doesn't even know she was pregnant. Ami wouldn't have told anybody but Karl."

I responded with a noncommittal grunt. He knew now, though I was willing to grant the possibility that he hadn't known then.

I paused to stick my head into the Dead Man's room. "We're going now."

Take care of yourself, Garrett. And mind your manners with your betters.

"The same to you, Chuckles. Want to tell me Glory Mooncalled's secret now? Just in case the worst happens? I'd hate to check out still mystified."

With you entering a Stormwarden's lair? No. We'll consider it after this is done and the break is complete.

He had a point.

I gave Dean some unnecessary instructions about locking up behind me. Then we left.

48

I decided to make a brief detour to Lettie Faren's. Maybe it was wrong. There are times when ignorance *is* bliss.

The man on the door knew me and knew my presence was considered undesirable, but he made only a token effort to keep us out. Inside, Amber gawked and whispered that she wouldn't have believed it if she hadn't seen it.

I gawked myself, but not for the same reasons.

The place wasn't open for business. Never, to my knowledge, had the house been closed before. Alarmed, I pushed past a barman and a swamper who made half-hearted efforts to stop us. I slammed into the pest hole Lettie calls home.

It only took one look. "Stay out there," I instructed Amber.

The mound of ruin that was Lettie Faren tried to glare with eyes blackened and swollen, and failed. She couldn't strike the spark. What remained was a feeble mask for fear.

I asked, "Chodo's boys?"

She croaked an affirmative.

"You should've told me where to find Donni when you knew, before the hard boys decided they wanted her too."

She just looked at me. Chances were she'd just looked at Chodo's boys too. For a while. She was damned near as tough as she thought.

"I'm working for Raver Styx these days. That's a tight crack to get caught in, between the Stormwarden and the kingpin."

"I didn't have nothing to tell them and I don't got nothing to tell you, Garrett. Bring on the old witch if you want."

"The wicked flee when no man pursueth. I'll wish you a speedy recovery. Good-bye."

As we headed for the exit, Amber asked, "Why didn't you want me to go in there?"

I gave it to her straight. "I'm not the only one looking for Donni Pell. Those other guys beat her up trying to find out where Donni went."

"Bad?"

"Very. They aren't nice people. In fact, I'm about convinced that you're the only nice person anywhere in this mess."

She laughed nervously and said, "You don't know me very well yet." Then, conversationally, "You're not so bad yourself, Garrett."

Perhaps she didn't know me very well yet either.

49

The man at the Stormwarden's gate was a stranger. He had a competent, professional look. "How was the vacation in the sunny Cantard?"

It bounced off. "Grim as usual, Mr. Garrett. The Stormwarden is expecting you and is waiting in her audience room. Miss daPena can show you the way."

"Yeah. Thanks. You guys going to do anything for Slauce?"

"Say what?"

"You going in on flowers or anything? I thought I'd kick in if I could. It never would've happened if he hadn't been coming to see me."

"We haven't decided what to do yet. We'll let you know. All right?"

"Sure. Thanks."

When we were out of earshot, Amber said, "See? I told you you weren't all bad."

"A cynical, manipulative gesture meant to incite a sympathetic attitude among the troops."

"Right, Garrett. Whatever you say."

Raver Styx sat alone in the gloom of an unlighted room about the size of the Dead Man's. Her eyes were closed. She was so still and unresponsive I suffered a chill. Had we lost yet another daPena?

No. Those supposedly terrible eyes opened and fixed on me. I saw nothing but a tired and beaten old lady. "Please have a seat, Mr. Garrett." Like a wolfman under a full moon, she began to change. "Amber, I believe you'd do better to isolate yourself here in the house, but if you feel more confident with Mr. Garrett and his associates, you have my blessing." She was becoming the Stormwarden Raver Styx—with a measure of concerned mother.

Amber was within reach and my feet were out of the Stormwarden's line of sight. I nudged her ankle. She started, figured it out, said, "Thank you, Mother. I'd feel better with Mr. Garrett, I think. For now."

That wasn't so hard. Often all we need to be civil with one another is the presence of a referee we don't want thinking us fools.

"As you wish. Where would you like to begin, Mr. Garrett?"

"With Domina Dount."

"Willa Dount, Mr. Garrett. Loss of her position and title is a foregone penalty. Let's not extend any false hopes."

"You're the boss. Whatever, I want to do her first. Then your husband. Then the staff—if that appears productive."

"Wouldn't it be a bit trifling?"

"Maybe. But a few trifles are all I need to fill the gaps in the picture I already have."

"I'm tempted to invoke penalties on the lot and let the gods distinguish between the wicked and the merely incompetent."

Sometimes I felt that way about our ruling class. I observed the Dead Man's advice, though, and kept my opinion to myself. "I know what you mean."

"How do you want to work it? In my presence? In Amber's?"

"In Willa Dount's case, with you present and Amber absent. To begin. I've already told Amber how long to stay away. After she comes in, I want you to find a reason to leave. Having dealt with Willa Dount, I doubt the footwork will do any good, but I want to try."

"Very well."

"I'll want to see all the documents she has. Especially the letters from the kidnappers. Have you seen those?"

"Yes, I have."

"Did you recognize the hand?"

"No. It seemed feminine."

"I thought so, too. So precise, what I saw. I feared the one-in-a-thousand chance that Amiranda had written them."

"Amiranda had the penmanship of a drunken troll. There was no reading it, but no mistaking or disguising it, either."

"Good. Now, with your husband I'd prefer to begin with you out of the room. As for the staff, I'll ask you and Amber person by person. If the intimidation factor inherent in your presence is counterproductive—"

"I understand. Let's get to it."

"Where is Willa Dount now?"

"In her office, doing the job that will be hers for a few more hours."

"Would you get her, Amber? Tell her she needs to bring the documents."

"Yes, master." She gave me a wink that her mother caught.

"I'd appreciate it if you'd hold off acting against Willa Dount or anyone else for another day, Stormwarden. Tomorrow I want to take everyone on a walk-through of what happened the night of the ransom payoff and the morning of Amiranda's death."

"Is that necessary?"

"Yes. Absolutely. Afterward there'll be no lingering doubts."

She didn't press for details, a courtesy I appreciated. Maybe she wasn't such a bad old gal after all.

We waited in silence.

50

Willa Dount marched in with a stack of papers. "You
sent for me, madam?" She didn't seem surprised to see
me—and shouldn't have since she had her agents among
the staff.

"I've hired Mr. Garrett to hunt down the person or
people responsible for the deaths of Amiranda, Karl,
and Courter Slauce. He wants to ask you questions,
Willa. Answer completely and truthfully."

I raised the eyebrow. Slauce too? Surprise, surprise.
But certainly a point for her.

"Give those papers to Mr. Garrett."

She did so with ill grace. "You're a vulture circling
this family, aren't you? You won't rest till you've picked
its bones."

"If you take a quick count of the number of noses on
your face, you'll come up with more than the number
of times I've approached the daPena family soliciting
employment."

"Your wit hasn't suffered any improvement."

"Willa. Sit down and be quiet. Restrain your prejudices and speak only when you're spoken to."

"Yes, madam."

Did the whip crack there, or did it crack?

Willa Dount planted herself in a chair, face blank
and cool.

If she was going to perch I was going to prowl. I rose, began moving, shuffling the papers. The kidnappers had gone to great lengths to make sure Domina Dount understood exactly what she was supposed to do. I slipped a finger behind the letters I'd met already, looked Willa Dount in the eye, and asked, "When did you first suspect that Karl's kidnapping was contrived?"

"When Amiranda disappeared. She'd been odd for weeks, and had her head together with Karl for days before he vanished."

Lie number one, straight out of the chute? Willa Dount should have been on the road to her payoff appointment before Amiranda made her break. Unless . . .

Unless she'd known beforehand what Amiranda planned.

"When did you begin to suspect the game had become real?"

"When I reached the place where I was supposed to hand the gold over. Those people weren't playing. They were deadly real. I'm afraid I almost lost my composure. I've never been that afraid."

"Describe the people you met there."

She frowned.

I told her, "I've asked you before about the payoff. You wouldn't talk. It was your right at the time. But not now. So tell me about those people, and about that night." I thumbed the first letter I hadn't yet read.

"There were two closed coaches and at least four people. Two coachmen of mixed parentage, probably ogre and human. The ugliest man I've ever seen. And a fairly attractive young woman. The ugly man was in charge."

"You said at least four. What does that mean? Was there somebody else?"

"There might have been someone inside the woman's coach. Twice I thought I saw movement in there, but they made me stay on the wagon. I wasn't close enough to be sure."

"Uhm." I picked a spot near a good light and adjusted a chair. "From the beginning of that night. Every trivial detail."

She began. And soon I was hearing what I expected, a tale with no significant deviations from the one Skredli had told me.

I lent her both ears and one eye while I skimmed the letters. Then I went over a few again. Then again. And finally I thought I saw what I'd half expected to see, though I'm no expert on forgery.

Willa Dount reached her departure from the bridge over Cedar Creek. I didn't figure anything interesting happened after that. "Hold it there."

She stopped dead. And dead is the way I'd describe the voice she'd been using. She'd been under so much strain for so long she had very little fire left.

"That payoff setup was as queer as a nine-foot pixie. No swap on the spot—though I admit there wasn't a lot you could do once you got there. You couldn't run away. But they let you see them. And then they let you go without killing you. Knowing who you worked for. At a time when at least one of them knew there'd be a murder within a few hours."

"I can't explain that, Mr. Garrett. Death is all I expected when I realized that Karl wasn't there."

Unless you took out some kind of insurance, I thought. Like maybe not delivering the whole ransom, and, maybe, refusing to let the balance go until you and Karl were safe. Maybe even not knowing where the rest was, or saying you didn't, so they wouldn't try anything rough. There was something or you wouldn't be here now.

I thought it but didn't say it.

"Did you hear any names mentioned? Did you get a good look at any of them?"

"No names. There was moonlight. I saw all four well enough to recognize again, though the woman and the ugly man stayed back. I have excellent night vision. Maybe they didn't realize how clearly I saw them."

"Maybe. It probably doesn't matter now, anyway. They're all dead but the woman."

She just looked at me. You couldn't crack her with a sledgehammer.

I had everything I wanted to get with the Stormwarden watching. I was wondering how I could stall just as Amber let herself in.

Raver Styx made no pretenses and no excuses. She stood and left.

Amber whispered, "I didn't find anything in her quarters. She doesn't keep a journal or—"

"You don't have to talk behind my back in front of me, Amber. Spit it out."

I nodded.

"The accounts didn't look jiggered. The silver was sold for anywhere from seven to fifteen percent below market. I'm not sure, but I'd guess that would be reasonable in the circumstances. Whatever, the price of silver has fallen enough that now the buyers are the losers."

That was my Amber, keeping up with the metals market despite everything.

"Who did the buying?"

She handed me a list.

"Interesting. The top name here, Lyman Gameleon, is down for a hundred twenty thousand at the maximum discount. Gameleon is one of our big-three suspects."

Even that didn't rock Willa Dount. She said only, "It was an emergency and I went where I had to go to get enough gold. The Stormwarden has examined the accounts of these transactions and expressed no disapproval."

A thought. Maybe even an inspiration. "Do you recall the dates and times of the transactions, Amber?" She had not noted those.

"No. Should I go get them?"

Willa Dount said, "That won't be necessary. I remember." She rattled off every deal as though she was reading from the record.

The timing made it conceivable that the deals themselves had initiated the chain of complications. Or, at least, could have led to intensive recomplication.

"Did Gameleon know what the gold was for?"

"Lord Gameleon, Garrett," Domina scolded.

"Look, I don't care if you call him Pinky Porker. Just answer the question."

"Yes. He had to be told before he'd deal."

I'd already established, to my own satisfaction, a link between Gameleon and Donni Pell. "Was that wise?"

"In retrospect, probably not. But at the time Lord Gameleon was a last resort."

"Hardly. But let's not fight about it. That's it for tonight."

"Tonight?"

"I'll need you again tomorrow. Early. We're all going to walk this through."

She gave me a puzzled look as she rose. What chicanery was I planning?

"Find the Baronet and send him in," I said.

I'd grown impatient and irritable by the time the door opened. And that opening didn't make anything better.

Willa Dount and Raver Styx came in, the Stormwarden looking like one of the tempests she brewed. "Will you want to question the staff, Mr. Garrett?"

"Where's your husband?"

"I don't doubt the answer to that question would be quite interesting. He left the house shortly after you arrived. When last seen he was entering the house of Lord Gameleon, his half-brother, who lives across the street. Lord Gameleon admits that he was there earlier but denies that he is now. About the staff?"

There was no juice left. My candle had begun to gutter. "The hell with them. I can tie the knot on it without them. I'm going home to get some sleep. Meet me at my place at eight, ready for a trek upcountry. Don't let anybody else wander off. Make a production of leaving so anyone interested will know something is up."

"As you will, Mr. Garrett. That will be all for tonight, then, Willa."

I asked, "Amber, are you coming or staying?"

Staring at the floor, she replied, "I'll go with you. But I need to get some things first."

I guess that was as close as she could come to telling her mother to pick her nose with her elbow. The Stormwarden developed a severe tick in her left cheek but she said nothing. She understood battles lost as well as battles won.

The first thing I did when we got to the house was write a letter to Morley Dotes. I had one of the neighbor kids deliver it. Then I brought the Dead Man up to date and feigned an effort to pry a few secrets out of him just to keep him feeling wanted. I joined Amber in the kitchen, where we shared one of Dean's finer productions. Then I stashed myself away for the night.

My dreams, which I usually don't recall, weren't the kind I'll treasure forever.

51

Dean rousted me out in plenty of time to get ready. We breakfasted well and packed our field rations. I took a look at my arsenal and picked a couple of lethal engines suitable for a lady. I made Amber practice with them until her mother's cavalcade arrived.

A thoughtful woman, the Stormwarden. She had somehow ascertained that I didn't have transportation of my own. She rolled up with a coach, a carriage, and a spare horse. She was in the coach. Willa Dount was driving the carriage. Amber stepped up on the seat beside her. What a lighthearted and friendly drive that would be.

I went around the front of the horse and looked him in the eye. He looked back. I saw none of the tribe's usual malice. He obviously hadn't heard of me.

The Stormwarden had shown some sense in another direction. I had expected to have to nag her into sending her army home, but she'd brought only the two men atop her coach. I couldn't squawk about them.

I suppose when you're a stormwarden, you only need guards for show.

"You lead the way," I told Domina Dount. Her face was old stone as she nodded and started her team. Amber settled facing backward when she saw that I would ride rear guard, though most of the time the Stormwarden's coach obscured our views of one another.

Willa Dount set a brisk pace, occasionally slowing so her boss could catch up. I stayed fifty yards behind the coach. In the city I watched the citizenry watch it. In the country I watched farmers. And as we moved up-country I kept mentally reviewing my maps.

I didn't see a single place that looked suitable for what I suspected had happened.

I thought about moving up beside Willa Dount. She might have given something away.

Sure. Like stones flinch.

But I had a reason for lying back.

Morley overtook me two thirds of the way to the deadly crossroads. At that point the road passed among trees and travelers couldn't be watched from afar. He dared rein in and talk.

"They're back there," he told me. "Gameleon and six men. They won't be easy."

"They trying to catch up?"

"No."

"Good. We'll put everybody in the sack at once."

"You're crazy, Garrett. Seven of them and no telling what up ahead and you're talking like you've got them by the shorthairs?"

"All they've got is numbers. I've got a stormwarden. Hustle on up and tell Saucerhead."

Morley resumed his lone-rider act in a hurry.

It was coming together beautifully. I just hoped I wouldn't be in the middle when it crunched.

I wasn't the most pleased of men when we reached the crossroads. I hadn't spotted one place that fulfilled the criteria for my concept of what had become of most of the ransom gold—though I'd seen a few side roads and whatnot that would later bear further examination. If there was a later. If Amber wasn't more defeatist than I was becoming.

I made the mistake, for a short time, of thinking I saw a chance for the big hit. You don't want to fall into that trap. It can shatter your perspective. It can narrow your focus until the rest of the world slides out of touch.

"Hold up!" I yelled at Willa Dount. She had turned west without pausing. My fault. I hadn't told her we would be stopping.

We got out of traffic's way. I dismounted. Where was Saucerhead? I'd expected him to be waiting.

He stepped out of the woods on the south side of the road. From the corner of my eye I noted Willa Dount's surprise. I joined him. "What have we got?"

"You were right. She's down there."

"Alone?"

"Nope. Company, and plenty of it. One guy by himself showed up about midnight last night. Then a mob of ogre breeds got there just before I left."

"Skredli?"

He nodded.

"How many?"

"Fifteen."

"Crask and Sadler behaving?"

"They aren't stupid, Garrett. They know their limitations."

"I suppose. I'd better tell the Stormwarden. You scout out a workable approach?"

"Sure. What about those guys behind you?"

"They can take care of themselves." I waited while a string of goat carts trundled past, trotted to the Stormwarden's coach, and invited myself inside.

"Why have we stopped, Mr. Garrett?"

I explained. "I didn't expect it to turn into so large a party. Otherwise, everything's come together. Any suggestions?"

"The man who arrived last night. My husband?"

"Probably. My friend wouldn't know him by sight."

"Does Lord Gameleon know where he's going?"

"I don't know."

"He may need someone to follow."

"We can't sneak up on anybody going straight in."

"I realize that, Mr. Garrett."

"I've got a little help but not enough to handle four-to-one odds."

"You have me."

What was that worth? I didn't ask. "All right. My friend and I will sneak up through the woods. You be careful."

"Take Amber. And *you* be careful, Mr. Garrett. I have to salvage something from this disaster."

"She'll be all right." I left the coach. "Amber. You come with me."

The Stormwarden left the coach on the other side. She said something to the men on top. The driver nodded. The other descended. He and Raver Styx boarded the carriage. It rolled away as Amber joined Saucerhead and me.

"What are we doing?" she asked.

"Going for a walk in the woods." I tied my mount's reins to the coach. We ducked into the trees.

Just in time. Lord Gameleon and his boys trotted past. They weren't in livery and made a big deal of ignoring the coach.

When they were gone Saucerhead asked, "She's going straight in?"

"I guess. We'll have to hurry. Where's Morley? With Crask and Sadler?"

"Right. Follow me. Miss daPena?"

"Just lead, Mr. Tharpe. I'll keep up."

52

Our timing was perfect.

We were near the edge of the clearing when Morley appeared out of nowhere. "Not bad for a city boy," I told him. Crask and Sadler popped up as suddenly. If we'd been unfriendly, we would have been in big trouble. "Anything happening over there?"

"Lot of screaming."

"What?"

"Started right after I got here. Somebody's asking some questions. Somebody else isn't giving the answers they want to hear."

I wasn't surprised.

Crask said, "Something's happening."

I joined him. From where he stood the farmhouse could be seen plainly. Ogre breeds boiled out, raced across the weedy field toward the gap where the road left the woods. "Their lookout must have spotted the Stormwarden."

Someone grunted.

"They been doing any patrols? Or just watching the road?"

"Watching the road," Sadler said. "They're ogres."

"Stupid. The Stormwarden may have overestimated herself. They might kill first and ask questions later."

"They're distracted now," Saucerhead said. "Be a good time to move up. If we keep low along the downhill side of that swale there, we can get pretty close. Maybe up to the foundation stones where the barn used to be."

I recalled a deer trail through the high grass that followed the route Saucerhead recommended. I looked but I couldn't see the stones. "You've been over there?"

"Yeah. I had to look in and make sure."

"Let's go."

Saucerhead went first, then Crask, then Morley. I told Amber to keep down and sent her next. I followed her. Sadler brought up the rear.

We were halfway across when the brouhaha broke out in the woods. We stopped. I said, "That doesn't sound like ogres running into surprise sorcery."

"No."

"Let's move."

As we crouched among the stones, thirty yards from the rear of the house, Skredli's gang emerged from the woods uphill. They had five or six prisoners.

"Gameleon," I said. "What happened to the Stormwarden?"

"There are twelve breeds up there, Garrett," Morley said. "In a minute they won't be able to spot us behind the house. Why don't we make our move? Be waiting for them inside when they get there?"

I didn't like it. But the odds weren't going to get any better. I checked the others. They all nodded. "Amber, stay put. I'll holler when it's safe."

She had developed a case of deafness. When we moved toward the back door, she moved with us. I cursed under my breath but there was nothing I could do short of bopping her and laying her out.

We reached the house unnoticed. Morley volunteered to lead. Nobody argued. He was the best.

We moved.

Inside there were three ogres, one woman and Karl daPena, Senior. Morley creamed two of the ogres before they knew they were in trouble. The third tried to yell and only got out a bark before Crask stuck a knife through his throat.

Sadler finished the other two.

Amber dumped her breakfast.

"I told you to stay out." I ground my teeth and examined our prizes. Neither seemed particularly pleased to see us.

"Frying pan into the fire, eh, Baronet?"

Both were strapped into chairs. DaPena was gagged. The woman wasn't, but she was yelled out. Both had been tortured, and with little finesse.

"You must be the marvelous Donni Pell. I've been anxious to meet you. Right now you don't look like something that men would kill for."

"Cut the sweet talk, Garrett," Morley said. "They're coming."

I peeked. "That clown Skredli must have raised an army."

"We can take them. They have to keep hold of their prisoners."

"I like a man with a positive attitude. Why don't I slide out the back way and you holler when you've got them?"

"You going to mouth your way through the gates of hell or are you going to decide what to do?"

"Crask, Sadler, you guys get out of sight down that hall. Saucerhead, wait behind the door. Let four or five get in, then slam it and bolt it. Morley and I will jump out from the kitchen. We ought to polish off the bunch before the rest bust in. Amber, you get out back."

This time she did what I told her. Nothing like a good scare.

"And you call me a tactical genius," Morley grumbled. But he ducked into the kitchen without offering a suggestion of his own.

Even tactical geniuses stumble. When Saucerhead went to slam the door, Skredli and two other breeds were on the transom. He had the strength to bounce two of them back into the yard, but the third got caught between the edge of the door and the frame. He did a lot of yelling and flailing while Saucerhead grunted and strained, trying to shut the door right through him. And Tharpe did manage to hang on while we thumped the five he'd let in.

Morley chuckled. "Seven to go. Let them in, Saucerhead."

Tharpe jumped back. Skredli and the guys stomped in.

We did expect them to have their cutlery out, ready for carving. We didn't expect Gameleon's brunos to help them. They did. "We been suckered, Garrett," Saucerhead said as he stumbled back past me.

Long knife in one hand and head thumper in the other, fending off two ogres and a man, I fell past a window and shot a quick look to see if help was coming.

No stormwarden.

Had the gang dealt with her already? Had they caught her in a pincer up in the woods?

I kicked one guy in the groin but not good enough to slow him much. The three pushed me toward the kitchen, keeping me too busy staying alive to keep track of what was happening to everybody else. Win or lose, Skredli and his bunch would get hurt. They were up against the best TunFaire offered.

Small consolation.

I got in a solid thump to an ogre's head as I backed through the kitchen doorway. He reeled, stalling his companions. I whirled and dove through a window.

I did not land well. The breath went out of me and didn't want to come back. But I got my feet under me in time to lay a whack on the skull of a guy trying to climb after me. It was no head breaker, but it discouraged him.

I limped to the front door, wound up and flung one of the witch's crystals. Then I held up a wall while my breath caught up with me and the crystal did its deed.

The uproar inside died.

When I went in, everybody was folded up puking. I

shambled around thumping heads. When I had the bad guys down I scrounged what I could and tied them up. I got done just before the spell wore off.

Sitting against a wall, Morley glared and croaked, "Thanks a bloody bunch, Garrett. I'm ruined."

"Ingrate. You're alive."

I don't dare describe the looks the ingrates Crask and Sadler gave me. It was a good thing they had stomachs and a few wounds to patch.

I heard sounds outside. I went to the door.

The Stormwarden was coming. Finally.

She left the carriage and strode toward me. I stepped out of her way. She entered, scanned the battleground, sniffed, looked at me suspiciously. I said, "We're all here now. I'll get things sorted out and we'll start."

"All right." She marched over to the Baronet. His chair had overturned during the struggle. She stared down at him briefly, then turned to Donni Pell. "Is this the infamous whore, Mr. Garrett?"

"I didn't ask yet. I think so."

"She doesn't look like much, does she?"

"With females you never know. She might be a whole different act cleaned up and set down where she thought she could work her magic."

That got me the darkest look she'd given yet.

Meanwhile, Domina Dount just stood in the doorway, for the first time in our acquaintance, at a loss.

"Saucerhead. Why don't you get Amber?"

He gave me a look as loving as the Stormwarden's, but nodded and went out back. I said, "Stormwarden, I don't know if it's within your expertise, but if you can, we'd all appreciate a little healing magic here."

"Everyone who faces the Warlords of Venageta must learn elementary field medicinal spells, Mr. Garrett."

"Maybe everyone of a certain class." Amber came in. Her face went gray. I thought she was going to upchuck again. "It gets rough sometimes, Amber. Gut it out. You all right, Saucerhead?"

"I'll live, Garrett. Why the hell don't you ever warn anybody when you're going to pull something out of

your sleeve?" He winced and clapped one hand to his
stomach.

I didn't bother explaining that if I'd warned him I'd
have warned the bad guys too.

53

We dumped the ogres and Brunos in the weeds, live or dead. The farmhouse was still as crowded as a rabbit warren. We found seats for everybody. Only Amber and I remained standing. She leaned against the doorframe, too nervous to sit. Though the Stormwarden's perch was no better than anyone else's, her manner turned it into a throne.

She said, "Proceed, Mr. Garrett."

"Let's start with my old buddy Skredli. Skredli, tell the nice people the story you told me at Chodo's place. Keep in mind that the lady there can make you hurt a lot worse than Chodo ever did."

Skredli got fatalistic again. He told his story. The same story.

Donni Pell was the villain of his piece. She was a wonder to watch as she tried working on him so he would cast her in a better light.

Gameleon and daPena were worth watching, too. And Domina Dount, for that matter, as she learned that some things she'd heard but not gut-believed were true.

When Skredli finished, I looked at Gameleon. "You think you can talk your way out of here?"

"I'll have your head."

Morley asked, "You want me to knock him around a

little to improve his attitude, Garrett? I always wanted to see if blue-blood bones sound different when they break."

"I don't think we'll need to."

"Let me twist his arm a little. How about you, Saucerhead? We could hang him up by the ankles and break him like a wishbone."

I snapped, "Knock it off!"

Raver Styx lifted her left hand and extended it toward Gameleon, palm forward, fingers spread. Her face was bland. But lavender sparks danced between her fingers.

Gameleon yelled, "No!" Then he screamed a long, chilly one. I wouldn't believe anybody had that much breath in him. He went slack.

"So much for him. For now. Baronet? How about you? Want to sing your song?"

Hell no, he didn't. His old lady was sitting right there. She'd have his nuchos on a platter.

She said, "Karl, whatever you're thinking, the alternative will be worse." She raised her left hand again. A few sparks flew. He flinched, whimpered. She dropped her hand into her lap, smiled a cruel smile. "I'd do it, too, you know." And she would. *I* was convinced.

There were some bleak faces in that place.

I looked at Gameleon, at daPena, at Domina Dount, at Amber, who sincerely regretted having come. Poor old Skredli was damning himself for not running instead of trying to make a last score.

Donni Pell . . . Well, I concentrated on the spider woman for the first time. I had avoided that because even I, a bit, was subject to whatever made her so dangerous.

She didn't look dangerous. She was a small woman, fair, well into her twenties, but with one of those marvelous faces and complexions that make some small, fair women look adolescent for years beyond their time. She was pretty without being beautiful. Even ragged, filthy, and abused, she had a certain something that touched both the father and the lech in a man, a something that made a man want to protect and possess.

I don't play with little girls, but I know the feeling a man can get looking at a ripening fifteen-year-old.

In my time I have encountered several Donni Pells. They are conscious of what they do to men—manipulate it like hell. The sensual frenzy is balanced by manipulating the fatherly urge as well. Usually they come across as being empty between the ears, too. In desperate need of protection.

Donni Pell, I suppose, was an artist, having turned an essentially patriarchal society's stereotype of a woman's role into a bludgeon with which she worked her will upon the male race. She was still trying to do it, bound and gagged.

Under it all she was tough. As hard and heartless as a Morley Dotes, who might qualify as the male counterpart of a Donni Pell. Skredli and his boys hadn't broken through.

The Stormwarden said, "Will you get on with it, Mr. Garrett?"

"I'm trying to decide where to poke the hornet's nest. Right now these people have no incentives."

"How about staying alive?" She rose and joined me. "Somebody here had Amiranda killed. Somebody here had my son killed. Somebody here is going to pay for that. Maybe a lot of somebodies if the innocent don't convince me of their lack of guilt. How's that for motivation, Mr. Garrett?"

"Excellent. If you can convince a couple men who figure their place in the world entitles them to immunity from justice."

"Justice has nothing to do with it. Stark, bloody, screaming, agonizing vengeance is what I'm talking about. I'm not concerned about political repercussions. I no longer care if I get pulled down."

Her intensity convinced me. I looked at her husband and Gameleon. DaPena was convinced, too. But Gameleon was holding his own.

Softly, I said, "Courter Slauce."

Equally softly, the Stormwarden replied, "I haven't forgotten him. Continue."

I scanned them all again—then turned on Domina Dount. "You feel like modifying anything you've said before?"

She looked blankly at me.

"I don't think you're directly repsonsible for any deaths, Domina. But you helped turn a scam into something deadly."

She shivered. Willa Dount *shivered!* She was ready to break. The blood had reached her when she'd had to see it firsthand. Amber sensed it, too. Despite the state of her nerves, she glared at me. I winked.

"Nobody wants to kick in?"

Nobody volunteered to save himself.

"All right. I'll reconstruct. Correct me if I get it wrong, or if you want somebody else to get the shaft."

"Mr. Garrett."

"Right, Stormwarden. So. It started a long time ago, in a house on the Hill, when a woman who shouldn't have had children did so."

"Mr. Garrett!"

"My contract is for a job done without interference, Stormwarden. I was going to walk lightly. But since you're impatient, I'll just spit it out. You made life such hell for them that your whole family was ready to do anything to get away. Nobody worked up the guts to try till you went to the Cantard, though. It's unlikely anybody would have then if your husband hadn't, in the course of continued unwanted attentions, gotten Amiranda pregnant."

Amber glared daggers. Domina Dount squeaked. The Stormwarden glared, too, but only because I was making public something she already suspected. The Baronet fainted.

"As soon as she knew, Amiranda went to the only friend she had, your son. They cooked up a scheme to save her from shame and get them both away from a house they loathed. Junior would get kidnapped. They would use the ransom to start a new life.

"But they couldn't work it out by themselves. They wanted it to look so real the Stormwarden Raver Styx would believe that her son had been done in by dishonorable villains. Why? Because whatever else they felt, the daPena brats loved their father and didn't want him crucified. They wanted to cover for him."

"Mr. Garrett—"

"I'm going to do it my way, Stormwarden." I faced Donni Pell. "They couldn't pull it off without help. So Junior went to his girlfriend. She said she'd arrange everything. And things started going wrong right away, because Donni Pell can't do anything straight.

"She told the guys she hired what was happening, figuring she could work it for a profit. She told the Baronet, figuring she could get something out of him. She told Lord Gameleon, maybe. Or maybe he got it from another direction. There are several ways he could have known.

"Donni planned to do the stunt using ogres who were stealing from the daPena warehouse and selling to Gameleon. That was a big screw-up. Domina Dount already had Junior investigating shortages at the warehouse." I spoke directly to Donni. "And you knew it.

"Meanwhile, Karl Senior let Domina Dount in on the news."

Willa Dount registered an inarticulate protest.

"Karl got grabbed on schedule and taken here, where Donni grew up. Then Willa Dount, to keep it looking good at her end, asked me to put my stamp of approval on what she was doing to get him back. The kidnappers thought I'd been hired to poke into the warehouse business. They tried to convince me to keep out.

"Now it gets confusing as to who did what to who and why. None of the principals understood what they were doing because they were all being pulled in several directions. Everybody at the Stormwarden's house thought they had a chance for a big hit and a break with Raver Styx. Everybody outside saw the big hit. But the pregnancy and warehouse might come out if the kidnapping was investigated. Junior had to be sent home and kept quiet so the trails could get stale before the Stormwarden got back. But then I was suddenly in the middle of the thing. Nobody knew what I was doing, and I wouldn't go away.

"So. The ransom demand was made. The delivery was set. Domina raised the money. And Amiranda, who sensed that it wasn't going according to plan, headed for her rendezvous with Junior.

"But Donni had gotten other folks involved. And they fancied a hunk of ransom. The hell with the kid. What could he do? Go cry to his mother?

"But Karl Senior, who figured to get half of Donni's half of the ransom, warned her that Ami was tough enough to blow the whole thing." I glared at the Baronet. He was awake now, and bone white. "So Donni arranged for Ami to do what she had planned: disappear forever. I guess Junior was supposed to think it was Ami who left him without his share."

Donni Pell made noise and shook her head. The Stormwarden stared at her with the intensity of a snake sizing up supper.

I didn't know if I had that part right. Amiranda's death, otherwise, benefited no one but the Baronet. But I couldn't figure him for the order. He wouldn't have done it for his piddling share of the ransom. Or maybe he never got it, because he hadn't made tracks when he should have had cash in hand.

I glared into Donni's eyes. "You going to tell us who wanted the girl killed? Or are you just going to tell us it wasn't you?"

She had a very dry throat. I don't think anybody heard her but me. "It was the kid. He said—"

I don't bash women often. When I backhanded her I told myself it was because she wasn't one. Not in the lady sense.

With her talent she might have sold the idea to somebody. But I'd been back and forth with it from the beginning, and if there was one thing I'd learned from it all, it was that the son wasn't guilty of that one. His big crime was stupidity compounded by gutlessness.

"Better come up with a more likely sacrifice, kid. Or you're it."

The trouble with Donni Pell was that she had no handles. She knew exactly where she stood and exactly what her chances were. She was the only person alive who really knew what had happened. I could guess, and spout, and maybe come close, but I couldn't get more than seventy-five percent.

The Stormwarden said, "Mr. Garrett, I'm willing to be patient in the extreme, but this approach isn't unmasking anything. With what you've already given me I've reached several conclusions. One: that my brother-in-law, Lord Gameleon, for reasons he considered adequate, had my son killed. In his instance my only interest is to determine the extent to which my husband had knowledge of that and was involved in the effort to financially weaken me by siphoning my sources of income."

She wasn't stupid. And just because she wasn't in the trade didn't mean she had to be blind. "All right. I would've gotten to that eventually. I was hoping friend Donni would nail it down when the flood started."

"There won't be a flood with her, Mr. Garrett. You know that. The woman has the soul of a . . . a . . ."

At a loss for words? I would have suggested "Stormwarden" to fill her metaphor, but she was already unhappy with me. It was no time to press my luck.

She said, "I'm also certain that my husband killed Courter Slauce. That much detecting I could manage myself. He was away from the house when it happened. He left on Slauce's heels, in a panic according to the men on the gate."

The Baronet tried to protest. Nobody listened. I asked, "Why?"

"Slauce knew something. Karl was frightened enough to murder him to keep him from telling you. Courter would have been easy for him. Comparatively. Karl hated the man, and Slauce wouldn't have felt he was in any danger from such a coward. That leaves Amiranda."

54

Who *did* kill Amiranda Crest?

It was the question of the case. I'd begun to suspect we'd never get an answer. Only one person knew—maybe—and he or she wasn't talking.

"I have a suggestion, Mr. Garrett," the Stormwarden said in a tone that made it clear it was a command. "You take your friends, and the ogre, and Amber, and go back to TunFaire. I'll finish here. When you've settled your accounts, bring the ogre to my home."

From the corner of my eye I caught Morley making a little jabbing motion with his thumb. He thought it was time to go and he was probably right. I said, "You were going to work on our wounds."

"Yes." No sooner said than done. Crask and Sadler were awed. With Saucerhead's help they grabbed Skredli and dragged him out the front door. He hollered and carried on like he thought the Stormwarden was going to save him.

"Into the carriage," I told them.

Morley raised an eyebrow and jerked his head toward the house.

"Her problem. You, get down," I told the man who had driven down the Stormwarden and Willa Dount. "Amber. Get up on the seat. No. Don't argue. Just do it. Shut him up, Saucerhead." The Stormwarden's man backed away from us, looking at me like he was looking death in the eye. He went around the side of the house instead of going inside. "Sadler, you drive. Crask, keep the ogre under control."

They gave me dark looks. I didn't care. I wanted words with Morley and Saucerhead as we walked up the slope.

"Roll."

They rolled. We trudged along behind. I looked back once. The Stormwarden's man was headed across the clearing. Evidently he understood what was going on and wanted to be far away.

Morley spoke first. "I don't like the way she took over all of a sudden, Garrett."

And Saucerhead. "You don't ever want to go to her place again."

"She'd hand me my head. I know." We walked until we reached the woods. I told Sadler to stop. "You guys understand what was happening down there? What the old bitch was thinking?"

Crask knew. "She's going to rub them. Then she's going to arrange something for us because she don't want nobody around who knows she did it to guys like her old man and Gameleon."

I looked up at Amber. She wanted to argue, but she shivered. After a moment, she said, "I think I saw the change come over her before you did, Garrett. What are you going to do?"

"If we took a vote, none of us would go for letting her do what she wants."

Morley said, "Kill them all and let the gods sort them out."

Saucerhead said, "It isn't like they're innocent. Except maybe the Dount woman."

"Amber. Where will Willa Dount stand?"

"I don't know. She's been into things like this with Mother before. Mother would trust her to keep her mouth shut. But Mother seemed a little crazy. She might include Willa with the others. She had to be guilty of something, even if she didn't kill anybody."

"Yeah. She was guilty of a lot. But not the killings. I don't think."

Friend Skredli flopped in the back of the carriage.

A scream came from the farmhouse. "Gameleon," Morley said. "I figured she'd start with him."

"She'll stay with him for a long time. Amber. Do you see the position we're in?"

She didn't want to.

"Your mother plans to kill those people, then kill us so we can't accuse her," I reiterated. "Right?"

Weakly, "Yes. I think so."

"What options does that leave us?"

She shrugged.

I let her stew it awhile. "You think she thinks we're dumb enough not to see that?"

Nobody thought that.

Skredli thumped around again. Nobody paid any attention.

"Does she think we'll go back to town and try to insure ourselves? Or does she figure we'll do something about it now?"

"How well does she know us?" Morley asked.

"I don't know. She told me she checked me out when she hired me."

"She expects us to move now, Garrett."

Saucerhead said, "She'll never be more vulnerable."

Amber snapped, "Wait a damned minute!"

"Sweetheart, you said yourself—"

"I know. But you can't—"

"You think we should let her hunt us down instead?"

"You could get out of TunFaire. You could—"

"So could she. But she won't. And neither will we. TunFaire is home. Crask. Sadler. What do you think?"

They huddled and muttered for half a minute. Crask elected himself spokesman. "You're right. We're in it with you for whatever you have to do. If it looks practical."

Gameleon had stopped yelling. He'd probably passed out. After a pause, the Baronet took up the song. I moved downhill a little, to where I could see the farmhouse. "I wish I knew more about her skills. Can she tell we're up here? Does she know exactly where we are?" I looked at Amber.

"Don't expect me to help you, Garrett. Even if she does plan murder."

I surveyed the others. They were waiting on me. "I have a suggestion. You take the carriage and go home. Or to my house, if you want. Then you won't be involved. You won't know anything."

"I'll know who came home."

"But that's all you'll know. Get along now. Saucerhead, drag the ogre out before she leaves. You can drive the damned thing, can't you, Amber?"

"I'm not completely helpless, Garrett."

"Scoot, then."

She scooted.

The Baronet had stopped yelling. Donni Pell was tuning up. I said, "We've got to assume she knows we're here. It makes no sense to bet the other way."

Crask asked, "So how you figure to get to her?"

"Something will come to one of us."

Morley gave me a hard look. It said he knew I had something in mind already. I did, but the seed hadn't yet sprouted.

"It's going to be dark soon," Saucerhead predicted. "That what you're waiting for?"

"Maybe. Let's have a chat with friend Skredli."

We set him up against a tree. The others stood behind me, baffled, as I squatted. "Here we are again, Skredli. Me with an idea how you can get out of this with your butt still attached."

He didn't believe there was any such idea. I wouldn't have in his place.

"I'm going to give you a chance to bail me out of a jam. You do it, the worst off you can be is with a head start from here to the farmhouse. I hear you can pick them up and put them down when you want."

A flicker of interest betrayed itself. "Untie him while I explain," I said. "He'll need to get loosened up."

Saucerhead did the honors, not gently.

"Here it is, Skredli. You go down in the field and get your buddies loose. Then you hit the Stormwarden. Take her out. Then give a holler and light out. I have business in that house so I won't be after you. No promises about Saucerhead, but you'll have your head start."

He looked at me hard.

"What do you say?" I asked stonily.

"I don't like it."

"How does it stack up against your current chances?"

I never knew an ogre with a sense of humor. Skredli stunned me when he said, "You talked me into it, you smooth-talking son of a bitch."

"Good. Get up. Work the kinks out." I took one of the witch's crystals from my pocket. This one didn't need to be stomped for activation. "This little treasure here," I said. "It's from the same source as the spell that had everybody puking awhile ago. And that had everybody spinning when we raided your place in Ogre Town. Just so you know it's the real thing, Skredli." I shoved it into his pocket, said the proper word. "If you try to take it out, or if you do anything that makes me want to repeat that word, it'll blow up. It'll tear you in half."

"Hey! We made a goddamn deal!"

"It stands. I'm just trying to make sure your side does. The spell isn't good for more than an hour, and the crystal won't activate if you're too far away for it to hear me yell. I figure the farmhouse is barely in yelling distance. You follow me?"

"Yeah. You human bastards never let up, do you? Never give a guy a break."

"That's the way you want to look at it, Skredli, that's all right with me. Long as you whack the witch."

Skredli drained a long, put-upon sigh from his long-suffering body. "When?"

"As soon as it's dark." Minutes away. I could distinguish the farmhouse only by looking to one side of it.

Five minutes later I told Skredli, "Anytime you feel like getting started."

"How about next New Year's?" He started down the slope.

55

Skredli apparently had an honest streak. If somebody had tried that stunt on me, I would have tested the trick somehow. Unless they were better talkers than I.

"You guys gather around close," I said, after I'd given the breed fifteen minutes to get started. "I've got two tricks left. This one is the best." I took out a crystal bigger than the others the witch had given me. It gave off the minutest amount of soft orange light. I suspect it had stretched her limits to create it—if it did what she claimed it would.

"When I break this, we'll be invisible to the second sight, or whatever you call it, for about ten minutes. We'll still be visible to regular eyes. Once I crack it, don't waste any time."

"You fibbed to Skredli, you bad boy," Saucerhead said.

"Sideways. Sort of. Maybe. If he runs after he makes his diversion, I won't chase him."

"What about me?"

"I warned him. You do what you want when we have the Stormwarden wrapped up."

He grinned big enough to see in the dark.

"Everybody got it?"

They said they did. Morley asked, "What else have you got?"

"What?"

"You said you had a couple of things. I know you, Garrett. What are they?"

"Just one more. A crystal from the same family I used before. This one causes violent muscle cramps."

"Please yell or something this time, Garrett."

"All right. Here goes."

I broke the glowing crystal.

Skredli found half a dozen guys to back him and made his move when we were a hundred-fifty yards from the farmhouse. It wasn't a happy move for the most. The attack was over before we were two-thirds of the way to the house. Worms of blue light snapped and snarled around the place. Men yelled. A couple staggered away ablaze. But nothing reached us.

I watched Skredli brush off a patch of fire and head for the woods beyond the house. Saucerhead saw him too. He growled but stuck.

The Stormwarden stepped out the front door. We dropped down in the grass. There was enough light cast by burning men to show her grinning. She turned back into the darkened house.

I flung my last crystal. I hit the dirt.

Tinkle. And a long scream.

I charged. The others damn near stomped on my heels. They knew as well as I that we had to get her wrapped up in the few seconds when the pain distracted her too much to protect herself.

She was fighting it when we arrived. I tried to clap a hand over her mouth. She ducked me. Morley let her have a fist in the temple that loosened her up, then Crask and Sadler pinned her to the floor. I got back around and clamped my hand over her mouth. "Get the damned light going, Saucerhead."

The woman couldn't remain still. The spasms racking her were as violent as convulsions.

A lamp came to life. But Morley had lighted it. Saucerhead was nowhere to be seen.

Morley set the lamp down and brought a rag that I

stuffed into the Stormwarden's mouth. In seconds he returned with rope. We bound her. Her spasms began to ease. "Where did you come up with rope all of a sudden?"

"They didn't need it anymore."

I looked. He was right. Gameleon and the Baronet had checked out. Donni Pell was alive but that was about all. Domina Dount was unbound but standing in a corner, her face a mask of horror, eyes wide but unseeing, skin as pale and cold as a human's can get. I don't think she knew we were there. "Not a very nice lady at all," I said. I sort of wished Amber could be there to see what had happened to her father.

There wasn't a lot left of him or his half-brother. I understood why he'd been scared enough to murder Courter Slauce. Had he foreseen this, I could see him being scared enough to ice Amiranda.

Even Sadler and Crask were impressed. And they weren't the types one impresses with human messes.

The Stormwarden was recovering. Her eyes were open, hard, unfriendly. "What now?" Sadler asked.

Our next move was obvious. There was only one way to save our butts: do unto others first. But that was a hell of a giant step, even after we'd started taking it. I've got no use for our masters from the Hill, and the others had none either, but we'd been conditioned to think them immune to our ire.

A wish came true.

A sound. I thought it was Saucerhead. But Sadler and Crask, nearer the door, whipped out blades and got set for trouble.

Amber walked in. And right behind her was Saucerhead's witch.

I gawked.

Shaggoth stuck his head in the door while Morley muttered something elvish, sniffed disgustedly, and withdrew into the night.

Morley finally managed, "What the hell was that?"

"A troll."

Amber didn't react physically this time. She looked at

her father's remains. She looked at her mother. She looked at Gameleon and Donni Pell. She looked at her mother again. She looked at Willa Dount, then she looked at me. Her lips were tight and white. She shook her head, took Willa Dount into her arms and began making soothing sounds.

"What now?" Sadler asked again.

I looked at the witch. "Your stuff came in handy."

"I guessed it might." She looked like *she* might lose her most recent meal.

"What're you doing here?"

"Shaggoth came upon this child on the road, in hysterics. He brought her to me. I wheedled some of her story out of her and guessed some more and thought you might be in trouble. We've been on the hill behind you for the past hour."

"Ran into Amber just by chance, eh?"

She smiled. "We like to keep track." She glanced around. "Your associate has asked twice what you want to do now."

"It isn't a matter of what I want to do. It's what I have to do to stay healthy. I was planning to dump them down the well and fill it. By the time anyone digs them up they won't be identifiable."

"You tend to think as grimly as those you oppose today, Garrett. You're the knight in the nighted land, remember? A rage for justice? That's what you brought with you when you visited me. Not kill or be killed."

"Show me the way. My head's locked in. It's gotten too bloody and too brutal."

"Amber. Come here."

Amber left Willa Dount, who had begun to show some color. "Yes?"

"Explain to Garrett what we discussed while we waited on the hillside."

"Discussed? You told me . . . Garrett, all we have to do now is get some people from the High Council to come and see what's happened. Nobody else has to get killed. We can just sit tight and keep things the way they are. Answer questions honestly. My mother has overstepped her rights. They'll take appropriate steps. Including making certain Mother never hurts anybody again. You and your friends included."

I thought about it. I thought about it some more. Maybe they were too damned idealistic. But if the right bunch came out, some of the Stormwarden's enemies, we might come up smelling like roses. They could tie it in a knot and make a good show, get what they wanted, and come out looking like champions of justice themselves. "It's worth a think. Let's take a walk." I grabbed her hand and went outside.

"What is it?" she asked.

"The gold?"

"It's gone. Isn't it? Anyway, if it turns out the way the witch said, it won't matter. I'll get everything that belonged to my mother and father and *she* won't be there to—"

"The gold isn't gone. Not most of it. Willa Dount hid it somewhere. Skredli's bunch weren't after two hundred thousand. They asked for twenty thousand. Domina forged an extra cipher into all those letters."

"Oh. I see. You want your half."

"Not really. I never counted on getting it. I just want you to keep it in mind if you bring in a tribunal. They get a sniff of that, they could get itchy to grab."

"It's all right with you? To do it this way?"

"It's fine with me. It's you I'm asking about."

"She said it would be."

"The witch?"

"Yes. She knows you better than I do, I guess."

"Let's go inside." We went. I told Crask and Sadler, "You guys got any reason to hang around?"

Crask was leaning against a wall, watching the witch. He said, "Yeah." He pointed. "Her." He meant Donni Pell. "Chodo wants her. When you're done with her. If she's still breathing."

"What for?"

"An ornament. Like the broads that hang around the pool. He thinks she'd be interesting, all he's heard."

"I see." I liked an aspect of the idea. I examined my

conscience. Better than killing her. Maybe. "It's all right with me. Take her now."

The witch gave me an unreadable look. Then she stepped over and did something to Donni Pell. The girl began breathing easier.

Saucerhead came strolling in. He saw the witch and looked sheepish immediately. I got the distinct impression the world would be plagued by an ogre breed named Skredli no more.

Morley said nothing. In fact, he did one of the fanciest fades ever. I paid no attention while Crask and Sadler started out with Donni Pell on a crude stretcher. And when I looked, Morley was nowhere in sight.

56

The investigators came in a body of eight. They were painfully thorough, yet there was never any doubt of their ruling. The final decision found Lord Gameleon, Baronet daPena, and the Stormwarden Raver Styx all guilty of murder. Amiranda's death they ascribed to person or persons unknown.

On the Hill they don't hang each other. Raver Styx was sentenced to be stripped of her property and sorcerous powers and ejected from the Hill, to make her way alone in the world. Except she didn't exactly go alone. Willa Dount vanished, and the last I heard Raver Styx was trying to hunt her down. One hundred eighty thousand marks gold!

I wonder if Raver Styx will have any luck. I never managed to locate Willa Dount or the gold, despite months of searching whenever I had free time.

I did figure out that she had kept it with her all the time. She hadn't been late to the payoff meet because she'd stopped on the way, but, as Skredli had thought, she'd miscalculated the speed a heavily loaded wagon could make. The cut she'd forged for herself had been concealed under a false bottom. I found the very wagon and the man who had modified it for her. Whatever she did with the gold, she did it after the payoff.

I did all right, though. I found ways to recover most of the rest, and Amber made sure I got ten percent.

I've had no direct contact with Amber since we got back to TunFaire. She's been too busy muscling into her mother's place in the scheme of the Hill to visit me. I haven't dared go there.

I looked like I'd spent six weeks in the wild islands when I got home. Dean took one look and rolled up his nose. He said, "I'll put some water on to heat, Mr. Garrett."

I heard a woman say something in the kitchen. I was not up to coping with one of his nieces. "What have I told you about . . ."

Tinnie stepped into the hallway, an angry red-haired vision. "I'm going to give you one chance to explain, Garrett," she said, and went back into the kitchen.

"What the hell is that?"

"She saw you coming out of Lettie Faren's place with a woman the afternoon she got back to town." Dean looked smug.

"And you, knowing who I was with and why, didn't bother to explain because you figured it would serve me right to get on her shit list. Eh?"

He refused to look abashed. The rat.

Tinnie took my word. More or less. After I explained everything six times and showed her that, yes, I'd even made money on this one. But it took some doing, and some of the money had to be spent in fancy eating places and whatnot, before she decided to forgive me for whatever it was she imagined I might have done.

She finally relented when I started muttering about marrying one of Dean's nieces. She wanted to save me from a fate worse than death.

A week had passed when Crask came to the door. I wasn't in a good mood. Dean and the Dead Man and Tinnie were all riding me for one reason or another. Saucerhead was avoiding me because of what he'd gone through during the investigation. Morley's boys wouldn't let me get anywhere near his place. Every time I left the house, Pokey Pigotta followed me. For no special reason, just because he wanted to hone his skills to the point where he could do it without me getting wise. I wasn't in a good mood.

"Yeah?" I saved my nastiest tone. I'm not so stupid I'd lay that on one of Chodo Contague's head breakers. The next one that came around might not be somebody I recognized—and he might play a few drumrolls on my skull with pieces of lead pipe.

"Chodo wants to see you."

Wonderful. I didn't want to see Chodo. Not unless I got into a pinch so bad it was time to collect my favor. "Social?"

Crask smiled. "You could say that."

I didn't like it. I hadn't seen Crask smile since he'd turned up in my life.

He said, "He has a gift for you."

Oh boy. A gift from the kingpin. The way those boys operate, that could mean anything. With my imagination it couldn't mean anything good. But what could I do? I'd been summoned. I have enough enemies without adding the kingpin just to snub him. "Let me tell my man. So he can lock up."

I told Dean. I glanced in on the Dead Man. The fat son was still asleep. He'd dozed off while we were out at the damned farm. He still hadn't told me how Glory Mooncalled was working his military magic.

I had a surprise for him.

57

Chodo could put on a show. Crask took me out there in a coach as fancy as anything off the Hill. Maybe the same one we had used going into Ogre Town.

The kingpin met me by his pool. He was in his wheel-chair, but they had just dragged him out of the water. The girls finished setting him up and bounced off, giggling. What a good life they had. Until their knockers started to sag.

One cutie stayed.

I didn't recognize her at first. When I did, I was startled.

This wasn't the Donni Pell I'd known so briefly. Not the Donni who had been so tough on that farm. This Donni had been broken down and rebuilt. She looked as eager to please as a puppy.

Chodo noticed my surprise. He looked me in the eye and smiled. His smile was like Crask's. That was like looking Death in the face and having him grin. "A gift, Mr. Garrett. Not to be considered for the favor I owe. Just a token of my esteem. She's quite tame now. Quite pliable. I have no more use for her. I thought you might. Take her."

What could I do? He was who he was. I said thank you and told Donni Pell to get dressed. Then I let Crask take us back to my place.

What the hell was I going to do with her?

What had he done to her? She wasn't really Donni Pell anymore.

She spoke only when spoken to.

I took her into the Dead Man's room, sat her down, woke him up.

Garrett, you pustule on the nose of . . . Heavens! Not another one. You have had that redhaired trollop in and out for—

"How would you know? You've been snoring."

You truly believe I can sleep through—

"Can it, Chuckles. This one is the famous Donni Pell. A few weeks with the kingpin has given her a whole new attitude."

Yes. He seemed mildly distressed. Maybe even pitying, though the gods knew the woman didn't deserve that.

"I think she'll give me answers if I ask questions."

She will. Yes. Does that mean you have not unraveled the last few for yourself?

"Sort of." It meant I'd been trying to put the mess out of mind. With a little help from Tinnie, it had begun to recede. "You going to claim you figured out who killed Amiranda?"

Yes. And why. You never cease to amaze me, Garrett. It is quite obvious, actually.

"Illuminate me."

Illuminate yourself. You have all the information. Or ask that tortured child.

He meant tormented. Only "tormented" really described Donni Pell.

I tried, running it right through from the beginning. I didn't get it. Maybe I was just lazy because the answer was there for the asking. "Donni, who killed Amiranda Crest?"

"The Domina Willa Dount, Mr. Garrett."

"What? No!" But . . . Wait. "Why?"

"Because Amiranda helped Karl make up the ransom notes I wrote out and sent. Because Amiranda knew we were going to ask for twenty thousand marks gold, and when she saw the notes, they said two hundred thousand. Because as soon as she met Karl she was going to find out that it wasn't because he'd gotten greedy or I'd made a mistake."

Right. And I had to believe the Dead Man had come to that conclusion. Because I'd given him the details of my interview with Willa Dount with the Stormwarden standing by, when I'd gotten an indication that the Domina'd had prior knowledge that Amiranda was going to run. . . .

But I'd had my mind made up another way. Damn me.

I'd had her and I'd let her get away. She'd pulled it off. She had all that gold now.

I'd closed my mind and she was home free. Nothing to worry about the rest of her life—except staying a step ahead of Raver Styx.

I felt like a moron. The Dead Man was greatly amused at my expense.

He was even more amused because now I was stuck with Donni Pell. I had no idea what the hell to do with her. I couldn't keep her. I couldn't kick her out in the street in her condition. I sure as hell wasn't going to give her back to Lettie Faren. . . .

"All right, Old Bones. Before you doze off, you tell me how Glory Mooncalled is getting away with all these amazing triumphs because he's worked some kind of deal with the centaur tribes."

I can figure some things out, given a few hints. I grinned. I'd stolen his big thunder.

Both sides in the Cantard use centaur auxiliaries for almost all their scouting. They are almost entirely dependent upon them. If the centaurs decided not to see something, the warlords would be blind. I wondered *what* the deal was, and if maybe someday it might not embarrass Karenta as much as it was embarrassing the Venageti right now.

It can't be too long before the Venageti War Council gets a handle on it. Even when you have your mind made up, you can't stay blind to reality forever.

I left the Dead Man fuming and took Donni Pell to the kitchen so Dean could feed her.

If Garrett is a sucker for a damsel in distress, Old Dean is a sucker for one who is hurting. He never did tell me where, but he got her a good position as housekeeper and companion to an older, handicapped woman. They were supposedly very good for one another.

Sometimes I think about changing my line of work. Nobody emerged happy from this one except the worst villain of the piece.

Maybe I should just thank the gods that I got out of it alive with a few friends—and a profit.

That's why you do a job, isn't it? To survive?

ABOUT THE AUTHOR

Glen Cook was born in 1944 in New York City. He has lived in Columbus, Indiana; Rocklin, California; and Columbia, Missouri, where he attended the state university. He attended the Clarion Writers Workshop in 1970, where he met his wife, Carol. "Unlike most writers, I have not had strange jobs like chicken plucking and swamping out health bars. Only full-time employer I've ever had is General Motors, where I am currently doing assembly work in a light-duty truck plant. Hobbies include stamp collecting, and wishing my wife would let me bring home an electric guitar so my sons and I could terrorize the neighbors with our own homegrown, head-banging rock 'n' roll."

Glen Cook

WHISPERING NICKEL IDOLS

In TunFaire, a city of gorgeous women, powerful sorcerers and dangerous magic, the beautiful, criminally insane daughter of a comatose crime boss has some lascivious designs on private investigator Garrett—who now has to figure out why everyone is suddenly after him.

0-451-45974-1

Available wherever books are sold or at penguin.com

THE ULTIMATE IN
SCIENCE FICTION AND FANTASY!

From magical tales of distant worlds to stories of
technological advances beyond the grasp of man, Penguin has
everything you need to stretch your imagination to its limits.

penguin.com

ACE
Get the latest information on favorites like
William Gibson, T.A. Barron, Brian Jacques,
Ursula K. LeGuin, Sharon Shinn, and Charlaine Harris,
as well as updates on the best new authors.

ROC
Escape with Harry Turtledove, Anne Bishop,
S.M. Stirling, Simon R. Green, Chris Bunch, Jim Butcher,
E.E. Knight, and many others—plus news on the
latest and hottest in science fiction and fantasy.

DAW
Mercedes Lackey, Kristen Britain, Tanya Huff,
Tad Williams, C.J. Cherryh, and many more—
DAW has something to satisfy the cravings of any
science fiction and fantasy lover.
Also visit dawbooks.com.

*Get the best of science fiction and fantasy
at your fingertips!*

Penguin Group (USA) Online

What will you be reading tomorrow?

Tom Clancy, Patricia Cornwell, W.E.B. Griffin,
Nora Roberts, William Gibson, Robin Cook,
Brian Jacques, Catherine Coulter, Stephen King,
Dean Koontz, Ken Follett, Clive Cussler,
Eric Jerome Dickey, John Sandford,
Terry McMillan, Sue Monk Kidd, Amy Tan,
John Berendt…

You'll find them all at
penguin.com

*Read excerpts and newsletters,
find tour schedules and reading group guides,
and enter contests.*

Subscribe to Penguin Group (USA) newsletters
and get an exclusive inside look
at exciting new titles and the authors you love
long before everyone else does.

PENGUIN GROUP (USA)
us.penguingroup.com